PRAISE FOR JENNIFER LYNN BARNES

The Naturals Series

"*The Naturals* is *Criminal Minds* for the YA world, and I loved every page." —Ally Carter, *New York Times* bestselling author

★ "[A] tightly paced suspense novel that will keep readers up until the wee hours to finish." —*VOYA*, starred review

"It's a stay-up-late-to-finish kind of book, and it doesn't disappoint." —*Publishers Weekly*

"Even a psychic won't anticipate all the twists and turns." —*Booklist*

The Inheritance Games Series

"Barnes is a master of puzzles and plot twists. *The Inheritance Games* was the most fun I've had all year." —E. Lockhart, #1 *New York Times* bestselling author of *We Were Liars* and *Again Again*

"A thrilling blend of family secrets, illicit romance, and a high-stakes treasure hunt, set in the mysterious world of Texas billionaires. The nonstop twists kept me guessing until the very last page!" —Katharine McGee, *New York Times* bestselling author of *American Royals*

"Impossible to put down." —Buzzfeed

★ "Part *The Westing Game*, part *We Were Liars*, completely entertaining." —*Kirkus Reviews*, starred review

★ "This strong, *Knives Out*–esque series opener... provides ample enjoyment." —*Publishers Weekly* starred review

"Not to be missed." —

ALSO BY JENNIFER LYNN BARNES

The Inheritance Games
The Inheritance Games
The Hawthorne Legacy
The Final Gambit

The Brothers Hawthorne

Coming next: *The Grandest Game*

The Naturals
The Naturals
Killer Instinct
All In
Bad Blood
Twelve: A Novella

The Debutantes
Little White Lies
Deadly Little Scandals

The Lovely and the Lost

ALL IN

A NATURALS NOVEL

#1 *New York Times* bestselling author

JENNIFER LYNN BARNES

LITTLE, BROWN AND COMPANY

New York   Boston

This book is a work of fiction. Names, characters, places, and incidents are the product of the author's imagination or are used fictitiously. Any resemblance to actual events, locales, or persons, living or dead, is coincidental.

Copyright © 2015 by Jennifer Lynn Barnes
Excerpt from *Bad Blood* copyright © 2016 by Jennifer Lynn Barnes
Excerpt from *The Inheritance Games* copyright © 2020 by Jennifer Lynn Barnes

Cover art copyright © 2023 by Katt Phatt. Cover design by Karina Granda.
Cover copyright © 2023 by Hachette Book Group, Inc.

Hachette Book Group supports the right to free expression and the value of copyright. The purpose of copyright is to encourage writers and artists to produce the creative works that enrich our culture.

The scanning, uploading, and distribution of this book without permission is a theft of the author's intellectual property. If you would like permission to use material from the book (other than for review purposes), please contact permissions@hbgusa.com. Thank you for your support of the author's rights.

Little, Brown and Company
Hachette Book Group
1290 Avenue of the Americas, New York, NY 10104
Visit us at LBYR.com

Originally published in hardcover and ebook by Hyperion, an imprint of Disney Book Group, in November 2015
Revised Trade Paperback Edition: May 2023

Little, Brown and Company is a division of Hachette Book Group, Inc. The Little, Brown name and logo are trademarks of Hachette Book Group, Inc.

The publisher is not responsible for websites (or their content) that are not owned by the publisher.

Little, Brown and Company books may be purchased in bulk for business, educational, or promotional use. For information, please contact your local bookseller or the Hachette Book Group Special Markets Department at special.markets@hbgusa.com.

Library of Congress Control Number: 2023932767

ISBNs: 978-0-316-54084-1 (pbk.), 978-1-4847-1958-9 (ebook)

Printed in New Jersey, USA

CCR, 04/25

*For Anthony, my partner
in crime, now and always.*

YOU

Anything can be counted. The hairs on her head. The words she's spoken to you. The number of breaths she has left.

It's beautiful, really. The numbers. The girl. The things you have planned.

The thing you're destined to become.

CHAPTER 1

New Year's Eve fell on a Sunday. This would have been less problematic if my grandmother hadn't considered "Thou shalt gather thy family for Sunday dinner" an inviolable commandment, or if Uncle Rio had not appointed himself the pourer of wine.

There was a lot of wine.

By the time we were clearing away the plates, it was pretty clear that none of the adults would be driving themselves home anytime soon. Given that my father had seven siblings, all of them married, several with kids a decade or more my senior, there were a lot of "adults." As I carried a stack of plates into the kitchen, the dozen or so arguments brewing behind me were almost, but not quite, drowned out by the sound of boisterous laughter.

Viewed from the outside, it was chaos. But viewed with a profiler's eye, it was simple. Easy to understand. Easy to make sense of. This was a family. The *kind* of family, the individual personalities—those were there in the details: shirts tucked and un-tucked, dishes chipped but handled with love.

"Cassie." My great-uncle bestowed upon me a beatific, bleary-eyed smile as I came into the kitchen. "You miss your family, eh? You come back to visit your old Uncle Rio!"

As far as anyone in this house knew, I'd spent the past six months at a government-sponsored gifted program. Boarding school, more or less. Parts of that were true.

More or less.

"Bah." My grandmother made a dismissive noise in Uncle Rio's general direction as she took a stack of plates from my hands and transferred them to the sink. "Cassie did not come back for old fools who drink too much and talk too loud." Nonna rolled up her sleeves and turned on the faucet. "She came back to see her nonna. To make up for not calling like she should."

Two guilt trips, one stone. Uncle Rio remained largely unfazed. I, on the other hand, felt the intended twinge of guilt and joined Nonna at the sink. "Here," I said. "Let me."

Nonna harrumphed, but slid over. There was something comforting about the fact that she was exactly the same as she'd always been: part mother hen, part dictator, ruling her family with baked ziti and an iron fist.

But I'm not the same. I couldn't dodge that thought. *I've changed.* The new Cassandra Hobbes had more scars—figuratively and literally.

"This one gets cranky when she does not hear from you

for too many weeks," Uncle Rio told me, nodding at Nonna. "But perhaps you are busy?" His face lit up at the prospect, and he studied me for several seconds. "Heartbreaker!" he declared. "How many boyfriends you hide from us now?"

"I don't have a boyfriend."

Uncle Rio had been accusing me of hiding boyfriends from him for years. This was the first and only time he'd ever been right.

"You." Nonna pointed a spatula—which had appeared in her hand out of nowhere—at Uncle Rio. "Out."

He eyed the spatula warily, but held his ground.

"Out!"

Three seconds later, Nonna and I were alone in the kitchen. She stood there, watching me, her eyes shrewd, her expression softening slightly. "The boy who picked you up here last summer," she said, "the one with the fancy car . . . He is a good kisser?"

"Nonna!" I sputtered.

"I have eight children," Nonna told me. "I know about the kissing."

"No," I said quickly, scrubbing at the plates and trying not to read too much into that statement. "Michael and I aren't . . . We don't . . ."

"Ahh," Nonna said knowingly. "His kisses, not so good." She patted me consolingly on the shoulder. "He is young. Room for improvement!"

This conversation was mortifying on so many levels, not the least of which was the fact that *Michael* wasn't the one

I'd been kissing. But if Nonna wanted to think that the reason my phone calls home had been so few and far between was because I was caught in the throes of young romance, let her.

That was an easier pill to swallow than the truth: I'd been subsumed into a world of motives and victims, killers and corpses. I'd been held captive. Twice. I still woke up at night with memories of zip ties digging into my wrists and the sound of gunfire ringing in my ears. Sometimes, when I closed my eyes, I saw light reflected off of a bloody blade.

"You are happy at this school of yours?" Nonna made her best attempt at sounding casual. I wasn't fooled. I'd lived with my paternal grandmother for five years before I'd joined the Naturals program. She wanted me safe, and she wanted me happy. She wanted me *here*.

"I am," I told my grandmother. "Happy." That wasn't a lie. For the first time in my life, I felt like I belonged somewhere. With my fellow Naturals, I never had to pretend to be someone I wasn't. I couldn't have, even if I'd wanted to.

In a house full of people who saw things the rest of the world missed, it was impossible to hide.

"You look good," Nonna admitted grudgingly. "Better now that I have fed you for a week." She harrumphed again, then gently shoved me to the side and took over washing the dishes. "I will send food back with you," she declared. "That boy who picked you up, he is too skinny. Maybe he will kiss better with a little meat on his bones."

I sputtered.

"What's this about kissing?" a voice asked from the doorway. I turned, expecting to see one of my father's brothers. Instead, I saw my father. I froze. He was stationed overseas, and we weren't expecting him for another couple of days.

It had been over a year since the last time I'd seen him.

"Cassie." My father greeted me with a stiff smile, a shade or two off from the real deal.

My thoughts went to Michael. He would have known exactly how to read the tension in my father's face. In contrast, I was a profiler. I could take a collection of tiny details—the contents of a person's suitcase, the words they chose to say hello—and build the big picture: who they were, what they wanted, how they would behave in any given situation.

But the exact meaning of that not-quite-a-smile? The emotions my father was hiding? Whether he felt a spark of recognition or pride or anything fatherly at all when he looked at me?

That, I didn't know.

"Cassandra," Nonna chided, "say hello to your father." Before I had a chance to say anything, Nonna had latched her arms around him, squeezing tightly. She kissed him, then smacked him several times, then kissed him again.

"You are back early." Nonna finally pried herself away from the prodigal son. She gave him a look—probably the same look she'd given him when he'd tracked dirt in on her carpet as a little boy. "Why?"

My father's gaze flitted back to me. "I need to talk to Cassie."

Nonna's eyes narrowed. "And what is it you need to talk to our Cassie about?" Nonna poked him in the chest. Repeatedly. "She is happy at her new school, with her skinny boyfriend."

I barely registered that assertion. My attention was fully focused on my father. He was slightly disheveled. He looked like he hadn't slept at all the night before. He couldn't quite look me in the eye.

"What's wrong?" I asked.

"Nothing," Nonna said, with the force of a sheriff declaring martial law. "Nothing is wrong." She turned back to my father. "You tell her nothing is wrong," she ordered.

My father crossed the room and took my shoulders gently in his hands.

You're not normally this gentle.

My brain ran through everything I knew about him—our relationship, the type of person he was, the fact that he was here at all. My stomach felt like it had been lined with lead. I knew with sudden prescience what he was going to say. The knowledge paralyzed me. I couldn't breathe. I couldn't blink.

"Cassie," my father said softly. "It's about your mother."

CHAPTER 2

There was a difference between *presumed dead* and *dead*, a difference between coming back to a dressing room that was drenched in my mother's blood and being told that after five long years, there was a body.

When I was twelve, thirteen, fourteen years old, I had prayed every night that someone would find my mother, that the police would be proven wrong, that somehow, despite the evidence, despite the amount of blood she'd lost, she'd turn up. Alive.

Eventually, I had stopped hoping and started praying that the authorities would find my mother's body. I had imagined being called in to identify the remains. I'd imagined saying good-bye. I had imagined burying her.

I hadn't imagined this.

"They're sure it's her?" I asked, my voice small, but steady.

My father and I were sitting on opposite sides of a porch

swing, just the two of us, the closest thing to privacy Nonna's house could afford.

"The location's right." He didn't look at me as he replied, staring out into the night. "So is the timing. They're trying to match dental records, but you two moved around so much. . . ." He seemed to realize, then, that he was telling me something I already knew.

My mother's dental records would be hard to come by.

"They found this." My father held out a thin silver chain. A small red stone hung on the end.

My throat closed up.

Hers.

I swallowed, pushing the thought down, like I could unthink it by sheer force of will. My father tried to hand me the necklace. I shook my head.

Hers.

I'd known my mother was almost certainly dead. I'd *known* that. I'd believed it. But now, looking at the necklace she'd worn that night, I couldn't breathe.

"That's evidence." I forced the words out. "The police shouldn't have given it to you. It's evidence."

What were they thinking? I'd only been working with the FBI for six months. Almost all of that time had been spent behind the scenes, and even I knew you didn't break chain of evidence just so a halfway-orphaned girl could have something that had belonged to her mother.

"There weren't any prints on it," my father assured me. "Or trace evidence."

"Tell them to keep it," I ground out, standing up and walking to the edge of the porch. "They may need it. For identification."

It had been five years. If they were looking for dental records, there probably wasn't anything left for me *to* identify. *Nothing but bones.*

"Cassie—"

I tuned out. I didn't want to listen to a man who'd barely known my mother telling me that the police had no leads, that they thought it was all right to compromise evidence, because none of them expected this case to be solved.

After five years, we had a body. That was a lead. *Notches in the bones. The way she was buried. The place her killer had laid her to rest.* There had to be *something*. Some hint of what had happened.

He came after you with a knife. I slipped into my mother's perspective, trying to work out what had happened that day, as I had so many times before. *He surprised you. You fought.*

"I want to see the scene." I turned back to my father. "The place where they found the body, I want to see it."

My father was the one who'd signed off on my enrolling in Agent Briggs's gifted program, but he had no idea what kind of "education" I was receiving. He didn't know what the program really was. He didn't know what I could do. Killers and victims, UNSUBs and bodies—this was my language. *Mine.* And what had happened to my mother?

That was mine, too.

"I don't think that's a good idea, Cassie."

It's not your decision. I thought the words, but didn't say them out loud. There was no point in arguing with him. If I wanted access—to the site, to pictures, to whatever scraps of evidence there might be—Vincent Battaglia wasn't the person to ask.

"Cassie?" My father stood and took a hesitant step toward me. "If you want to talk about this—"

I turned around and shook my head. "I'm fine," I said, cutting off his offer. I pushed down the lump rising in my throat. "I just want to go back to school."

"School" was overstating things. The Naturals program consisted of a grand total of five students, and our lessons had what you would call *practical applications*. We weren't just pupils. We were resources to be used.

An elite team.

Each of the five of us had a skill, an aptitude honed to perfection by the lives we'd lived growing up.

None of us had normal childhoods. Those were the words I kept thinking, over and over again, four days later as I stood at the end of my grandmother's drive, waiting for my ride to arrive. *If we had, we wouldn't be Naturals.*

Instead of thinking of the way I'd grown up, going from town to town with a mother who conned people into thinking she was psychic, I thought about the others—about Dean's psychopath of a father and the way Michael had learned to read emotions as a means of survival. About Sloane and Lia and the things I suspected about their childhoods.

Thinking about my fellow Naturals came with a particular brand of homesickness. I wanted them here—all of them, any of them—so badly that I almost couldn't breathe.

"Dance it off." I could hear my mother's voice in my memory. I could see her, wrapped in a royal blue scarf, her red hair damp from cold and snow as she flipped the car radio on and turned it up.

That had been our ritual. Every time we moved—from one town to the next, from one mark to the next, from one show to the next—she turned on the music, and we danced in our seats until we forgot about everything and everyone we'd left behind.

My mother wasn't a person who'd believed in missing anything for long.

"You're looking deep in thought." A low, no-nonsense voice brought me back to the present.

I pushed back against the memories—and the deluge of emotions that wanted to come with them. "Hey, Judd."

The man the FBI had hired to look after us studied me for a moment, then picked up my bag and swung it into the trunk. "You going to say good-bye?" he asked, nodding toward the porch.

I turned back to see Nonna standing there. She loved me. Fiercely. Determinedly. *From the moment you met me.* The least I owed her was a good-bye.

"Cassandra?" Nonna's tone was brisk as I approached. "You forget something?"

For years, I'd believed that I was broken, that my ability

to love—fiercely, determinedly, freely—had died with my mother.

The past few months had taught me I was wrong.

I wrapped my arms around my grandmother, and she latched hers around me and held on for dear life.

"I should go," I said after a moment.

She tapped my cheek with a little more oomph than necessary. "You call if you need anything," she ordered. "Anything."

I nodded.

She paused. "I am sorry," she said carefully. "About your mother."

Nonna had never met my mother. She didn't know the first thing about her. I'd never told my father's family about my mom's laugh, or the games she'd used to teach me to read people, or the way we'd said *no matter what* instead of *I love you*, because she didn't just love me—she loved me forever and ever, no matter what.

"Thanks," I told my grandmother. My voice came out slightly hoarse. I tamped down on the grief rising up inside me. Sooner or later, it would catch up to me.

I had always been better at compartmentalizing than ridding myself of unwanted emotions altogether.

As I turned away from Nonna's prying eyes and walked back to Judd and the car, I couldn't banish the memory of my mom's voice.

Dance it off.

CHAPTER 3

Judd drove in silence. He left it to me to break it, if and when I was ready to do so.

"The police found a body." It took me ten minutes to push those words past the edge of my lips. "They think it's my mother's."

"I heard," Judd said simply. "Briggs got a call."

Special Agent Tanner Briggs was one of the Naturals program's two FBI supervisors. He'd been the one to recruit me, and he'd used my mother's case to do it.

Of course he'd gotten a call.

"I want to see the body," I told Judd, staring out at the road in front of us. Later, I could process. Later, I could grieve. Answers, facts, *that* was what I needed now. "Pictures of the crime scene," I continued, "anything Briggs can get from the locals, I want to see it."

Judd waited a beat. "That all?"

No. That wasn't all. I wanted, desperately, for the body

the police had found not to be my mother. And I wanted it to be her. And it didn't matter that those things were contradictory. It didn't matter that I was setting myself up to lose, no matter what.

I bit down, my teeth digging into the inside of my cheek. After a moment, I answered Judd's question out loud. "No, that's not all. I also want to take down the person who did this to her."

That, at least, was simple. That was clear. I'd joined the Naturals program to put killers behind bars. My mother deserved justice. I deserved justice, for everything I'd lost.

"I ought to tell you that hunting down the person who killed her won't bring her back." Judd switched lanes, seemingly paying more attention to the road than to me. I wasn't fooled. Judd was a former marine sniper, always aware of his surroundings. "I ought to tell you," he continued, "that obsessing over this case won't make it hurt any less."

"But you won't," I said.

You know what it's like to have your world torn apart. You know what it's like to wake up each day to the awareness that the monster who tore it apart is still out there, free to do it again.

Judd wouldn't tell me I needed to let this go. He couldn't.

"What would you do," I said softly, "if it were Scarlett? If there were a lead, no matter how small, on her case?"

I'd never spoken Judd's daughter's name in his presence before. Until recently, I hadn't even been aware she existed. I didn't know much about her, other than the fact that she'd been the victim of a serial killer known as Nightshade.

The one thing I did know was how Judd would have felt if there were a development in that case.

"It was different for me," Judd said finally, his eyes fixed out on the road. "There was a body. Don't know if that makes it better or worse. Better, probably, because I didn't have to wonder." His teeth clamped together for a moment. "Worse," he continued, "because that's something no father should ever see."

I tried to imagine what Judd must have gone through when he saw his daughter's body and immediately wished that I could stop. Judd was a man with a high tolerance for pain and a face that hid nine-tenths of what he felt. But when he saw his daughter's lifeless body, there would have been no hiding, no gritting his teeth through the pain—nothing but the roar in his ears and a devastation I knew all too well.

If it were Scarlett whose body had just been found, Scarlett whose necklace had just turned up, you wouldn't sit idly by. You couldn't—no matter the cost.

"You'll tell Briggs and Sterling to get me the files?" I said. Judd wasn't an FBI agent. His first and only priority was the well-being of the Bureau's teenage assets. He was the final word on our involvement in any case.

Including my mother's.

You understand, I thought, staring at him. *Whether you want to or not—you do.*

"You can look at the files," Judd told me. He pulled the car into a private airstrip, then fixed me with a look. "But you're not doing it alone."

CHAPTER 4

The private jet seated twelve, but when I stepped onto the plane, only five of those seats were filled. Agents Sterling and Briggs sat at the front of the plane, on opposite sides of the aisle. She was looking at a file. He was looking at his watch.

All business, I thought. Then again, if it had really been all business between them, they wouldn't have needed the space provided by the aisle.

Behind them, Dean sat with his back to the front of the plane. There was a table in front of him and a deck of cards on the table. Lia was sprawled across two seats, catty-corner from Dean. Sloane was perched, cross-legged, on the edge of the table, her white-blond hair pulled into a lopsided ponytail on top of her head. If she'd been anyone else, I would have been seriously concerned that she was about to topple over, but knowing Sloane, she'd probably already done the math on her current position and taken whatever steps necessary to ensure the laws of physics fell in her favor.

"Well," Lia said, shooting me a lazy grin, "look who finally decided to grace us with her presence."

They don't know. The realization that Briggs hadn't told the rest of the team about my mother—about the body—washed over me. If he had, Lia wouldn't have been lazily poking at me; she would have been jabbing. Some people comforted. Lia prided herself on providing distractions—and not the kind you wanted to thank her for.

My assumption was confirmed when Dean turned to look at me. "Don't mind Lia," he said. "She's in a mood because I beat her at Chutes and Ladders." A small smile played around the edges of his lips.

Dean wasn't crossing the plane. He wasn't putting a calming hand on my shoulder or neck. And that meant that he *definitely* didn't know.

In that moment, I didn't want him to.

The smile on his face, the way he's teasing Lia—Dean was healing. Each day we were together, the barriers came down a little. Each day, he inched out of the shadows and became a little more himself.

I wanted that for him.

I didn't want him thinking about the fact that my mother was a victim. I didn't want him thinking about the fact that his father was a killer.

I wanted to hold on to that smile.

"Chutes and Ladders?" I repeated.

Lia's eyes glittered. "My version is *much* more interesting."

"That is concerning on so many levels," I said.

"Welcome back," Agent Briggs told me. Across from him, Agent Sterling looked up from the file she was reading and met my eyes. Briggs's ex-wife was a profiler. She was my mentor.

If Briggs knows, Sterling knows. Within a heartbeat, my eyes went to the file in her hand.

"Grab a seat," she told me.

I took that to mean, *We'll talk later.* Sterling was leaving it up to me to decide what I wanted to tell the others—and when. I knew that I wouldn't be able to keep this a secret indefinitely. Lia's specialty was deception detection. Lying was out of the question, and no matter how firmly I locked this away, it wouldn't take Dean long to realize that something had happened.

I had to tell them. But I might be able to put it off for a couple of hours—especially since the one person who would have known immediately that something was wrong wasn't on this plane.

"Where's Michael?" I asked, sliding into the seat next to Dean.

"Fifteen miles southeast of Westchester, due north of Long Island Sound." Sloane tilted her head to one side, like her slightly off-center ponytail was weighing it down.

"He went home for Christmas," Dean translated. Underneath the table, his hand found its way to mine. Initiating physical contact wasn't easy for Dean, but slowly, he'd begun to reach out more.

"Michael went home for Christmas?" I repeated. My eyes darted to Lia's. She and Michael had been on-again, off-again long before I'd arrived on the scene. We both knew—*everyone* on this plane knew—that "home" wasn't a place Michael should be.

"Michael wanted to go home for a visit." Agent Briggs inserted himself into the middle of the conversation, coming to stand in the aisle just behind Sloane. "It was his request and his choice."

Of course it was. My stomach twisted. Michael had told me once that if you couldn't keep someone from hitting you, the best thing to do was *make* them hit you. When Michael was hurting, when there was even a chance he might be hurt, he sought out conflict.

He'd taken my choosing Dean like a backhanded slap.

"He wanted to see his mom," Sloane chirped up innocently. "He said he hadn't seen her in a really long time."

The rest of us understood people. Sloane understood facts. Whatever Michael had told her, she would have believed.

"I gave him a list of conversation starters before he left," Sloane told me seriously. "In case he and his mom need something to talk about."

Knowing Sloane, that probably meant she'd encouraged Michael to break the ice by informing his family that the last word in the dictionary was *zyzzyva*, a form of tropical weevil.

"Michael," Briggs cut in, "will be fine." Something about

the way the agent's jaw clenched told me that Briggs had made sure that Michael's father knew his continued freedom depended on Michael's continued well-being.

We'd all come to the Naturals program in different ways. Michael's father—the one who'd taught him all about being hit—had traded Michael to the FBI for immunity on white-collar crimes.

"There, there," Lia cut in flatly, "everyone's fine, Kumbaya. If the comforting-Cassie portion of our daily ritual is over, can we get on with something a bit less tedious?"

One good thing about Lia: she didn't let you indulge in worry or angst for long.

"Wheels up in five," Briggs replied. "And Sloane?"

Our resident numbers expert bent her head back so she was staring up at Briggs. "There's a high probability you're going to tell me to get off the table," she said.

Briggs *almost* smiled. "Get off the table."

CHAPTER 5

We'd been airborne for about twenty minutes when Briggs and Sterling started briefing us on where we were going—and why.

"We have a case." Sterling's voice was calm and cool. Not too long ago, she would have insisted that there was no *we*, that minors—no matter how skilled—had no place in an FBI investigation.

Not too long ago, the Naturals program had been restricted to cold cases.

A lot had changed.

"Three bodies in three days." Briggs picked up where Sterling had left off. "Local police didn't realize they were dealing with a single UNSUB until an initial autopsy was done on the third victim this morning. They immediately requested FBI assistance."

Why? I let the question take hold. *Why didn't the police connect the first two victims? Why request FBI intervention so quickly after victim number three?* The busier my brain was, the easier it would be to keep it from going back to the body the police had found.

Back to a thousand and one memories of my mother.

"Our victims seem to have very little in common," Briggs continued, "aside from physical proximity and what appears to be our UNSUB's calling card."

Profilers used the term *modus operandi*—or MO—to refer to the aspects of a crime that were necessary and functional. But leaving a calling card? That wasn't functional. It wasn't necessary. And that made it a part of our Unknown Subject's signature.

"What kind of calling card?" Dean asked. His voice was soft and had just enough of a hum in it to tell me that he was already shifting into profiling mode. It was the tiny details—what the calling card was, where the police had found it in each case, what, if anything, it said—that would let us understand the UNSUB. Was our killer signing his work, or delivering a message? Tagging his victims as a sign of ownership, or opening a line of communication with the police?

Agent Sterling held up a hand to stave off questions. "Let's back up." She glanced over at Briggs. "Start from the beginning."

Briggs gave a curt nod, then flipped a switch. A flat screen near the front of the plane turned on. Briggs hit a button, and a crime scene photo appeared. In it, a woman with long, dark hair lay on the pavement. Her lips had a bluish tint. Her eyes were glassy. A sopping wet dress clung to her body.

"Alexandra Ruiz," Agent Sterling narrated. "Twenty-two years old, college student majoring in pre-occupational therapy at the University of Arizona. She was found about twenty minutes after midnight on New Year's Eve, floating facedown in the rooftop pool at the Apex Casino."

"The Apex Casino." Sloane blinked several times. "Las Vegas, Nevada."

I waited for Sloane to tell us the square footage of the Apex, or the year it was founded. Nothing.

"Pricey." Lia filled the void. "Assuming our victim was staying at the Apex."

"She wasn't." Briggs brought up another photo, inset to one side of Alexandra's, this one of a man in his early forties. He had dark hair with just a dusting of silver. The photo was a candid one. The man wasn't looking at the camera, but I got the distinct feeling that he knew it was there.

"Thomas Wesley," Briggs told us. "Former internet mogul, current world poker champion. He's in town for an upcoming poker tournament and rented the penthouse suite at the Apex, with exclusive access to the rooftop pool."

"I'm guessing our boy Wesley likes to party?" Lia asked. "Especially on New Year's Eve?"

I stopped examining Thomas Wesley's picture as my eyes were drawn upward toward Alexandra's. *You and some friends thought it would be a blast to spend New Year's Eve in Vegas. You got invited to a party. Maybe even* the *party.* Her dress was turquoise. Her shoes were black, high-heeled. One heel had been snapped off. *How did you break your heel?*

25

Were you running? Did you struggle?

"Did she have any bruises?" I asked. "Any sign that she'd been held under the water?"

Any sign that she fought back?

Agent Sterling shook her head. "There were no signs of a struggle. Her blood alcohol level was high enough that police assumed it was an accident. Tragic, but not criminal."

That would explain why the police hadn't connected their first two victims. They hadn't even realized Alexandra *was* a victim.

"How do we know it *wasn't* an accident?" Lia swung her legs over the side of her seat, letting them dangle off.

"The calling card." Dean and I answered at the exact same time.

I turned my mind from Alexandra to the UNSUB. *You made it look like an accident, but left something to tell the police that it wasn't. If they were smart enough, if they connected the pieces of the puzzle, they'd see. See what you were doing. See the elegance in it.*

See how clever you are.

"What was it?" I voiced the question Dean had asked earlier. "What did the UNSUB leave?"

Another click from Briggs, another picture on the screen, this one a close-up of a wrist. *Alexandra's.* Her arm lay palm-up on the pavement. I could see the veins beneath her skin, and just above them, on the outside edge of her wrist, were four numbers, inked into her skin in fancy script: *3213.* The ink was dark brown, with a slight orange tint to it.

"Henna," Sloane offered, playing with the edge of her sleeve, judiciously avoiding eye contact with the rest of us. "A dye derived from the flowering plant *Lawsonia inermis*. Henna tattoos are temporary and, at any given time, less common than permanent tattoos by a factor of about twenty to one."

I could feel Dean beside me, processing this information. His gaze was locked onto the picture, as if he could will it to tell him the full story. "The tattoo on her wrist," he said. "That's the calling card?"

You're not just leaving messages. You're leaving them inked onto the bodies of your victims.

"Is there any way to get a time stamp on the tattoo?" I asked. "Did he mark her, then drown her, or drown her, then mark her?"

Briggs and Sterling exchanged a look. "Neither." Sterling was the one who answered the question. "According to her friends, she got the tattoo herself."

As we processed that information, Briggs cleared the screen and brought up a new photo. I tried to look away, but couldn't. The corpse on the screen was covered in blisters and burns. I couldn't tell if the victim was male or female. There was only one patch of unmarred skin.

The right wrist.

Briggs gave us a close-up.

"4-5-5-8." Sloane read out loud. "3-2-1-3. 4-5-5-8." She stopped talking, but her lips kept moving as she went over and over the numbers.

Meanwhile, Dean and I were staring at the photograph.

"Not henna this time," he said. "This time I had the numbers burned into my target's skin."

My preferred pronoun for profiling was *you*. I talked *to* the killer, *to* the victims. But when Dean slipped into an UNSUB's head, he imagined *being* the killer. *Doing* the killing.

Given who and what his father was—and the way Dean couldn't shake the fear that he'd inherited some trace of monstrousness—that didn't surprise me. Every time he profiled, he faced that fear head-on.

"I suppose you're going to tell us victim number two burned the numbers into his own arm?" Lia asked Briggs. She did a good job of sounding unaffected by the gruesomeness of what we were seeing, but I knew better. Lia was an expert at masking her true reactions, showing only what she wanted the world to see.

"In a manner of speaking." Briggs brought up another picture, side by side with the wrist. It looked like some kind of wristband. Set back into the thick material it was made of were four metal numbers: 4558, but flipped—a mirror image of the numbers on the victim's skin.

Agent Sterling enlightened us. "Fire-retardant fabric. When our victim caught fire, it heated the metal, but not the fabric, leaving a legible brand underneath."

"According to our sources, the victim received the bracelet with a parcel of fan mail," Briggs continued. "The envelope it was mailed in is long gone."

"Fan mail?" I said. "And that makes the victim . . . who?"

Another picture flashed onto the screen in response to my question, this one of a twentysomething male. His face was striking and gaunt, sharp angles offset by violet eyes—probably contacts.

"Sylvester Wilde." Lia let one of her feet fall to the floor. "Modern-day Houdini, illusionist, hypnotist, and jack-of-all-trades." She paused, then translated for the rest of us. "He's a stage magician—and like most of his kind, an *excellent* liar."

From Lia, that was a compliment.

"He had a nightly show," Briggs said, "at the Wonderland."

"Another casino." Dean mulled that over.

"Another casino," Agent Sterling confirmed. "Mr. Wilde was in the midst of his evening performance on January second when he—to all appearances—accidentally set himself on fire."

"Another *accident*." Dean bowed his head slightly, his hair falling into his face. Already, his concentration was so intense, I could see it in the lines of his shoulders, his back.

"Or so the authorities believed," Agent Briggs said. "Until . . ."

One last picture, one last victim.

"Eugene Lockhart. Seventy-eight. He was a regular at the Desert Rose Casino. He came once a week with a small group from a local retirement home." Briggs didn't say anything about how Eugene had died.

He didn't need to.

There was an arrow protruding from the old man's chest.

CHAPTER 6

How did a killer go from staging accidents to shooting someone with an arrow in broad daylight?

As the jet descended into Las Vegas, that was the question I kept coming back to. Our briefing hadn't stopped with the picture of Eugene Lockhart, skewered through the heart, but that was the moment when every assumption I'd made about this killer had started to change.

Beside me, I could feel Dean mulling over what we'd been told, too. Part of being a Natural was not being able to turn off the parts of our brains that worked differently than other people's. Lia couldn't choose to stop recognizing lies. Sloane would always see numbers everywhere she looked. Michael couldn't help picking up on every last micro-expression that crossed a person's face.

And Dean and I compulsively pieced people together like puzzles.

I couldn't have stopped if I'd tried—and knowing what my brain would cycle back to the second I stopped thinking about this case, I didn't fight it.

Behavior. Personality. Environment. There was a rhyme and reason to the way even the most monstrous killers behaved. Decoding their motivations meant trying to step into the UNSUB's shoes, trying to see the world the way he or she saw it.

You wanted the police to know that Eugene Lockhart was murdered, I thought, starting with the obvious. People didn't get "accidentally" shot with hunting arrows in the middle of busy casinos. Compared to the earlier murders, that was definitely an attention-getter. *You wanted the authorities to take notice. You wanted them to see. See what you were doing. See you.*

Are you used to going unnoticed?

Are you sick of it?

I went back over what we'd been told. In addition to the four-digit number written in permanent marker on the old man's wrist, the medical examiner had also found a message inscribed on the arrow that had killed him.

Tertium.

Latin, meaning "for the third time."

Hence the police looking back over all recent accidental deaths and homicides and the discovery of the numbers tattooed on Alexandra Ruiz's wrist and burned into Sylvester Wilde's.

Why Latin? I turned that over in my head. *Do you consider yourself an intellectual? Or is the use of Latin ritualistic?* A slight shiver ran down my spine at that possibility. *Ritualistic how?*

Without meaning to, I leaned into Dean's body. Brown eyes met mine, and I wondered what he was thinking. I wondered if climbing into this killer's mind was giving him chills, too.

Dean laid a hand on my arm, his thumb tracing along the back of my wrist.

Across from us, Lia eyed our hands and then brought her own to her forehead in a melodramatic motion. "I'm a dark and angsty profiler," she intoned. "No," she countered in a falsetto, bringing her other hand up, "*I'm* a dark and angsty profiler. Ours is a star-crossed love."

Toward the front of the plane I heard Judd cough. I deeply suspected he was covering a laugh.

"You never did tell us why the locals called in the FBI so quickly," I told Agent Briggs, easing my body away from Dean's and trying to redirect Lia's attention before she did a reenactment of our *entire* relationship.

The plane landed. Lia stood and stretched, arching her back before taking the bait. "Well?" she prompted the agents. "Care to share with the class?"

Briggs kept his answer brief and to the point. "Three murders at three different casinos in three days. The casino owners are obviously concerned."

Lia grabbed her bag and slung it neatly over one shoulder. "What I'm hearing," she said, "is that the powers that be at the casinos, worried that murder might be bad for business, used their substantial political capital to get local law enforcement to call in the experts." A slow, dangerous smile spread over Lia's lips. "Dare I hope this means those same casino owners will also see to it that we get the Vegas VIP treatment?"

I could practically see visions of nightclubs and VIP rooms dancing in Lia's head.

Briggs must have been thinking the same thing, because he grimaced. "This isn't a game, Lia. We're not here to play."

"And," Agent Sterling added sternly, "you're underage."

"Too young to party, just old enough to participate in federal investigations of serial murder." Lia let out an elaborate sigh. "Story of my life."

"Lia." Dean leveled his own version of Briggs's look at her.

"I know, I know, don't agitate the nice FBI agents." Lia waved away Dean's objection, but dialed it back a notch anyway. "Are we at least getting our rooms comped?" she asked.

Briggs and Sterling glanced briefly at each other.

"The FBI has been given a complimentary suite at the Desert Rose," Judd said, stepping in and answering on their behalf. "I, on the other hand, have secured two rooms at a modest hotel just off of the Strip."

In other words: Judd wanted to keep some distance between us and the FBI's base of operations. Considering that I'd been taken captive by not one, but *two* UNSUBs in the past six months, I certainly wasn't going to complain about the idea of keeping our visibility low.

"Sloane," Dean said suddenly, drawing my attention in her direction. "Are you okay?"

Sloane's teeth were bared in what was, quite possibly, the largest, fakest smile I'd ever seen. She froze like a deer in headlights. "I'm not practicing smiling," she said quickly. "Sometimes people's faces just do this."

That statement was met with silence from every single person on the plane.

Sloane hastily changed the subject. "Did you know that New Hampshire has more hamsters per capita than any other state?"

I was used to Sloane spitting out statistics at random, but given that we were getting ready to disembark in Vegas, I would have expected something a little more thematically applicable. That was when I realized—*Vegas.*

Sloane had been born and raised in Las Vegas.

If we'd had normal childhoods, we wouldn't be Naturals. I didn't know much about Sloane's background, but I'd caught pieces here and there. Sloane hadn't gone home for Christmas. Like Lia and Dean, that meant she had nowhere to go.

"Are you okay?" I asked her quietly.

"Affirmative," Sloane chirped. "I'm fine."

"You're not fine," Lia said bluntly. Then she reached over and pulled Sloane to her feet. "But put me in charge of your life decisions for the next few days, and you will be." Lia punctuated those words with a glittering smile.

"Your statistical track record for decision-making is somewhat concerning," Sloane told her seriously. "But I'm willing to take this under advisement."

Briggs brought one hand to his temple. Sterling opened her mouth—probably to decree that Lia not be allowed to make *anyone's* Vegas-related decisions, including her own—but Judd caught the female agent's eyes and shook his head slightly. He had a soft spot for Sloane, and it was clear to everyone on this plane that she wasn't happy to be home.

Home isn't a place, Cassie. The memory crept up on me. *Home is the people who love you most, the people who will always love you, forever and ever, no matter what.*

I stood and pushed back against the memory. I couldn't dwell on my mother. We were in Vegas for a reason. There was work to do.

The door to the jet opened. Agent Briggs turned to Agent Sterling. "After you."

YOU

Three is the number. The number of sides on a triangle. A prime number. A holy number.

Three.

Three times three.

Three times three times three.

You run your fingertips over the edge of an arrowhead. You're a good shot. You knew you would be. But killing the old man brought you no joy. You prefer the long game, the careful planning, lining up dominoes in loops and rows until all you have to do is knock over one—

The girl in the pool.

The flames burning the skin from number two.

Perfect. Elegant. Better, by far, than skewering the old man.

But there is an order to things. There are rules. And this was how it had to be. January third. The arrow. An old man in the wrong place at the wrong time.

Have you gotten their attention yet?

You pocket the arrowhead. In another life, in another world, three would be enough. You could be happy with three.

Three is a good number.

But in this life, in this world, three is not enough. You can't stop. You won't.

If you don't have their attention yet, you will soon.

CHAPTER 7

I'd spent most of my childhood in motels and apartment buildings where rent was paid by the week. Compared to some of the places my mother and I had stayed, the hotel Judd had booked for us looked nice enough—if a bit run-down.

"It's everything I dreamed it would be." Lia sighed happily. In addition to detecting lies, she also had an aptitude for telling them. With every appearance of sincerity, she eyed the building's exterior like she had stumbled across a long-lost love.

"It's not that bad," Dean told her.

Like a switch had been flipped, Lia dropped the act and tossed her long black hair over one shoulder. "This is Las Vegas, Dean. 'Not bad' isn't exactly what I was aiming for."

Judd snorted. "It'll do, Lia."

"What if I told you it didn't have to?" That question

came from the parking lot behind us. I recognized the voice instantly.

Michael.

As I turned to face him, I wondered which Michael I would see. The boy who'd recruited me to the program? The raw, unguarded Michael who'd shown me brief glimpses of his oldest wounds? The careless, indifferent one who'd spent the past three months acting like nothing and no one could touch him?

Especially me.

"Townsend," Dean greeted Michael. "Nice car."

"Aren't you a bit young for a midlife crisis?" Lia said.

"Life in the fast lane," came Michael's reply. "You have to adjust for inflation."

I looked at the new car first, then at Michael. The car was a classic—a convertible in deep cherry red with a style I associated with the fifties or sixties. It was in mint condition. Michael gave every appearance of being in mint condition, too. There were no bruises on his face, no marks on the arm resting on the back of the passenger seat.

Michael's eyes lingered on my face, just for an instant. "Don't worry, Colorado," he told me, a sharp smile pulling at the edges of his lips. "I'm all in one piece."

That was the first time he'd responded to something I hadn't said in weeks. The first time he'd acted like I was a person worth reading.

"In fact," Michael announced, "I'm feeling like a new man. An incredibly generous, incredibly well-connected new man." He glanced around at the others, his gaze coming to rest on Judd. "I hope you don't mind," he said, "but I made us a reservation of my own."

Michael's reservation was at the Majesty, the most expensive luxury hotel and casino in the city. Sloane hesitated as we approached the grand entrance, bobbing back and forth slightly like a magnet repelled by an invisible field. Her lips moved rapidly as she rattled off the digits of pi under her breath.

Some children had security blankets. I was fairly certain Sloane had grown up with a security number.

As I tried to figure out what about the Majesty had triggered this particular episode, our expert statistician forced her lips to stop moving and stepped over the threshold. Lia met my eyes and raised an eyebrow. Clearly, I wasn't the only one who'd noticed Sloane's behavior. The only reason Michael hadn't noticed was that he was several yards ahead, sauntering through the lobby.

As the rest of us followed, I stared up at the sixty-foot ceiling. Judd hadn't put up a fight about moving. The profiler in me said Judd had sensed that Michael needed this—not the luxury offered by the Majesty.

Control.

"Mr. Townsend." The concierge greeted Michael with all of the formality of a diplomat greeting a foreign head of state. "We're so pleased you and your party will be joining us. The Renoir Suite is one of the finest we have to offer."

Michael took a step toward him. Months after being shot in the leg, Michael still had a noticeable limp. He made no attempt at hiding it, his hand coming to rest on his thigh, daring the concierge to let his gaze drop.

"I do hope the suite has elevator access," Michael said.

"Of course," the concierge replied nervously. "Of course!"

I caught Dean's eyes. His lips twitched slightly. Michael was messing with the poor guy—and enjoying it just a little bit too much.

"I believe the Renoir Suite has private elevator access, does it not, Mr. Simmons?" A blond-haired man in his twenties smoothly interjected himself into the conversation as he came to stand beside the concierge. He was wearing a dark red shirt—silk, from the looks of it—under a black sports jacket. As he raked assessing blue eyes over Michael, his fingers casually fastened the top of two buttons on the jacket—less of a nervous gesture than one that called to mind a soldier readying himself for battle.

"I'll take it from here," he told the concierge.

The concierge nodded his head slightly in response. The interplay told me a few things. First, the concierge had no problems taking orders from a man at least twenty years his junior. And second, the man in question had no problems whatsoever giving them.

"Aaron Shaw." He introduced himself to Michael, holding out a hand. Michael took it. At second glance, I realized Aaron was younger than I'd initially thought—twenty-one or twenty-two.

"If you'll follow me," he said, "I'd be glad to personally show you to your rooms."

My mind arranged and rearranged what I knew about Aaron Shaw. *Behavior. Personality. Environment.* Aaron had come to the concierge's rescue. As he walked through the lobby, he nodded and smiled at various people, from bellhops to guests. He clearly knew his way around.

With each step he took, people got out of his way.

"Your family owns the casino?" I asked.

The rhythm of Aaron's stride faltered, just for a second. "Am I that obvious?"

"It's the silk shirt," Michael told him in a conspiratorial whisper. "And the shoes."

Aaron came to a stop in front of a glass elevator. "Outed by my footwear," he deadpanned. "There goes my future in espionage."

You expect other people to take you seriously, I thought, *but you're capable of laughing at yourself.*

Beside me, Sloane was staring at the hotelier's son like he'd just reached into her rib cage and ripped out her heart.

"I was joking about the espionage," Aaron told her with a smile more genuine than any he'd offered Michael. "Promise."

Sloane searched her store of mental heuristics for an appropriate response. "There are 4,097 rooms in this hotel," she told him, an oddly hopeful tone in her voice. "And the Majesty serves over twenty-nine thousand meals a day."

I turned back to Aaron, ready to run interference, but he didn't bat an eye at Sloane's version of "conversation."

"Have you stayed with us before?" he asked her.

For some reason, that question hit Sloane hard. Silently, she shook her head. Belatedly, she remembered to smile at him—the same painfully large smile she'd been practicing on the plane.

You're trying so hard, I thought. But for the life of me, I wasn't sure exactly what it was that Sloane was trying to do.

The elevator doors opened. Aaron stepped on and held the door for the rest of us. Once we were all on, he glanced at Sloane. "Everything okay, miss?"

She nodded furtively. As the elevator doors closed, I bumped my hip lightly into Sloane's. After a moment, she snuck a hesitant look at me and bumped back.

"Did you know," she said brightly, making another attempt at conversation, "that elevators only kill about twenty-seven people per year?"

CHAPTER 8

The much-touted Renoir Suite had five bedrooms and a living area large enough to host the majority of a football team. Floor-to-ceiling windows lined the far wall, giving us a panoramic view of the Vegas Strip, neon and glowing, even during the day.

Lia hopped up on the bar, her legs dangling down as she considered our digs. "Not bad," she told Michael.

"Don't thank me," Michael returned easily. "Thank my father."

A ball of unease began to unfurl in my stomach. I didn't want to thank Michael's father for anything—and under normal circumstances, neither did he. Without another word, Michael sauntered toward the master bedroom, claiming it for his own.

Dean came up behind me. He laid one arm lightly on my shoulder.

"This doesn't feel right," I told him softly.

"No," Dean said, staring after Michael. "It doesn't."

Sloane and I ended up sharing a room. As I peered out our balcony window, I wondered how long it would take her to tell me what was wrong.

How long will it take me to tell her? To tell all of them? I pushed back against the questions.

"Did you have many nightmares while you were home?" Sloane asked softly, coming to stand behind me.

"Some," I said.

I'd have more now that there had been a break in my mother's case. And Sloane would be there. She'd tell me factoids and statistics until I fell back asleep.

Home isn't a place, I thought. My throat muscles tightened.

"We shared a room for forty-four percent of the last calendar year," Sloane said wistfully. "So far this year, we're at zero."

I turned to look at her. "I missed you, too, Sloane."

She was quiet for a few seconds, and then she looked down at her feet. "I wanted him to like me," she admitted, like that was some terrible thing.

"Aaron?" I asked.

Instead of answering, Sloane walked over to a shelf full of blown-glass objects and began sorting them, largest to smallest, and for objects of similar size, by color. *Red. Orange. Yellow.* She moved with the efficiency of a speed-chess player. *Green. Blue.*

"Sloane?" I said.

44

"He's my brother," she blurted out. Then, on the off chance that I might not have understood her meaning, she forced herself to stop sorting, turned, and elaborated. "Half brother. Male sibling. We have a coefficient of relatedness of point-two-five."

"Aaron Shaw is your half brother?" I tried to make that compute. What were the chances? No wonder Sloane had behaved so strangely around him. As for Aaron, he'd noticed Sloane. He'd smiled at her, talked to her, but she could have been anyone. She could have been a stranger on the street.

"Aaron Elliott Shaw," Sloane said. "He's 1,433 days older than I am." Sloane looked back at the glass objects, perfectly arrayed in front of the mirror. "In my entire life, I've seen him exactly eleven times." She swallowed. "This is only the second time he's seen me."

"He doesn't know?" I asked.

Sloane shook her head. "No. He doesn't."

Sloane's last name isn't Shaw.

"Forty-one percent of children born in America are illegitimate." Sloane lightly traced her index finger along the edge of the shelf. "But only a minority of those are born as a result of adultery."

Sloane's mother wasn't her father's wife. Her father owns this casino. Her half brother doesn't even know she's alive.

"We don't have to stay here," I told her. "We can go back to the other hotel. Michael would understand."

"No!" Sloane said, her eyes wide. "You can't tell Michael, Cassie. You can't tell anyone."

I'd never known Sloane to keep a secret. She didn't have much of a brain-to-mouth filter, and what little she had disappeared under the influence of even the smallest bit of caffeine. The fact that she wanted to keep this between us made me wonder whether those were her words or someone else's.

You can't tell anyone.

"Cassie—"

"I won't," I told Sloane. "I promise."

Looking at her, I couldn't keep from wondering how many times Sloane had been told, growing up, that she was a secret. I wondered how many times she'd watched Aaron or his father from afar.

"There's a high probability that you're profiling me," Sloane stated.

"Occupational hazard," I told her. "And speaking of occupational hazards, the numbers on the victims' wrists—any thoughts?"

Sloane's brain worked in ways that were incomprehensible to most people. I wanted to remind her that here, with us, that was a good thing.

Sloane took the bait. "The first two victims were 3213 and 4558." She caught her bottom lip between her teeth, then plowed on. "One odd number, one even. Four digits. Neither are prime. 4558 has eight divisors: 1, 2, 43, 53, 86, 106, 2279, and, of course, 4558."

"Of course," I said.

"In contrast, 3213 has *sixteen* divisors," Sloane continued.

Before she could tell me all sixteen of them, I interjected, "And the third victim?"

"Right," she said, turning to pace the room as she spoke. "The number on the third victim's wrist was 9144." Her blue eyes got a faraway look in them that told me not to expect decipherable English any time soon.

The numbers matter to you, I thought, turning my mind to the killer. *The numbers are the most important thing.*

Very few aspects of this UNSUB's MO had remained constant. Victimology was a wash. *You've killed one woman and two men. The first two were in their twenties. The third was almost eighty.* Our killer had killed in a different location each time, using a different methodology.

The numbers were the only constant.

"Could they be dates?" I asked Sloane.

Sloane paused in her pacing. "4558. April fifth, 1958. It was a Saturday." I could see her searching through her encyclopedic store of knowledge for details about that date. "On April fifth, 1951, the Rosenbergs were sentenced to death as Soviet spies. In 1955 on that date, Churchill resigned as England's prime minister, but in 1958 . . ." Sloane shook her head. "Nothing."

"Knock, knock." Lia announced her presence the way she always did, without giving anyone time to object before she sauntered into the room. "I come bearing news."

Lia slipped personas on and off as easily as most people switched clothes. Since we'd arrived, she'd changed into a red dress. With her hair pulled back into a complicated swirl, she looked sophisticated and a little bit dangerous.

That did not bode well.

"The news," Lia continued with a slow smile, "involves some *fascinating* revelations about how our very own Cassandra Hobbes spent her Christmas vacation."

Lia knew. *About my mother. About the body.* I felt like there was a vise around my chest, tightening centimeter by centimeter until I couldn't manage more than shallow breaths.

After a few seconds, Lia snorted. "Honestly, Cassie. You go away for two weeks and it's like you've forgotten everything I taught you."

She was lying, I realized. *When Lia said the news she'd heard was about me, she was lying.* For all I knew, there might not even *be* news.

"Interesting, though," Lia continued, her eyes eagle sharp, "that you believed me. Because that seems to suggest that something interesting *did* happen while you were home."

I said nothing. Better to stay silent in Lia's presence than to lie.

"So *was* there news?" Sloane asked Lia curiously. "Or were you just making conversation?"

That's one term for it.

"There's definitely news," Lia declared, turning back toward the door and walking out of the room. I glanced at Sloane, and then we hurried to catch up with her. As we rounded the corner, Lia finally shared.

"We have a visitor," she said airily. "And the news is that she's *very* unhappy."

CHAPTER 9

Agent Sterling stood in the middle of the Renoir Suite's sprawling living room, her eyebrows arched so high, they practically disappeared into her hairline. "This is your idea of low-key?" she asked Judd.

Judd walked into the kitchen and started a cup of coffee. He'd known Agent Sterling since she was a kid. "Relax, Ronnie," he said. "No one is going to connect five spoiled teenagers and an old man in a four-thousand-dollar-a-night suite to the FBI."

"Given the average yearly salary of an FBI agent," Sloane interjected before Agent Sterling could say anything, "that seems true."

Michael strode into the room, dressed in what appeared to be a swimsuit and a fluffy white robe. "Agent Sterling," he said with a tip of an imaginary hat. "So glad you could join us." He made quick work of studying her. "You're annoyed, but also concerned and a bit peckish." He crossed the room and picked up a bowl of fruit. "Apple?"

Sterling gave him a look.

Michael took the apple for himself and crunched into it. "You don't have to worry about our cover." Dean entered the room, and Michael gestured first toward him, then toward the rest of us. "I'm a VIP. They're my entourage."

"Four teenagers and a former marine," Agent Sterling said, folding her arms over her chest. "That's your entourage."

"The fine folks at the Majesty don't *know* they're teenagers," Michael countered. "Dean and Lia could pass for early twenties. And," Michael added, "I may have led them to believe Judd was my butler."

That got nothing more than a slight eyebrow raise out of Judd, who poured himself a cup of coffee without responding.

"If anyone asks," Michael called to him, "your name is Alfred."

Agent Sterling seemed to realize that she'd lost control of the situation. Rather than argue with Michael, she crossed the room and perched on the arm of the sofa. She nodded to the seats and waited for us to follow the unspoken order. We sat. The position she'd taken up meant she was seated higher than the rest of us, looking down.

I doubted that was an accident.

"Persons of interest." Agent Sterling laid a thick file folder down on the coffee table in front of her, then reached back into her briefcase. "Schematics of the first two crime

50

scenes." She passed those to me, and I passed them to Sloane. Finally, she held up a DVD. "The Desert Rose's security footage from the casino floor for the hour before and the hour after Eugene Lockhart was shot."

"That's it?" Lia asked. "That's all you brought us?" She leaned back in her chair and put her feet up on the mahogany coffee table. "It's like you *want* me to entertain myself."

The evidence Agent Sterling had just handed over gave Sloane plenty to work with. Dean and I could weave through the information they'd collected on the persons of interest. Even Michael could scan the security footage for any emotional outliers.

But Lia needed witness interviews—or at the very least, transcripts.

"We're working on it," Agent Sterling told her. "Briggs and I will be conducting interviews of our own. I'll make sure they're recorded. If there's something we need a consult on, you'll be the first to know. In the meantime"—she stood up and glanced around the massive, sprawling suite—"enjoy your accommodations, and stay out of trouble."

Lia's expression was all innocence—and all too convincing.

Sterling headed for the door. She stopped to talk to Judd on the way out. After a quiet exchange, Sterling called back to me. "Cassie?" she said. "A word."

Hyperaware of the fact that the others were watching, I met Agent Sterling at the door. She pressed a USB drive into my hand. "That's everything we have on the developments in your mother's case," she said softly.

No matter what. I hadn't let myself think those words in years. And now, they were the only thing I could think. *Forever and ever, no matter what.*

"You've been through the files?" I asked Agent Sterling, my mouth going dry.

"I have."

My hand closed tighter over the drive, as if part of me was afraid she'd take it away.

"Judd said he told you not to look at the files alone. If you want me with you when you look at them, Cassie, you have my number." With those words, Sterling slipped out the door, leaving me to face the inquisition alone.

I forced myself to ignore the looks I was getting from Michael and Lia, the look I was getting from Dean. Part of me wanted to walk past them, shut myself in my room, and look at the contents of the drive in my hand, to read it, memorize it, devour it whole.

Part of me wasn't sure I was ready for what I would find.

Trying my hardest to keep those thoughts from my face, I made my way back to the others and to the files Agent Sterling had brought us on the current case. "Let's get to work."

CHAPTER 10

The FBI had collected the local police department's notes on five persons of interest in the deaths of Alexandra Ruiz and Sylvester Wilde. I started with the first file.

"Thomas Wesley," I said, hoping the others would follow my lead and focus on the case. I laid a finger on the man's picture—the same one Agent Briggs had put up on the screen on the plane.

"Self-satisfied," Michael declared, studying the photo for a moment. "And hyperaware."

Filing Michael's observations away for reference, I skimmed the file. Wesley had created and sold no fewer than three internet start-up companies. His net worth was eight figures, nearing nine. He'd been playing poker professionally for about a decade—and in the past three years, he'd ascended the ranks, winning multiple international competitions.

Intelligent. Competitive. I took in the way Wesley was

53

dressed in the picture and processed Michael's read on the man. *You like to win. You like a challenge.*

Based on the party he'd thrown on New Year's Eve, he also liked women, excess, and living the high life.

"What are you thinking?" I asked Dean. He was a warm, steady presence by my side, reading over my shoulder, not asking the questions I knew he had to be thinking about the exchange between Sterling and me.

"I think our UNSUB likes a challenge," Dean answered quietly.

Just like Thomas Wesley.

"How many of our POIs are here for the poker tournament?" I asked. Picking out potential suspects was significantly easier when there was variation among the people you were profiling. By definition, anyone capable of playing poker at an elite level was highly intelligent, good at masking their own emotions, and amenable to taking calculated risks.

Lia thumbed through the files. "Four of the five," she said. "And the fifth is Tory Howard, stage magician. Four bluffers and an illusionist." Lia smiled. "I do like a challenge."

You're methodical, I thought, my brain turning back to the UNSUB. *You plan six steps ahead. You get a rush out of seeing those plans come to fruition.*

In most of the cases we'd worked in the past few months, the killers' assertions of dominance over their victims had been direct. The victims had been overpowered. They'd been chosen, they'd been stalked, and they'd died looking at the faces of their killers.

This UNSUB was different.

"Persons of interest two, three, and four." Michael drew my attention back to the present as he spread the files out one by one on the coffee table. "Or, as I like to call them," he continued, glancing at each POI's picture for less than a second, "Intense, Wide-Eyed, and Planning-Your-Demise."

The one Michael had referred to as *Planning-Your-Demise* was the only woman of the three. She had strawberry blond hair with a slight curl to it and eyes that looked several sizes too big for her face. At first glance, she could have passed for a teenager, but the dossier informed me that she was twenty-five.

"Camille Holt." I paused after reading her name. "Why does that sound familiar?"

"Because she's not just a professional poker player," Lia replied. "She's an actress."

The dossier confirmed Lia's words. Camille was classically trained, had an undergraduate degree in Shakespearean literature, and had played small but critically acclaimed roles in several mainstream films.

She didn't exactly fit the profile of your typical professional poker player.

You don't like being put in boxes, I thought. According to the file, this was Camille's second major poker tournament. She'd gone far enough in the first to surpass expectations, but hadn't won.

I thought about what Michael had said about her facial

expression. To the untrained eye, she didn't look like she was plotting anything. She looked *sweet*.

You like being underestimated. I rolled that over in my mind as I made my way through the next two files, skimming the information the FBI had gathered on Dr. Daniel de la Cruz (Intense), and the supposedly wide-eyed Beau Donovan, who looked more like he was scowling to me.

De la Cruz was a professor of applied mathematics. True to Michael's assessment, he seemed to approach both poker and his field of study with laser focus and an intensity unmatched by his peers.

For maximal contrast, Beau Donovan was a twenty-one-year-old dishwasher who'd entered the qualifying tournament here at the Majesty two weeks before. He'd won, giving him the amateur spot in the upcoming poker championship.

"Shall we role-play?" Lia asked. "I'll be the actress. Dean can be the dishwasher from the wrong side of the tracks. Sloane is the mathematics professor, and Michael is the billionaire playboy."

"Obviously," Michael replied.

I picked up the final file, the one that belonged to Tory Howard, the only POI who *wasn't* an elite poker player.

The magician.

"I'm bored and approaching *really* bored," Lia announced when it became clear that none of us were going to take her up on the role-play suggestion. "And I think we all know that's not a good thing." She stood, smoothing one hand over her red dress while the other grabbed for the DVD. "At least on a security video, something might actually happen."

Lia popped the DVD into a nearby player. Sloane looked up from her spot on the floor just as the security footage began to play. A split screen showed the view from eight cameras. Sloane stood, her eyes moving rapidly back and forth, as she took in the data, tracking hundreds of people, some stationary, some moving from one frame to the next.

"There." Sloane reached for the remote and paused it. It took me a moment to zero in on what she'd seen.

Eugene Lockhart.

He was sitting in front of a slot machine. Sloane fast-forwarded the footage. I kept my eyes locked on Eugene. He stayed there, playing the same slot again and again.

But then, something shifted. He turned around.

Sloane set the DVD to play in slow motion. I skimmed each of the other cameras' footage. A blur of motion passed first through one, then through another.

The arrow.

We watched as it buried itself in the old man's chest. I didn't let myself look away.

"The angle of entry," Sloane murmured, "the placement of the cameras . . ." She rewound the footage and played it again.

"Stop," Michael said suddenly. When Sloane didn't pause the footage, he reached for the control himself and toggled back, bit by bit. "See anyone familiar?" he asked.

I scanned the various camera shots.

"Bottom right." Dean found her first. "Camille Holt."

CHAPTER 11

We spent the next six hours buried in the evidence. Sloane and Michael went over and over the video. Dean and I made our way through the final dossier, then worked back through all of them in more detail. We found everything we could online about Camille Holt. I watched interview after interview with her. She was a self-professed method actor, who embodied her characters the entire time she was filming a role.

You like trying different people's skin on for size. You're fascinated by the way the mind works, the way it breaks, the way people survive things no one should be able to survive.

It was there, in the roles she chose: a mentally ill woman on death row, a single mother weathering the loss of her only child, a homeless teenager turned vigilante after an assault.

So, Camille, I wondered, *what role are you playing now?* According to our files, she'd been at the party where

Alexandra was killed. That meant she was present at a minimum of two of the three murders.

"Enough." Judd had stayed mostly out of our way, observing, but unobtrusive. Now, he reached for the remote control and turned the television off. "Your brains need time to process," he said gruffly. "And your stomachs need food."

We objected. That didn't go well for us.

After we pried ourselves away from the evidence, Lia "suggested" Sloane and I change for dinner, which I took as a threat that she would pick out an outfit for me if I didn't comply. Unwilling to tempt fate—and Lia's fashion sense—I put on a dress. When I went to fold my jeans, the USB drive Agent Sterling had given me fell out of the pocket. I bent to pick it up, half expecting Sloane to come out of the bathroom and catch me in the act.

She didn't.

I forced myself to open my hand and stared at the drive. No amount of throwing myself into the Vegas case could make this matter less. I'd wanted to see the files—*needed* to see them—but now that I held the answers in my hand, I was paralyzed.

When people ask me why I do what I do, Locke's voice whispered in my memory, *I tell them that I went into the FBI because a loved one was murdered.*

Sensory detail broadsided me: the light reflecting off the knife, the glint in Agent Locke's eyes. There wasn't always a rhyme or reason to what triggered my flashbacks—and there was nothing I could do except ride it out.

I was supposed to kill her, Locke continued in my memory, manic with the desire to have been the one to end my mother's life. *I was supposed to be the one.*

I shuddered. When I came back to the present, my palms sticky with sweat, I couldn't keep from slipping into Locke's mind. *If you were here, if you had access to new information on my mom's case,* I thought, *you'd find the person who killed her. You'd kill him, for killing her.*

I swallowed back the emotion rising up inside of me, grabbed my computer, and made my way out into the suite. Judd had forbidden me from looking at my mother's file alone. *I'm not alone,* I told myself. I was never really alone.

Part of me would always be in that blood-spattered dressing room with my mother. Part of me would always be at the safe house with Locke.

I made it to the door to the suite and began to open it, planning to slip out into the hallway. *I just need a few minutes to look at—* My thought cut off abruptly as I realized the hallway outside our suite was already occupied.

Lia was leaning against one wall, four-inch heels on her feet, one leg crossed over the other at the ankles. "We both know that when you told Cassie you were in one piece, you were lying."

From where I was standing, with the door only partially ajar, I couldn't see Michael, but I could imagine his facial expression exactly as he replied, "Do I look like I'm in *multiple* pieces to you?"

Still leaning against the wall, Lia uncrossed her ankles. "Take off your shirt."

"I'm flattered," Michael replied. "Really."

"Take off the damn shirt, Michael."

There was silence then. I heard a light rustling, then Lia stepped out of my view.

"Well," Lia said, her voice light enough to send chills down my spine. "That's . . ."

"Leverage," Michael filled in.

Lia had a habit of sounding like things weren't important when they mattered the most. I eased the door open just far enough to see Michael, rebuttoning his shirt.

Underneath, his chest and stomach were mottled with bruises.

"Leverage," Lia repeated softly. "You don't tell Briggs, and in exchange, your father—"

"He's very generous."

Michael's words cut into me. The car he'd been driving, this hotel—that was the price Michael was exacting for the damage his father had inflicted?

You make him pay because you can. You make him pay because at least then you're worth something.

I swallowed down the ball of sorrow and anger rising in my throat and backed away from the door. I hadn't consciously thought of myself as eavesdropping until I'd heard something I had no right to hear.

"I'm sorry," I heard Lia say.

"Don't be," Michael told her. "It doesn't suit you."

The door clicked into place. I stood there, staring at it, until someone came up behind me. Without turning around, I knew it was Dean.

I always knew when it was Dean.

"Flashback?" he asked quietly. Dean knew the signs, the same way I could tell when he'd become absorbed in red-tinged memories of his own.

"A few minutes ago," I admitted.

Dean didn't touch me, but I could feel the warmth of his body. I wanted to turn toward him, toward that warmth. Michael's secret wasn't mine to share. But I could tell Dean my own—if only I could make myself turn around. If only I could make my mouth form the words.

I had a flashback because I was thinking about my mother. I was thinking about my mother because the police found a body.

"You're good at being there for people," Dean murmured behind me. "But you don't have much practice at letting people be there for you."

He was profiling me. I let him.

"When you were a kid," he continued, his voice even and low, "your mother taught you to observe people. She also taught you not to get attached."

I hadn't told him that—not in words. Finally, I turned toward him. Brown eyes held mine.

"She was your whole world, your alpha and your omega, and then she was gone." His thumb gently traced the line of my jaw. "Letting your father and his family be there for you would have been the worst kind of betrayal. Letting *anyone* be there for you would have been a betrayal."

I'd been thrust into a family of strangers—loud and affectionate and overbearing *strangers*. I hadn't been able to share my grief. Not with them. Not with anyone.

You're not doing it alone. This time, Judd's words didn't seem as much like an order. They were a reminder. I wasn't twelve years old anymore. I wasn't alone.

I leaned into Dean's touch. I closed my eyes, and the words finally came.

"They found a body."

CHAPTER 12

"If I could make this better for you, I would." Dean's voice caught slightly on the last word. He had dark places and horrible memories of his own. He had scars—visible and invisible—of his own.

I brought my hand to the side of his neck, felt his pulse, slow and steady beneath my touch. "I know."

I knew that he would feel this for me if he could.

I knew that he knew "better" wasn't even a blip on my radar.

Dean couldn't erase the marks my past had left on me, any more than I could do that for him. He couldn't take away my pain, but he saw it.

He saw me.

"Dinner?" Sloane popped into the room, oblivious to the depth of emotion on my face, on Dean's.

I dropped my hand to my side, held Dean's dark eyes for a moment longer, and nodded. "Dinner."

— — —

As the hostess led us to our table at the Majesty's five-star sushi restaurant, I tried to keep all hints of my conversation with Dean off my face.

Lia was the first to claim a chair at our table, her fingers drawing lazy rings around the base of an empty wineglass. Michael helped himself to the seat next to her. They both had a natural aura of fearlessness and self-possession, like if someone dropped a cobra in the middle of the table, they'd both just sit there, Lia continuing to circle her wineglass and Michael artfully slumped in his chair.

I took a seat across from them and hoped Michael's eyes wouldn't meet mine. Between overhearing his conversation with Lia and telling Dean about the update in my mother's case, I felt drained, empty, but for a dense ball of emotion, barely contained in the pit of my stomach, like a grenade.

Get it under control, Cassie. If you feel it, he'll see it. So don't feel it.

"Can I tell you about our specials?" A waitress appeared beside our table. The six of us managed to place both drink and food orders before Michael turned his attention to my side of the table. I could feel him working his way up and down my face. He glanced briefly at Dean, then back at me.

"Well, Colorado," Michael mused out loud. "Slight tension in your neck and jaw, eyes cast downward, brows pulled together ever so slightly."

I felt naked under his gaze, laid bare.

I'm angry. I'm angry that the police found a body and angry that it took them five years to find it. I'm angry about what your father did to you.

"You're sad and you're angry and you feel sorry for me." An edge worked its way into Michael's voice. He wasn't a person who let other people feel sorry for him.

Nothing hurts you unless you let it.

"And you," Michael said, pointing a chopstick lazily at Dean, "are having one of those oh-so-Dean moments: self-loathing and inadequacy, *check*. Longing and fear, *check*. Constant, seething anger, bubbling just under the surface—"

"When you lose the remote control to your television, four percent of the time it ends up in the freezer!" Sloane blurted out loudly.

Michael glanced at Sloane. Whatever he saw there must have convinced him that now wasn't a good time to be stirring things up with Dean and me. He turned back to Judd and said, "I believe your line is 'This is why we can't have nice things.'"

Beside me, Dean snorted, and the tension that had settled over the table dissolved.

"Check out the company." Lia nodded to the bar. I turned to look. *Camille Holt.* She was sitting at the bar, wearing black shorts and a backless top, sipping a red drink and talking with another woman.

"Person of interest number five," Dean murmured, eyeing Camille's friend. "Tory Howard."

Next to Camille, Tory Howard—stage magician and rival of our second victim—drank beer from a bottle. Her dark hair was wavy and damp, like she'd come here straight from jumping out of the shower. *No muss. No fuss.* I tried to reconcile that with the fact that she was a performer, an illusionist, pulling off tricks that were larger-than-life.

"This," Judd muttered, "is why we can't have nice things."

He'd tried to tear us away from our work—and there work was, sitting at the bar.

"Mr. Shaw." The hostess's voice broke into my thoughts. I glanced toward the front of the restaurant, expecting to see Aaron. Instead, I saw a man who looked the way Aaron would in thirty years. His thick blond hair was tinged silver. His lips were set in a permanent half smile. He wore a three-piece suit as comfortably as other people wore a T-shirt and jeans.

Aaron's father. My stomach twisted, because if this was Aaron's father, he was Sloane's father, too.

Beside him, there was a woman with light brown hair coifed at the nape of her neck. She was holding a little girl, no older than three or four. The child was Korean, with beautiful dark hair and eyes that took in everything. *Their daughter,* I realized. *Aaron's little sister.* As the hostess led the trio to a table near ours, I wondered if Sloane knew her father had adopted a child.

I knew the exact moment Sloane saw them. She went very still. Underneath the table, I reached for her hand. She squeezed mine, hard enough to hurt.

Several minutes later, our food was deposited on the table. With great effort, Sloane let go of my hand and pulled her gaze away from the happy threesome, just as Aaron slid into the empty seat at the table to join his family.

His family. Not hers.

I tried to catch Sloane's eye, but she wouldn't look at me. She concentrated all of her attention on the sushi in front of her, carefully disassembling it and dividing each roll into its parts. *Avocado. Salmon. Rice.*

At the bar, Camille and Tory finished their drinks. As they gathered their possessions and turned toward us, I noticed two things. The first was the thick silver chain Camille wore looped multiple times around her neck.

The second thing was Aaron Shaw noticing Camille.

CHAPTER 13

Five minutes after Camille Holt and Tory Howard exited the restaurant, Aaron excused himself from his family's table. Half an hour after that, Mr. Shaw carried his delighted little girl through the room to get a cherry at the bar. As father and daughter returned to their seats, I saw Shaw register Sloane's presence. He never faltered, never altered the pace of his stride.

But my gut told me he recognized her.

This was a man who oozed power and control. Based on the son he'd raised, I was willing to bet he knew everything that went on in this casino. *Aaron might not know that Sloane is your daughter, but you do. You've always known.*

Beside me, Sloane looked so nakedly vulnerable that my eyes stung for her.

"Sloane?" Michael said quietly.

She forced her lips upward in a valiant attempt at a smile. "I'm digesting," she told Michael. "This is my digesting face, that's all."

Michael didn't press her on it, the way he would have if it were Dean or Lia or me. "And what a pleasant digesting face it is," he declared.

Beside me, Sloane developed an intense interest in her lap. By the time dessert arrived, she was moving her finger back and forth over the surface of her skirt. It took me a moment to realize that she was tracing out numbers.

3213. 4558. 9144.

I wondered how much of Sloane's fascination with numbers had arisen during moments like this one, when numbers were easy and people were hard.

"Well," Lia said, snagging a bite of mint ice cream with her spoon. "I, for one, am ready for bed. I'm also considering joining a nunnery and have no interest whatsoever in hitting the shops."

"I'm not going shopping with you," Dean said darkly.

"Because you're afraid I might try to introduce actual colors into your wardrobe?" Lia asked innocently.

Beside me, Sloane was still going, number after number drawn with the tip of her finger on the surface of her skirt.

"How many shops are there in Las Vegas?" Lia said. "Do you know, Sloane?"

The question was a kindness on Lia's part—though she wouldn't have liked me thinking of her as kind.

"Sloane?" Lia repeated.

Sloane looked up from her lap. "Napkins," she said.

"Not going to lie," Michael put in. "I had no idea that was a number."

"I need napkins. And a pen."

Judd fished a ballpoint pen out of his pocket and handed it to her. Dean grabbed some cocktail napkins off the bar.

3213. 4558. 9144. The second that Dean handed her the napkins, Sloane scrawled out the numbers, each sequence on its own napkin.

"It's not three," she said. "It's thirteen. He cut off the one. I don't know why he cut off the one."

He as in the UNSUB. Sloane wasn't a profiler. She'd never been trained to use *I* or *You*.

"That's why I didn't see it before." Sloane added a vertical line to the left of the first number. "It's not 3213," she said. "It's *1*3213." She moved on to the next napkin. "4558. 9144." With the pen, she began grouping the numbers into pairs. "Thirteen. Twenty-one. Thirty-four. Fifty-five. Eighty-nine." Finally, she circled the last three digits. "One hundred and forty-four." She looked up from the napkins, her eyes bright, as if she expected this to clarify everything. "It's the Fibonacci sequence."

There was a long pause. "And the Fibonacci sequence is what exactly?" Lia asked.

Sloane frowned, her forehead wrinkling. Clearly, it hadn't occurred to her that the rest of us might not know what the Fibonacci sequence was. "It's a series of numbers, derived from a deceptively simple formula where each subsequent integer is calculated by adding together the two previous numbers in the series." Sloane sucked in a breath, but babbled on. "The Fibonacci sequence appears throughout the biological world: the arrangement of pinecones, the family tree of honeybees, nautilus shells, flower petals. . . ."

Across the room, a man wearing a suit and an earpiece walked straight past the hostess. Even if I hadn't spent the past few months interacting with FBI agents, I would have recognized him as security.

People walk differently when they're the only ones in the room carrying a gun.

"The Fibonacci sequence is everywhere," Sloane was saying. The man in the earpiece approached Mr. Shaw and bent to whisper something in his ear. The casino owner's face remained carefully controlled, but when Michael followed my gaze, he must have seen something I didn't. His eyebrows shot up.

"It's beautiful," Sloane continued. "It's perfection."

I met Michael's eyes across the table. He held my gaze for a few seconds, then he raised one finger. "Check, please."

CHAPTER 14

The UNSUB's calling card had just taken on a whole new meaning. I'd assumed the numbers might have personal significance to the killer. But if they really were part of some famous mathematical sequence, there was a chance the point of the numbers was less about fulfilling our killer's emotional needs and more about sending a message.

What message? I smoothed a hand over my dress as we began the long walk back toward the main body of the hotel and casino. *That your actions aren't emotional? That they're as predetermined as numbers plugged into an equation?*

I barely noticed the lights and sounds that bombarded our senses when we hit the casino floor.

That you're a part of the natural order, like pinecones and seashells and bees?

Judd, Dean, and Sloane hung a left toward the lobby. Michael began veering right. "Shopping?" he asked Lia.

Somehow, I doubted that Michael and Lia, if left to their own devices in Sin City, would spend their time perusing the shops. Judd must have been thinking the same thing, because he gave the two of them a look.

"I'll have you know I'm very fashionable," Michael told Judd.

You saw something when security came for Sloane's father, Michael. You asked for the check an instant later. You're not going shopping.

Dean knew me well enough to recognize when I was profiling someone. "I'll go with Sloane to call Sterling and Briggs," he told me. I heard what he wasn't saying: *Go.*

Whatever Michael and Lia were about to do, I wanted in on it—and if part of the reason was that going back upstairs meant going back to the information that awaited me on that drive, Dean didn't begrudge me that.

When I was ready, he would be there.

"Fair warning." Lia eyed Dean and me before turning back to Judd. "If you make me go up to the suite right now, there's a very good chance that I will give a full-length performance of *The Ballad of Cassie and Dean.* Complete with musical numbers."

"And there is a very good chance," Michael added, "that I will be forced to accompany those musical numbers with a stunning display of interpretive dance."

Judd must have decided that it was in the best interest of team harmony to avoid that performance at all cost. "One hour," he told Michael and Lia. "Don't leave the building.

Don't separate. Don't approach anyone related to this case."

"I'll go with them," I volunteered.

Judd eyed me for a moment. Then he gave a brisk nod. "Make sure they don't burn the place down."

It took exactly thirty seconds after we parted ways with the others for Michael to confirm my assumption that he hadn't been overcome with a need to hit the shops. He came to a stop as we reached the edge of the casino floor. For several seconds, he stood there, his gaze moving methodically from one party of people to the next.

"What are you looking for?" I asked him.

"Curiosity. Irritation." He zeroed in on a group of women coming toward us. "That mollified look people get when they're offered free drinks in exchange for an inconvenience." He hung a right. "This way."

As Lia and I followed, Michael continued scanning faces. As we worked our way from the slots to the poker tables, I could sense an emotional shift in the air, even if I couldn't pinpoint it the way Michael could.

"Incoming," Michael murmured to Lia.

Seconds later, a bouncer was glaring down at us. "IDs, please," the man said. "You have to be twenty-one or over to be in this area."

"As luck would have it," Lia told him, "it's my twenty-first birthday." She said those words with a coy smile and just the right level of underlying giddiness.

"And your friends?" the bouncer asked Lia.

Lia linked an arm through Michael's. "*We,*" she said, "just met. And as for Miss Sweet-and-Innocent-Looking over there, I know for a fact that there are some pretty incriminating pictures of *her* twenty-first floating around on the interwebs, which is why *my* clothes will be staying on this evening."

Did she just . . . My cheeks flushed scarlet as I processed the fact that, yes, Lia had really just implied that my fictional twenty-first birthday had taken a Girls Gone Wild turn.

The bouncer leaned to one side to get a better look at me. If anything, the mortified expression on my face seemed to sell Lia's story.

"I'm going to hurt you," I muttered in Lia's general direction.

"You can't hurt me," she shot back brightly. "It's my birthday."

The bouncer grinned. "Happy birthday," he told Lia.

Chalk one up for the professional liar.

"But I'm still going to need to see some ID." The bouncer turned back to Michael. "Company policy."

Michael shrugged. He reached into his back pocket and removed a wallet. He flashed an ID at the bouncer, who examined it carefully. It must have passed muster, because then he turned to Lia and me. "Ladies?"

Lia opened her purse and handed him not one, but *two* IDs. He glanced at them and raised an eyebrow at Lia.

"It's not your birthday," he said.

Lia executed a delicate shrug. "What's the fun of only turning twenty-one once?"

With a snort, the bouncer handed the IDs back to her. "This area is closing," he said. "For maintenance. If you're looking for poker, you'll want to hit the tables on the south side."

When we were a good ten feet away, Michael turned to Lia. "Well?"

"Whatever this area's closing for," she replied, "it's not maintenance."

I tried to process the fact that Lia had fake IDs for *both* of us, then caught sight of something about a hundred yards away.

"There," I told Michael. "By the sign that says *restrooms*."

A half-dozen security personnel were directing patrons away.

"Come on," Michael said, looping around to come at the blocked-off area from behind.

"Back at the restaurant, a man came to get the hotel owner," I said, processing the situation as we walked. "I'd bet a thousand dollars that he's in private security."

There was a beat of silence during which I thought Michael might not reply. "Security was grim, but calm," he said finally. "Shaw Senior, on the other hand, looked shaken, calculating, and like someone had just offered him a plate of rotting meat. In that order."

We came out on the other side of the slot machines. From this angle, it was clear that they were redirecting foot traffic long before people could reach the area surrounding the bathroom.

January first, I thought suddenly. January second. January third.

"Three bodies at three different casinos in three days." I didn't realize I'd spoken the words out loud until I felt Michael and Lia staring at me. "Today's day four."

As if to mark my words, security parted to let Mr. Shaw past. He wasn't alone. Even from a distance, I recognized the suit-clad pair with him.

Sterling and Briggs.

YOU

1/1.
1/2.
1/3.
1/4.

You strip off your clothes and step into the shower, letting the scalding spray hit you in the chest. The water isn't hot enough. It should hurt. It should burn.

It doesn't.

There was blood this time.

1/1.
1/2.
1/3.
1/4.

It's her fault. If she'd done what she was supposed to do, there would have been no need for blood.

1/1.
1/2.
1/3.
1/4.

It's her fault for seeing through you.

It's her fault for resisting.

You close your eyes and remember coming up behind her. You remember closing your hands around the chain. You remember her fighting.

You remember the moment when she stopped.

You remember the blood. And when you open your eyes and look at the angry red surface of your own skin, you know that water this hot should hurt. You should burn.

But you don't.

The smile spreads slowly over your face.

1/1.

1/2.

1/3.

1/4.

Nothing can hurt you. Soon, they'll see. Everyone will see. And you will be a god.

CHAPTER 15

I stayed up until two in the morning, sitting on the couch with my phone on the coffee table, waiting for Sterling and Briggs to call, waiting for them to tell us what they'd found in that bathroom.

Maintenance issues, the bouncer had said.

You didn't call the FBI for maintenance.

My mind went to the UNSUB. *You do everything to a timetable. You're not going to stop. You're going to kill one a day, every day, until we catch you.*

"Can't sleep?" a voice asked me quietly. I looked up to see Dean silhouetted in the doorway. He was wearing a threadbare white T-shirt, thin enough and tight enough that I could see the steady rise and fall of his chest underneath.

"Can't sleep," I echoed. *You can't, either,* I thought. A light sheen of sweat on Dean's face told me that he'd been doing sit-ups or push-ups or some other form of physical exercise punishing enough in repetition to quiet the whispers in his own memories.

The things his serial killer father had told him again and again.

"I keep thinking about the fact that there was probably a body in that bathroom," I said, sharing the source of my sleepless night to keep him from dwelling on his own. "I keep thinking that Briggs and Sterling are going to call."

Dean stepped out of the shadows. "We're allowed to work active cases." He moved toward me. "That doesn't mean they're obligated to use us."

Dean was telling himself that, as much as telling me. When I profiled, it was like stepping into someone else's shoes. When Dean profiled, he gave in to a pattern of thought his early experiences had ingrained in him, a darkness he kept under lock and key. Neither one of us was good at pulling back. Neither one of us was good at waiting.

"I just keep thinking about the first three victims," I said, my voice rough in my throat. "I keep thinking that if we hadn't gone to dinner, if we'd worked harder, if I'd . . ."

"If you'd done what?"

I could feel the heat of Dean's body beside me.

"*Something.*" The word tore its way out of my mouth.

Agent Sterling had told me once that I was the biggest liability on the team because I was the one who really felt things. Michael and Lia were experts in masking their emotions and forcing themselves not to care. Dean had lived through horrors at the age of twelve that had convinced him that he was a ticking time bomb, that if he really felt things, he might turn into a monster like his father. And though Sloane wore her heart on her sleeve, she would always see patterns first and people second.

But I felt the loss of every victim. I felt my own lack every time an UNSUB killed, because every time that I didn't stop it, every time I didn't see it coming, every time I got there too late—

"If you'd done something," Dean said softly, "your mother might still be alive."

I knew what kept Dean up at night, and he knew what I was thinking before I did. He knew why I felt the weight of blood on my hands every time we lost a victim because I wasn't smart or fast enough.

"I know it's stupid." My throat closed in around the words. "I know what happened to my mom wasn't my fault."

Dean picked up my hand, holding it in his, sheltering it in his.

"I *know* it, Dean, but I don't believe it. I won't ever believe it."

"Believe me," he said simply.

I laid my hand flat on his chest. His hand closed around mine, holding on to it and on to me.

"It wasn't your fault," Dean said.

I could feel him willing me to believe that. My fingers curled inward, his shirt bunching in my hand as I pulled him toward me. My mouth came down over his.

The harder I kissed him, the harder he kissed back. The

closer we were, the closer I needed him to be.

You can't sleep, and I can't sleep, and we're here, in the dead of night—

I caught his lip in my teeth.

Dean was gentle. Dean was sweet. Dean was self-contained and always in control—but tonight, he buried his hands in my hair and pulled my head back. He captured my mouth with his.

Believe me, he'd said.

I believed that he knew what it was like to be broken. I believed that I wasn't broken to him.

"You're still thinking about what you saw downstairs." Dean ran his fingers gently through my hair, my head on his chest. The threadbare fabric of his shirt was soft against my cheek, the victim of too many washes.

I stared at the ceiling. "I am." The sound of his heartbeat filled the silence. I wondered if he could hear the sound of mine. "Assuming the Majesty's 'maintenance issue' really was another body, that's four murders in four days."

What happens on day five? We both knew the answer to that question.

"Why the Fibonacci sequence?" I asked instead.

"Maybe I'm the type of person who needs things to add up," Dean said. "Each number in the Fibonacci sequence is the sum of the two previous numbers. Maybe what I'm doing is part of a pattern—each kill exceeding the last."

"Do you like it?" I wondered out loud. "What you're doing? Does it bring you joy?"

Dean's fingers stilled in my hair.

Does it bring you joy?

I realized, then, how that question would have sounded to Dean. I sat up and turned to face him.

"You're nothing like him, Dean."

I ran my hand along his jaw. Dean's greatest fear was that he had something of his father in him. Psychopathy. Sadism.

"I know that," he told me.

You know it, I thought, *but you don't believe it.*

"Believe me," I whispered.

He cupped a hand around my neck, and he nodded—just once, just a little. My chest tightened, but inside me, something else gave.

You're nothing like your father.

What happened to my mother wasn't my fault.

My heart in my throat, I stood. I went to get the drive with my mother's files on it. And then I walked back and pressed it into his hand.

"You open the files," I told him, my voice dropping to a lower pitch as it got caught in my throat. "You open them, because I can't."

CHAPTER 16

The skeleton is wrapped in a royal blue shawl.

I sat in front of the computer with Dean beside me, scrolling from one picture to the next, my finger feeling heavier with each click.

There's a long-dead flower pressed into the bones of her left hand.

The necklace is around her neck, the chain tangled in her rib cage.

Empty sockets stared back at me from a skull devoid of human flesh. I stared at the contours, waiting for a spark of recognition, but all I felt was bile rising in the back of my throat.

You removed the flesh from her bones. Forensic analysis suggested the removal had been done post mortem, but that was cold comfort. *You destroyed her. You eradicated her.*

Dean brought his hand to rest on the back of my neck. *I'm here.*

I swallowed back the wave of nausea that threatened to overwhelm me. Once. Twice. Three times—and then I scrolled on to the next picture. There were dozens of them: pictures of the dirt road on which she'd been buried. Pictures of the construction equipment that had uncovered a plain wooden casket.

You wrapped her bones in a blanket. You buried her with flowers. You gave her a coffin. . . .

I forced myself to breathe and switched from the pictures to reading the official report.

According to the medical examiner, there was a notch on the outside of one of her arm bones, a defensive wound where a knife had literally cut her to the bone. Laboratory results indicated that the bones had been treated with some kind of chemical prior to burial. That made the remains hard to date, but crime scene analysis put the time of burial within days of my mother's disappearance.

You killed her, then you erased her. No skin on the bones. No hair on her head. Nothing.

Dean's fingers kneaded gently at the muscles at the back of my neck. I turned my gaze from the computer screen to him. "What do you see?"

"Care." Dean paused. "Honor. Remorse."

It was on the tip of my tongue to say that I didn't want to know if the killer had felt remorse. I didn't care that she'd mattered enough to him that he hadn't just flung her body down in some hole.

You don't get to bury her. You don't get to honor *her, you sick son of a bitch.*

"Do you think she knew him?" My voice sounded distant to my own ears. "That's one explanation for what we're seeing, isn't it? He killed her in a frenzy and regretted it after the fact."

The blood-splattered dressing room in my memory spoke of domination and anger, the burial site, as Dean had said, of honor and care. Two sides of the same coin—and taken together, the suggestion was that this wasn't a random act of violence.

You took her with you. I'd always known that my mother's killer had removed her from the room. Whether she was alive or dead when he'd done so, the police hadn't been able to say, though they'd known from day one that she'd lost enough blood that her chances of survival were next to nonexistent. *You took her because you needed her with you. You couldn't leave her behind for someone else to bury.*

"He might have known her." Dean's voice brought me back to the present. I noticed that this once, with this case, he didn't use the word *I.* "Or he might have watched her from afar and convinced himself that the interaction went both ways. That she knew he was watching. That he knew her the way no one else ever would."

My mom had made her living as a "psychic." Like me,

she'd been good at reading people—good enough to convince them that she had a line to "the other side."

Did she do a reading for you? Did you go to one of her shows?

I racked my memory, but it was a blur of faces in the crowd. My mother had done a lot of readings. She'd done a lot of shows. We'd moved around often enough that there was no point in forming connections. No friends. No family.

No men in her life.

"Cassie, look at this." Dean drew my attention back to the screen. He zoomed in on one of the pictures of the coffin. There was a design etched into the surface of the wood: seven small circles, forming a heptagon around what appeared to be a plus sign.

Or, I thought, thinking about remorse and burial rituals and the monster who'd carved that symbol, *a cross.*

CHAPTER 17

Sleep came for me in the dead of night. I dreamt of my mother's eyes, wide-set and rimmed in liner that made them look almost impossibly large. I dreamt of the way she'd shooed me out of the dressing room that day.

I dreamt of the blood and woke the next morning to something sticky dripping onto my forehead, one drop of liquid at a time. My eyes flew open.

Lia stood over me, a straw in one hand and a can of soda in the other. She eased her finger off the top of the straw and let another drop of soda hit my forehead.

I wiped it off and sat up, careful not to wake Dean, who lay beside me on the couch, still dressed in his clothes from the night before.

Lia put the straw in her mouth and sucked the remaining liquid out before plopping it back down in her soda.

Smirking, she eyed the sleeping Dean, then raised an eyebrow at me. When that failed to engender a response, she made a quiet tsk-ing sound with her tongue. I stood up, which forced her to take a step back.

"It's not what you think," I told her, my voice muted.

Lia twirled the straw contemplatively in between her middle finger and her thumb. "So you two weren't up until the wee hours of the morning looking at the information on that drive Agent Sterling gave you?"

"How did you—"

Lia cut off the question by turning my still-open laptop to face me. "Fascinating reading."

I felt a sinking sensation deep in my gut. *Lia knows. She read the file, and she knows.*

I waited for Lia to say something else about the files on that computer. She didn't. Instead, she strolled toward the bedroom she'd claimed as her own. After a long moment, I followed, just as she'd intended me to. We ended up out on the balcony.

Lia closed the door behind us, then hopped up on the railing. We were forty stories off the ground, and she sat there, perfectly balanced, staring me down.

"What?" I said.

"If you mention a word of what I'm about to tell you to Dean, I will disavow any knowledge of this conversation." Lia's tone was casual, but I believed every word of it.

I braced myself for an attack.

"You make him happy." Lia narrowed her eyes slightly. "As happy as Dean can be," she modified. "We'd have to ask Sloane for the exact numbers, but I'm estimating a two hundred percent reduction in brooding since the two of you embarked on . . . this *thing* of yours."

Dean was Lia's family. If she had a choice between saving every other person on the face of the planet and saving Dean, she would choose Dean.

She hopped off the railing and gripped my arm lightly. "I like you." Her grip tightened, as if she found that admission mildly distasteful to say.

I like you, too, I almost said, but didn't want to chance that she'd see those words as a shade short of the truth.

"I missed you," I said instead—the same words I'd said to Sloane. "You, Michael, Sloane, Dean. This is home."

Lia looked at me for a moment. "Whatever," she said, pushing down any emotion my words had wrought with a graceful little shrug. "The point is that I don't hate you," she continued magnanimously, "so when I say that you need to put on your big-girl panties and woman up, I mean that in the nicest possible way."

"Excuse me?" I said, pulling my arm from her grasp.

"You have Mommy issues. I get it, Cassie. I get that this is hard, and I get that you have every right to deal with the whole body-showing-up thing in your own way and time. But fair or not, no one here has the emotional bandwidth to deal with the Continuing Woes of Cassie's Murdered Mother."

I felt like she'd slammed the heel of her hand into my

throat. But even as I weathered the blow, I knew Lia had said those words for a reason. *You're not cruel. Not like that.*

"Sloane slipped two pairs of chopsticks into her sleeve last night at the end of the meal." Lia's statement confirmed my gut instinct. "Not disposable ones. The nice ones they had on the table."

In addition to being our resident statistician, Sloane was also our resident klepto. The last time I'd seen her take something, she'd been stressed out about a confrontation with the FBI. For Sloane, sticky fingers were a sign that her brain was short-circuiting with emotions she couldn't control.

"Let's call that Exhibit A," Lia suggested. "Exhibit B would be Michael. Do you have any idea what kind of absolute mind-warp going home is for him?"

I thought of the conversation I'd overheard between Lia and Michael the day before. "Yes," I said, turning back to face Lia again. "I do."

There was a beat of silence as she processed the truth she heard in those words.

"You think you do," Lia said softly. "But you couldn't."

"I heard you guys talking yesterday," I admitted.

I expected Lia to have a knee-jerk reaction to those words, but she didn't. "Once upon a time," she said, her voice even as she turned to stare out at the Strip, "someone used to give me gifts for being a good girl, the way Michael gets 'gifts' from his father. You might think you understand what's going on in Michael's head right now, but you don't. You can't profile this, Cassie. You can't puzzle it out."

When she turned back to face me, the expression on her face was flippant. "What I'm saying here is that Michael is about one downward spiral–induced bad decision away from eloping with a showgirl, and Sloane has been acting weird— even for Sloane—since we got here. We are officially at issue capacity, Cassie. So I'm sorry, but you don't get to be effed up right now." She tapped the tip of my nose with her finger. "It's not your turn."

CHAPTER 18

If Lia had done to Michael what she'd just done to me, he would have lashed back at her. If she'd done it to Sloane, Sloane would have been crushed—but I wasn't. Sooner or later, my grief would catch up to me. But Lia had given me a reason to fight it for that much longer. She wasn't wrong about Michael. She wasn't wrong about Sloane. Someone had to hold them together. Someone had to hold *us* together.

And I needed that person to be me.

My gut said Lia knew that. *You could have been nicer about it,* I thought—but if she had been, she wouldn't be Lia.

I stayed out on the balcony for another ten minutes after Lia sauntered off. When I finally made my way back inside, Michael, Lia, and Dean were gathered around the kitchen table—and so was Agent Briggs. He was dressed in plainclothes, which told me the FBI was making an effort at keeping these visits on the down low. The fact that Briggs's version of plain clothes *still* made him look like a cop was perfectly reflective of his personality: hyperfocused, ambitious.

Briggs played to win.

"There's been another murder." Briggs had apparently been waiting for my arrival to make that announcement. None of the four of us made an attempt at looking surprised. "That makes the Apex, the Wonderland, the Desert Rose, and the Majesty, all in a matter of four days. We may be looking at someone who has a grudge against the casinos or the people who profit from them."

Dean looked toward a file Briggs held in his hand. "The latest victim?"

Briggs tossed the folder down onto the kitchen table. I flipped it open. Glassy blue eyes stared back at me, impossibly large in a heart-shaped face.

"Is that . . ." Michael started to say.

"Camille Holt," I finished, unable to pull my eyes away.

You like being underestimated, Camille, I thought dully, bringing my hand to touch the edge of the picture. *You're fascinated by the way the mind works, the way it breaks, the way people survive things no one should be able to survive.*

Her skin was tinged a ghastly gray; the whites of her wide-set eyes were marked by blots of red—capillaries that had burst as she'd struggled against her assailant.

You struggled. You fought. She was lying on her back on

a white marble floor, strawberry blond hair spread out in a halo around her head—but I knew in my gut that she'd fought, viciously, with an almost feral strength her assailant wouldn't have been expecting.

"Asphyxiation," Dean commented. "She was strangled."

"Murder weapon?" I asked. There was a difference between strangling someone with a wire and strangling them with a rope.

Briggs took out a snapshot of an evidence bag. Inside was a necklace—the thick metal chain Camille had worn looped twice around her neck the night before.

In my mind, I could see her, sitting at the bar, one leg dangling off the stool. I could see her turning toward us and walking toward the exit.

I could see Aaron Shaw watching her go.

"You'll want to talk to the casino owner's son." Michael's thoughts were perfectly in line with my own. "Aaron Shaw. His interest in Ms. Holt wasn't professional."

"What did you see?" Briggs asked.

Michael shrugged. "Attraction. Affection. A sharp edge of tension."

What kind of tension? I didn't get the chance to follow up before Sloane popped into the kitchen and went to pour herself some coffee. Briggs eyed her warily. Sloane's tendency toward high-speed babbling when caffeinated was a thing of legend.

"I called you last night," Sloane told him reproachfully. "I called and called, and you didn't answer. Ergo, I get coffee, and you don't get to complain."

I thought about the chopsticks Sloane had stolen the night before. *You needed Briggs to pick up your call. You needed to be recognized. You needed to be heard.*

"There was another murder," Briggs told Sloane.

"I know." Sloane stared at the coffee in her hands. "Two. Three. Three. Three."

"What did you say?" Briggs asked sharply.

"The number on the corpse. It's 2333." Sloane finally came to sit at the table with the rest of us. "Isn't it?"

Briggs pulled a new picture out of the file. Camille's wrist: 2333 had been carved into it. Literally. The bloody numbers were slightly jagged. *From a henna tattoo to this.* The numbers had always been a message—but this? This was violent. Personal.

"Was she alive when the UNSUB did this?" I asked.

Briggs shook his head. "Postmortem. There was a compact in the victim's purse. We believe the UNSUB broke it and used one of the shards to carve the numbers in her wrist."

I shifted from Camille's perspective to her attacker's. *You're a planner. If this was what you'd intended all along, you would have brought something with you to do the job.*

That left me with two questions: first, what *had* the plan been, and second, why had the UNSUB deviated from it?

What went wrong? I asked the killer silently. *Did she thwart your plan somehow? Was she harder to manipulate than the others?* I thought about the fact that Camille had been present at the crime scenes for two of the victims. *Did you know her?*

"This is personal." Dean's thoughts were exactly in line with my own. "The other targets might have been selected for convenience. But not this one."

"That was Agent Sterling's take as well," Briggs said. He turned back to Sloane. "You decoded the numbers?"

Sloane grabbed a pen out of Agent Briggs's pocket, flipped the folder closed, and started scrawling numbers on the outside of the folder, talking as she wrote. "The Fibonacci sequence is a series of integers where each number is derived by adding the two that come before it. Most people believe it was discovered by Fibonacci, but the earliest appearances of the sequence are in Sanskrit writings that predate Fibonacci by hundreds of years."

Sloane set the pen down. There were fifteen numbers on the page:

0 1 1 2 3 5 8 13 21 34 55 89 144 233 377

"I didn't see it at first," she continued. "The pattern picks up mid-integer."

"Pretend for a moment," Lia told her, "that we're all very, very slow."

"I'm not very good at pretending," Sloane told her seriously. "But I think I can do that."

Michael choked back a snort.

Sloane picked the pen back up and put it down under

the number thirteen. "It starts here," she said, underlining four numbers, then inserting a slash before repeating the process.

0 1 1 2 3 5 8 <u>13 21 3/4 55 8/9 144/ 233</u> 377

2333. The image of Camille's wrist rose to the surface of my mind, like a drowned man bobbing to the surface of a lake. *You break the glass. You press the jagged edge to her flesh, carving in the numbers.*

"Why this sequence?" I said. "And why make it this hard to see? Why not start at the beginning, with 0112?"

"Because," Dean said slowly, "this knowledge has to be earned."

Briggs glanced at us, one after the other. "Agent Sterling and I will be spending the afternoon talking to potential witnesses. If you have any names to add to that list—besides Aaron Shaw—now would be the time to speak up."

At the mention of Aaron's name, Sloane's hands curved tightly around her cup of coffee. Michael cocked his head to the side and stared at her. An instant later, he caught me watching him and raised an eyebrow at me in an unspoken challenge.

You know something's up with Sloane, I thought, *and you know that I know what it is.*

"I assume you've gathered that Camille was out with Tory Howard last night?" Dean asked Briggs.

Briggs gave a brief nod. "We talked with Tory briefly yesterday. We'll go back for seconds today, then work our way through the rest of our list."

"I don't suppose you'd like to take me with you when you go to talk to this fine collection of potentially homicidal individuals?" Lia batted her eyes at Agent Briggs.

Briggs withdrew four earpieces from his pocket and laid them down on the table. They were joined, a moment later, by a tablet from his briefcase. "Video and audio feeds," he told us. "Agent Sterling and I are wired. Within a four-mile radius, you'll see what we see. You'll hear what we hear. If you pick up on something you think we might have missed, you can text or call. Otherwise, I want you studying up on our interrogation techniques."

Lia, Michael, Dean, and I reached for earpieces in unison.

Sloane turned to Briggs. "What about me?" she asked quietly.

There were four earpieces and five of us.

"Four casinos in four days," Briggs said. "I need you"—he put enough emphasis on those words to tell me he'd picked up on the vulnerability in Sloane's tone—"to figure out where this killer is going to strike next."

YOU

The roulette wheel spins. The players watch with bated breath. You watch the players. Like ants in an ant farm, they're predictable.

Some bet on black.

Some bet on red.

Some are hesitant. Some believe chance favors the bold.

You could tell them the exact odds of winning. You could tell them that chance favors no man. Red or black, it doesn't matter.

The house always wins.

You expel a breath, long and slow. Let them have their fun. Let them believe that Lady Luck might smile down on them. Let them keep their games of chance.

Your game—the one they don't even know they're playing—is a game of skill.

1/1.

1/2.

1/3.

1/4.

You know what comes next. You know the order. You know the rules. This is bigger than ants in an ant farm could ever imagine.

No one can stop you.

You are Death.

You are the house. And the house always wins.

CHAPTER 19

Lia perched on the back of the couch, one leg stretched out along its length, the other dangling over the side. Dean sat on the sofa in front of her, his forearms resting on his knees, staring at the tablet we'd propped up on the coffee table.

"Anything yet?" I asked, taking a seat beside him.

Dean shook his head.

"There." Lia's posture never changed, but her eyes lit up. On the tablet, a shot of a hand dominated the screen as Briggs reoriented the camera masquerading as a pen in his suit pocket.

"Michael—" I started to call out.

Michael appeared before I could say anything else. "Let me guess," he said, producing a flask and taking a swig. "Showtime."

My eyes lingered on the flask.

Dean put one hand on my knee. If Lia and I had noticed

Michael skating around the edges of the dark place, Dean almost certainly had as well. He'd known Michael for longer than I had, and he was telling me not to press the issue.

Without a word, I slipped in the earpiece Agent Briggs had given me and turned my attention back to the video feed.

On the screen, we saw what Agent Briggs saw—a stage with massive columns on either side. As he got closer to the stage, I recognized the person standing in front of it, examining the lighting.

Tory Howard was wearing a black tank and jeans, her hair pulled into a ponytail that was neither high nor low. *No muss. No fuss.* She either didn't care about the image she projected or she went out of her way to project an image centered on that ideal.

When she saw Briggs, she wiped her hands on the front of her jeans and met him in the middle aisle. "Agents," she said. "Can I help you with something?"

Agents, plural, I thought. That meant Sterling was there, too, just out of the frame.

"We have just a few more questions about last night for you." Briggs seemed to be taking lead on this one—which meant that Sterling had chosen to sit back and watch. Given that she was the profiler, that didn't surprise me. Sterling would want to get Tory's measure before she decided exactly which tack to take.

"I already told you," Tory replied to Briggs, a slight edge in her voice, "Camille and I went for drinks. We played a couple of hands of poker, and I called it an early night. Camille was looking for a party. I wasn't. I have a show today, and I like to be on my game."

"I understand your shows have been selling out," Agent Briggs said.

"Say what you mean, Agent." Tory leveled a look at him—and it was almost like she was aiming that same, dry look at us. "My show has been selling out ever since the Wonderland closed theirs down."

Ever since victim number two literally went up in flames, I corrected silently.

"You seem defensive." Agent Sterling was the one who said those words. I knew her well enough to know that she'd chosen that moment to speak up—and that observation—for a reason.

"This is the second time you've interviewed me in the past twelve hours," Tory retorted. "You came to my place of business. I hadn't known Camille for long, but I liked her. So, yes, when you come here, purportedly following up on what I told you last night, but also dropping oblique hints about my dead rival, I get a little defensive."

"Not just defensive," Michael opined. He didn't volunteer whatever else it was he saw in her face.

"I didn't hurt Camille," Tory said plainly. "And I wouldn't have wasted even one of my breaths on Sylvester Wilde. I'm sorry she's dead. I'm not sorry he is. Are we done here?"

Lia let out a low whistle. "She's good."

"At lying?" I asked, wondering which portion of the statement Tory had just made was untrue.

"She hasn't lied yet," Lia said. "But she will. The best liars start by convincing you either that they're straight shooters or that they can't lie. She's going with the former. And like I said, she's very, very good."

Tory was a magician. It was easy enough to believe that she was setting the stage so that when the misdirect came, Briggs and Sterling wouldn't see it coming.

Agent Sterling changed tactics. "Can you think of anyone who would want to hurt Camille? Anyone who might have a grudge against her?"

A flicker of sorrow crossed Tory's face. She pushed back against it. *No muss. No fuss.* "Camille was the only female likely to advance to the final round in a high-stakes competition dominated by egos and men. She was confident and manipulative, and she liked winning."

You identify with her, I realized as Tory spoke.

"Camille was also beautiful, borderline famous, and had no problems whatsoever telling people no," Tory continued unflinchingly. "There were probably a lot of people who wanted to hurt her."

Her tone was so matter-of-fact that I knew: *Someone—maybe multiple someones—hurt you.* Tory knew what it was like to be seen as weak, and she knew what it was like to be overpowered. I could see why Camille had chosen to spend time with her. If she'd been fictional, Tory Howard

106

was exactly the kind of character Camille Holt would have chosen to play.

"Did Camille ever say anything to you about Aaron Shaw?" Agent Briggs switched up the line of questioning again.

"Interesting," Michael murmured, leaning closer to the screen—and closer to Tory.

"Camille and I met at a New Year's party," Tory replied. "We hit it off. We went out for drinks a couple of times. I wasn't exactly her confidante."

I glanced back at Lia. *She's pelting them with truth again,* I thought.

"One more question," Agent Sterling said. "You and Camille went to the Majesty last night."

"The new sushi restaurant," Tory supplied. *More truth, easily verifiable.*

"Who picked the restaurant?" Sterling asked.

Tory shrugged. "She did."

Behind me, Lia swung her legs off the couch and stood. "And there we have it," she told us. "That's the lie."

CHAPTER 20

"I'll text Sterling." Dean reached for his phone. There was a good chance Sterling and Briggs might have picked up on the lie, but they'd want confirmation from Lia. "Anything to add?" Dean asked as he began typing.

By some miracle, Michael managed to stifle his long-held tendency to answer everything Dean said with a smart-mouthed barb. "Two things," Michael said. "First, defensiveness isn't an emotion. It's a combination of emotions that plays out in different ways in different people at different times. In this case, we've got a tantalizing cocktail of anger and self-presentation and guilt."

Tory feels guilty. I tried to reconcile that with what I knew about her. She struck me as pragmatic. Like Camille, she'd risen to the top of a male-dominated field. To have her own show in Vegas, she'd have to be ambitious.

She didn't strike me as a person who would let herself feel bad about anything for long.

"And the second thing?" Dean asked.

"Her reaction to Aaron Shaw." I beat Michael to the punch line.

Michael inclined his head slightly. "Temporary freezing of the facial muscles, brows fighting the urge to draw together, lips just barely stretching themselves back." He shifted his flask rhythmically from one hand to the other and back again, then clarified. "Fear."

What are you scared of, Tory? Why did you skirt the question when Briggs and Sterling asked you if Camille had said anything about Aaron Shaw?

My mind went to what I knew about Sloane's half brother. He'd grown up in a family where wealth and power were givens. I was betting he'd been raised to follow in his father's footsteps. It wouldn't be hard for someone like that to get used to blurring moral lines. But there had also been something gentle about the way he'd interacted with Sloane, and that something gave me pause.

Is it you Tory's scared of? I thought, picturing Aaron in my mind. *Or is it your father?*

Dean sent the text. A moment later, we heard Agent Sterling excuse herself from the interrogation. Dean got a text back less than a minute later. "Anything else?" he read out loud. "Cassie?"

The fact that Agent Sterling had directed that question to me told me that she was looking for something specific—a confirmation of her own hunch, or some aspect of Tory's personality that I would be more likely to pick up on than Dean.

"I'm not sure," I said quietly, "but we might be looking at a history of assault. Verbal, physical, sexual—or maybe just the ongoing threat thereof."

Saying those words felt like violating a confidence. Michael must have heard that in my voice, because he leaned over Dean and passed me the flask. I raised an eyebrow at him. He shrugged.

"I can't help you." The increase in volume drew my attention back to the tablet. Clearly, Tory had reached a breaking point. "If you have any more questions, you can address them to my attorney."

"Everything okay here?" Sterling reentered the conversation, stepping into the frame.

Briggs cleared his throat. "I was just asking Ms. Howard if anyone could verify her whereabouts after she parted ways with Ms. Holt." *And she asked for her attorney.* Briggs let the second half of that statement go unsaid.

She doesn't trust people in power, I told him silently. *And she certainly doesn't trust you.*

"I can." A male voice carried over the microphone several seconds before its owner appeared on-screen, stepping directly between the FBI agents and Tory. *Male. Young. Early twenties at most.* My brain started cataloging his demographics before my mind recognized his face.

"Beau Donovan," Dean said. "One of our persons of interest. The twenty-one-year-old dishwasher who won the amateur spot at the poker tournament."

"Tory was with me," Beau was saying on-screen. "Last night, after she and Camille parted ways, Tory was with me."

"Funny story," Lia mock-whispered. "She totally wasn't."

You're lying. That alone was enough for Beau to command my full attention. He was about the same height as Tory, but he stood slightly in front of her. *Protective.*

"You and Beau were together last night?" Agent Briggs pressed Tory.

"That's right," Tory said, staring down the agents. "We were."

"She really *is* good," Lia commented. "Even I might not have pegged that one for a lie."

"And how do you two know each other?" Sterling asked.

Beau shrugged, looking for a moment like the kid slumped in the back of the classroom, barely paying attention to what was said at the front. "She's my sister."

There was a beat of silence.

"Your sister," Agent Sterling repeated.

"Foster sister." Tory was the one who supplied that information. She was older than Beau by two years, maybe three. Something told me the protectiveness ran both ways.

"You still need help with fixing the lights?" Beau asked Tory, as if the FBI wasn't even standing in the room. "Or what?"

"Mr. Donovan," Agent Sterling said, forcing his attention back to her, "would you mind if we asked you a few questions?"

"Knock yourself out."

111

Tory isn't the only one who's not overly fond of people with power.

"I understand you've advanced to the finals of the Vegas multi-casino poker tournament," Agent Sterling said. "You're getting quite a bit of attention."

"Everyone likes an underdog story." Beau shrugged again. "I'm thinking of selling the rights to Hollywood," he deadpanned. "It'll be one of those really inspirational stories."

"Beau," Tory said, a warning note creeping into her voice. "Just answer the questions."

Interesting. She didn't want him to aggravate the authorities. For a split second, I felt like I was watching some alternate-universe version of Lia and Dean, where she was the older one and he had Michael's mouth.

"Fine," Beau told Tory, then he turned back to Agent Sterling. "What do you want to know?"

"How long have you been playing poker?"

"A while."

"You must be good at it."

"Better than some."

"What's your secret?"

"Most people are crappy liars." Beau let that sink in. "And for a high school dropout, I'm pretty good at math."

I saw Sterling filing those words away for future reference, and I did the same.

Agent Briggs took over the questioning. "Were you at the New Year's Eve party on the roof of the Apex?"

"Yeah," Beau said. "Thought I'd see how the other half lives."

"Did you know Camille Holt?" Agent Sterling asked.

"I did. She was a nice girl," Beau replied.

"Lie," Lia sing-songed.

"Well," Beau amended, as if he'd heard Lia, "Camille was nice to me. We were the outsiders in the inner circle. She was a chick. I'm a dishwasher." He managed a small, crooked smile. "A girl like that? She wouldn't normally give a guy like me two seconds. But once I joined the tournament, she went out of her way to make me feel welcome."

"She was trying to figure you out."

I recognized Agent Sterling's statement for what it was—an attempt to see how Beau dealt with rejection. *Tell him Camille was only nice to him because she was manipulating him, see what happens.*

Beau shrugged. "Of course she was."

"A swing and a miss," Michael said under his breath. In other words: Sterling's words hadn't gotten a rise out of her target. At all.

"Camille was competitive," Beau said. "I respected that. Besides, she decided pretty early on that I wasn't the one she needed to worry about."

Agent Sterling cocked her head to the side. "And who *was* Camille worried about?"

Beau and Tory both answered the question, and they both said the exact same thing. "Thomas Wesley."

CHAPTER 21

While Briggs and Sterling went to track down Thomas Wesley, the rest of us were left to entertain ourselves. Michael took out his earpiece and tossed it onto the carpet with no more care than one might use to throw away a crumpled napkin. "Call me when the show's back on," he said, reclaiming his flask and heading for his room. Lia shot me a look that said, *I told you we were at issue capacity. See?*

Yes, I thought, watching Michael go. *I do.*

"I'll go check on Sloane," I said. Michael wouldn't want my concern. Sloane, at least, might be glad for the company.

When I got to our room, I was greeted by the sound of upbeat techno music. I opened the door, half expecting Sloane to be wearing goggles and on the verge of blowing something up. *It helps me think,* Sloane had explained to me once, like explosives were an alternative form of meditation.

Luckily, however, in the absence of her basement lab, she'd taken a different—and less explosive—tack. She was lying upside down on the bed, the upper half of her body hanging over the end. Blueprints, schematics, and hand-drawn maps lay three-deep, covering the floor around her.

"Thirteen hours." Sloane yelled the words over the music, still hanging upside down. I went to turn the music down, and she continued, her voice softer, more vulnerable. "If our UNSUB is killing one a day, we have a maximum of thirteen hours until he kills again."

Briggs had told Sloane that he needed her to figure out where the UNSUB would strike next. She had clearly taken that request to heart. *You want to be needed. You want to be useful. You want to matter, even a little.*

I tiptoed around the papers and lay down on the bed next to Sloane. Hanging upside down, side-by-side, we turned to look at each other.

"You can do this," I told her. "And even if you can't, we'll love you just the same."

There was a beat of silence.

"She was wearing a dress," Sloane whispered after a moment. "The little girl." She shook her head slightly, then picked up a pen and began marking off distances on one of her maps, as easily as if the whole thing were right-side up.

My chest tightened. The grip Sloane had on the pen told me that even sinking herself into a project like this one wasn't enough to burn from her mind the memory of the doting father and his little girl.

"She was wearing a white dress." Sloane's voice was very small. "It was clean. Did you notice?"

"No," I said softly.

"Children stain white clothes within an hour of putting them on at least seventy-four percent of the time," Sloane rattled off. "But not her. She didn't ruin it."

The way Sloane said the word *ruin* told me that she wasn't just talking about *children* staining their clothing. She was talking about herself. And clothing was just the tip of the iceberg.

"Sloane—"

"He brought her to the bar to get a cherry." Her hand stilled, and she turned to look at me again. "He brought me cherries," she said. "Just once."

Sloane could have told me the number of cherries, the exact day and time, the number of hours that had passed since—I could *see* that information, repeating itself over and over again in her head.

"Does it help if I hate him for you?" I asked. *Him.* As in her father.

"Should it?" Sloane asked, wrinkling her forehead and sitting up. "I don't hate him. I think that maybe, someday, when I'm older, he could not-hate me."

When you're older—and better and normal and good, my brain filled in. Sloane had told me once that she said and did the wrong thing over eighty-four percent of the time. The fact that her biological father had played a role in teaching her that lesson—the fact that she still hoped that he might develop even the barest hint of affection for her someday, if only she could do things right—physically hurt me.

I sat up and latched my arms around her. Sloane leaned into the hug and rested her head on my shoulder for a few seconds. "Don't tell anyone," she said. "About the cherries."

"I won't."

She waited a moment longer, then pulled back. "Al Capone once donated a pair of cherry trees to a hospital as thanks for treating his syphilis." With those memorable words, Sloane lay back down, hanging upside down off the end of the bed and staring out at the maps and schematics she'd collected. "If you don't leave," she warned me, "there's a high probability that I'm going to tell you some statistics about syphilis."

I rolled off the bed. "So noted."

Back in the living room, Michael had apparently seen fit to return. For reasons I could not begin to fathom, he and Lia were arm wrestling.

"What—" I started to say, but before I could finish, Dean spoke up.

"Show's back on," he said.

Lia took advantage of Michael's distraction and slammed his hand down. "I win!" Before Michael could complain, she resumed her spot on the back of the couch. I sat next to Dean. Michael stared at us for a second or two, then picked his earpiece up off the floor and went to stand behind Lia.

On-screen, I saw a hand—probably Briggs's—reach out and knock on a hotel room door. I fit my earpiece back into my ear just in time to hear Thomas Wesley's assistant answer the door.

"May I help you?"

"Agents Sterling and Briggs," I heard Sterling say from off-screen. "FBI. We'd like a word with Mr. Wesley."

"I'm afraid Mr. Wesley isn't available at the moment," the assistant said.

The look on Lia's face called BS on that one.

"I would be happy to pass along a message or to put you in touch with Mr. Wesley's legal counsel."

"If we could just have a few minutes of Mr. Wesley's time—" Briggs tried again.

"I'm afraid that's impossible." The assistant smiled daggers at Briggs.

"It's fine, James," a voice called. A second later, Thomas Wesley appeared on-screen. His salt-and-pepper hair was slightly mussed. He was wearing a teal silk robe and very little else. "Agent Sterling. Agent Briggs." Wesley greeted them each with a nod, like a monarch graciously acknowledging his subjects. "What can I do for you?"

"We have just a few questions," Agent Sterling said, "concerning your relationship with Camille Holt."

"Of course."

"Mr. Wesley," the assistant—James—said, his voice tinged with displeasure. "You are under no obligation to—"

"Answer any questions I do not want to answer," Wesley finished. "I know. It just so happens I want to answer the agents' questions. And," he said, turning his attention back toward the screen, "I'm a man who's used to doing what he wants."

I had the oddest sensation, then, that he was addressing those words less to Agent Briggs than to the camera.

"You switched hotels," Agent Briggs said, dragging the man's gaze up. "Why?"

A benign question whose sole purpose was to keep the man from looking too closely at the pen in Agent Briggs's pocket.

"Bad juju at the other one," Wesley replied, "what with that whole murder business." His tone sounded flippant, but—

Michael filled in the blanks. "He's more disturbed than he wants to let on."

"You do realize," Agent Sterling replied to Wesley, "that there was—"

"Also a murder here at the Desert Rose?" Wesley said glibly. He shrugged. "Four bodies in four days at four different casinos. Given the choice between staying at a *fifth* casino on day five and staying at one of the four, I decided I liked my odds better at the latter."

You always play the odds, I thought, studying Wesley. *And based on your background in business, you usually win.*

"Can we come in?" Sterling was the one who asked that

question. She must have been playing the odds herself—specifically, that Wesley, a self-professed womanizer, was less likely to turn down a request from a female agent.

"Mr. Wesley actually has several commitments this morning," the assistant started to say.

"James, go organize the liquor cabinet," Wesley ordered lazily. "Alphabetically this time."

With one last dark look at the agents, Wesley's assistant did as he was bidden. Wesley opened the door to his suite wider and gestured. "Please," he said. "Do come in. I have an *excellent* view of the pool."

Three seconds later, Briggs and Sterling were inside the suite. I heard the door shut behind them. And then the feed went black.

CHAPTER 22

The sound of static was deafening in my ear. I jerked out my earpiece. The others did the same.

"What the . . ." When it came to swearing, Lia was both creative and verbally precise. She hit several buttons on the tablet.

Nothing.

Dean stood. "They're either out of range or something's blocking the signal."

Given that Thomas Wesley's most recent start-up had specialized in *security* tech, I was betting on the latter. I tried to text Sterling, but the message came back as undeliverable.

"Cell signal is blocked, too," I reported.

"You know," Michael said, a spark in his eye, "I'm feeling like a bit of a stroll. Possibly in the direction of the Desert Rose?"

"No," Dean said flatly. "Sterling and Briggs can handle Thomas Wesley, with or without us."

Lia twirled her ponytail contemplatively around her index finger. "Judd went to grab food," she commented. "And I did hear that the Desert Rose has the world's largest indoor swimming pool."

"Lia," Dean gritted out. "We're staying here."

"Of course we are," Lia told him, patting his shoulder. "And I am in no way planning to go no matter what you say, because I always do what I'm told. Goodness knows I have no real attachment to making my own decisions," she gushed. "Especially when the person issuing orders is you!"

We went to the pool.

Sloane chose to stay in the suite. Given how much she hated being left out, I took that to mean that she hated the idea of not delivering the answer Briggs had asked for more.

"Not bad," Lia announced, lying back on a lounge chair and casting her face toward the artificial sky. The Desert Rose's massive indoor swimming complex was bustling, both with families and with those who'd cordoned themselves off in the adults-only area—despite the fact that it wasn't even noon.

Dean gave Lia a much-abused look, but said nothing as he scanned the area for threats. I claimed the lounge chair next to Lia's. Thomas Wesley had said that his suite had a lovely view of the pool. I eyed the balconies with pool access, and my hand went to the earpiece hidden beneath my hair. I'd turned the volume down so that the static wasn't so deafening—but static was still the only thing I got.

"You're frustrated."

I looked up to see Michael staring at me.

He claimed the chair on the other side of Lia. His hands went to the bottom of his shirt, like he was about to take it off. Then he aborted the motion, running one hand through his hair and allowing the other to dangle over the side of the chair. He looked perfectly at ease, perfectly relaxed.

It took everything I had not to picture the bruises on his stomach and chest.

"Don't look at me like that," Michael said quietly. "Not you, Cassie."

I wondered what, exactly, he'd seen on my face. Was it my eyes or my lips or the tension in my neck that gave me away?

He knows that I know why he can't take his shirt off.

"Like what?" I said, forcing myself to lean back and close my eyes. Michael was an expert at pretending that things—and people—didn't matter. I wasn't quite so adept, but I wasn't going to force him to talk about this with me.

We don't talk about much of anything anymore.

Michael cleared his throat. "Well, this could get interesting."

I cracked my eyes open. Michael nodded toward the adults-only area of the pool. *Daniel de la Cruz. The professor. Person of interest number two.* I recognized the man a second before Lia did. After a moment's consideration, she rolled off her lounge chair, tossing her long ponytail over her shoulder.

As Lia strolled over and ducked under the rope and Dean grumbled something that sounded suspiciously like *bad idea* under his breath, I went back over what I knew about

Daniel de la Cruz. *Intense. Perfectionist.* And yet, there he was, holding a drink well before noon.

You're not drinking it, I realized after watching de la Cruz for a moment. This was a man who knew exactly how he was perceived—and exactly how to manipulate that perception. He made eye contact with a nearby woman.

She smiled.

To you, everything is an algorithm. Everything can be predicted. I couldn't pinpoint what precisely gave me that impression—the fit of his swimsuit? The attentiveness behind his eyes? *You have a PhD in mathematics. What kind of professor plays professional poker on the side?*

Before I could reason my way to any answers, Lia bumped into de la Cruz. He caught his drink an instant before he spilled it on her. *Good reflexes.*

Beside me, I could practically *hear* Dean gritting his teeth.

"She'll be fine," I murmured, even as I thought about our UNSUB, the Fibonacci sequence, the care with which the first two murders had been planned.

"She's going to be fine," Dean muttered. "*I'm* going to have a heart attack."

"What did I say, Jonathan?" A sharp voice cut into my thoughts. To my left, a man with perfect hair and a face riddled with barely masked displeasure stalked over to a little boy of maybe seven or eight. Whatever the boy said to him in response, the man didn't like it. He took another step toward the child.

Beside me, Michael's entire body tensed. A moment later, he was so relaxed that I wondered if I'd imagined it. He climbed lazily to his feet, brushing a speck of invisible dust from his shirt as he began weaving his way closer to the man and the boy.

"Dean," I said urgently.

Dean was already on his feet.

"I'll keep an eye on Lia," I told him. "Go."

Michael settled at a table adjacent to the boy and his father. He smiled pleasantly, staring out at the pool, but I knew better than to think the positioning was coincidental. Michael had learned to read emotions as a defense mechanism against his seemingly perfect father's volatile moods. Anger was the emotion that most set him on edge, but the kind of anger that hid behind masks, in the middle of seemingly perfect little families?

That wasn't just a trigger. It was a ticking bomb.

Dean took a seat at the table Michael had claimed. Michael propped his feet up on a spare chair, like he hadn't a care in the world.

True to my promise to Dean, I forced my attention back to Lia and the professor.

"You seem to be quite knowledgeable about the state of our investigation."

It took me a moment to realize that the audio had clicked back on in my earpiece. Briggs's voice was clear, but the reply was muffled. Angling my head down and letting my hair fall into my face, I adjusted the volume.

"—my business to know. The first girl died at my party, and Camille was a friend, of sorts. For a man in my position, it pays to keep track of one's friends."

I scanned the surrounding balconies. There, toward the top of the dome, I could make out three figures. Two of them were wearing suits. *Sterling and Briggs.*

I wasn't the only one who'd noticed them. Across the pool, the professor had locked eyes on Wesley and the agents as well. *You notice things, Professor. You pride yourself on it.*

I caught Lia's attention and held her gaze for a second. She said something to de la Cruz, then headed back toward me. In a fluid, choreographed motion, she pulled the ponytail holder from her hair, letting her jet-black tresses cascade down her back. As she took a seat beside me, she fit her own earpiece back into place.

"I don't suppose you could be persuaded to part with the source of your knowledge on Camille's case?" Agent Sterling asked. It was odd to be hearing her voice when I could only make out her silhouette on the balcony.

"Most likely not," Wesley replied smoothly. "However, James would be happy to furnish you with my alibis for each of the past four evenings."

Lia's expression eloquently communicated her skepticism that Assistant James would be at all *happy* to assist the FBI in any way. I turned to try to get the boys' attention, but neither Michael nor Dean was at the table where the two of them had been sitting a moment before.

Neither, I realized upon looking, were the young boy and his father.

As I scanned the crowd, Agent Sterling's voice provided the sound track. "You're an intelligent man," she was telling Wesley, playing to his ego. "What do you think happened to Camille Holt?"

I finally saw Michael, leaning against the side of a camel-themed snack bar. A few feet away, the young boy and his father reached the front of the line. I looked for Dean and found him caught behind a massive crowd of forty-something women, trying to make his way through them to Michael.

"What do I think?" Wesley was saying over the audio feed. "I think that were I in your shoes, I'd be particularly interested in Tory Howard's rather unique skill set."

A few feet away from Michael, the young boy reached up for an ice-cream cone. He smiled up at his father. His father smiled back.

I breathed an internal sigh of relief. Dean finally made his way through the crowd and began to close in on Michael.

At that instant, two things happened. On the audio feed, Agent Briggs asked Thomas Wesley to clarify his comment about Tory's skill set, and near the snack bar, the little boy stumbled and the ice cream fell from his cone and onto the ground.

The world fell into slow motion for me as the boy froze. The father made a grab for his son, his hand locking around the boy's arm as he jerked him roughly to the side.

Michael exploded forward. One second, he was a foot or two away from Dean, and the next, he was ripping the father's hand away from his son and throwing his body into a punch aimed at the man's face.

"I'm surprised you don't know." Wesley's voice broke through my horror. "Tory Howard is a decent magician, but her real talent is hypnosis."

CHAPTER 23

The man Michael attacked punched back. Michael went down. He didn't stay down.

I leapt forward, but Lia was in front of me in a heartbeat. "Dean's got this."

I tried to step around her.

"Back off, Cassie," Lia told me, her voice low, her face less than an inch from mine. "The last thing either of them needs is you caught in the middle of a brawl." She wove an arm through mine. To outward appearances, we looked like the best of friends, but her grip was iron-tight. "Besides," she added grimly, "someone has to do damage control."

That was when I realized that the audio feed had cut away again. The balcony where Sterling, Briggs, and Thomas Wesley had been standing moments before was empty.

Dean had to physically restrain Michael, pulling our fellow Natural back roughly against his own body. Security was called. Michael barely managed to avoid an arrest.

To say that our supervisors weren't pleased that we'd taken an unauthorized field trip would have been an understatement. To say that they were even *less* pleased with Michael's brush with the law would have been the understatement of the century.

Judd met us in the lobby of the Majesty. I could tell from the way he was standing, his feet spread slightly wider than usual, his arms crossed over his chest, that he'd gotten a call from Sterling and Briggs.

Beside me, Michael winced. Not because of his swollen lip or the cut over his quickly blackening eye, but because he could tell, from the slight hints of strain in Judd's face, *exactly* how much trouble we were in.

When we reached him, Judd turned without a word and started stalking toward the elevator. We followed on his heels. He didn't say a word until the elevator doors had closed.

"You're lucky that doesn't need stitches," Judd told Michael. I gathered from his tone that we were all somewhat less than lucky to be stuck on an elevator with a marine sniper who knew how to kill a grown man using nothing but his little finger.

"The audio feeds went out while Briggs and Sterling were questioning Thomas Wesley," Lia said. "We were just trying to stay in range."

I opened my mouth to confirm what Lia had said, but Judd stopped me. "Don't," he told me. "We're in Vegas. You're teenagers stuck in a hotel suite. If I were a betting man, I'd give myself excellent odds on guessing how this went down."

"If you were a betting man," Michael said lazily, "you'd be downstairs at the casino."

Judd reached out and pulled the emergency stop button. The elevator jerked to a halt. He turned and leveled a very calm stare at Michael, never saying a word.

Seconds ticked by, verging on a minute.

"Sorry." Michael addressed the apology more to the ceiling tiles than to Judd. "Sometimes, I just can't help myself."

I wondered if Michael was apologizing for the disrespect or for what he'd done at the pool.

"What do you think is going to happen," Judd said softly, "when the man you hit and his family go home tonight?"

The question sucked all of the oxygen out of the air. Judd pushed the stop button back in and the elevator jolted back into motion. I couldn't bring myself to look at Michael, because there was nothing—*nothing*—Judd could have said to devastate him more.

Eventually, the elevator doors opened. Judd and I were the last ones off. I couldn't help giving him a look as I stepped into the hall.

"May eighth," Judd said quietly. "Six years, this May." He gave me just enough time to process that date—process what it had to refer to—before he continued. "If I have to be a real bastard to keep from burying another kid, well then, Cassie, I can be a real bastard."

The muscles in my throat tightened. Judd walked past

me, past the others, and got to the door to our suite first. He opened it, then froze.

My heart pounding in my ears, I hurried to catch up. *What would it take to catch a battle-hardened marine completely off guard?* In the second or two before I saw for myself, my mind put forth the worst possible answer.

Sloane.

I made it to the entryway. Lia, Michael, and Dean were standing there, just as frozen in place as Judd. The first thing I saw was red.

Red dots. Red streaks. Red on the windows.

Sloane turned to beam at us. "Hi, guys!"

It took me a moment to process the fact that she was there, and she was *fine*. It was several seconds more before I realized that the red on the windows was a *drawing*.

"What the hell, Sloane?" Lia recovered her voice first.

"I needed a bigger surface to write on." Sloane popped the cap on and off the marker in her hand. "It'll come off," she told us. "Assuming I grabbed the dry-erase marker and not a permanent Sharpie."

Still processing what I was seeing, I walked toward the diagram Sloane had sketched onto the panoramic window's surface.

"There's a seventy-four percent chance it will come off," Sloane said, amending her prior statement. "On the bright side," she said, turning to survey her work, "I know where the killer is going to strike next."

CHAPTER 24

"I've drawn a to-scale map of the Strip, plotting out the locations of the first four murders." Sloane tapped on each red X as she rattled off the locations. "The rooftop pool at the Apex, the stage in the main theater at the Wonderland, the exact location where Eugene Lockhart was sitting when he was shot, and . . ." Sloane came to stand before the last X. "The east-most bathroom on the casino floor of the Majesty." She stared at us in anticipation. "The pattern isn't where the UNSUB struck as in *which casino*. It's the precise coordinates of the murder!"

An intense look settled over Dean's features. "Coordinates as in latitude and longitude?"

I could feel him starting to sink into the killer's perspective, integrating that information, when Sloane interjected.

"Not latitude. Not longitude."

She uncapped her pen and drew a straight line connecting the first two victims. Then she did the same, connecting the second victim to the third victim and the third to the fourth. Finally, she added five more marks, closely clustered inside the boundaries of the Majesty. She connected them to the rest, one after the other, then turned back to us, her eyes alight.

"Now do you see?"

I did.

"It's a spiral," Dean said.

At his words, Sloane went back over it and sketched an arc over each of the straight lines. The resulting pattern looked like a seashell.

"Not just *a* spiral," Sloane said, stepping back. "A Fibonacci spiral!"

Lia flopped down on the sofa and stared up at Sloane's diagram. "I'm going to go out on a limb and guess that has something to do with the Fibonacci sequence."

Sloane nodded emphatically. All energy, she looked at the window and, seeing no place left to write, bounded over to the adjacent wall.

"Let's try some paper this time," Judd interjected mildly.

Sloane stared at him very hard.

"Paper," she said, as if it were a word in another language. "Right."

Judd handed her a piece. She plopped unceremoniously down on the floor and began to draw. "The first non-zero number in Fibonacci's sequence is one. So you draw a square," she said, doing just that, "where each side is one unit long."

Beneath that square, she drew a second, identical square. "The next number in the sequence is also one. So now you have one and one. . . ."

"And one plus one is?" She didn't wait for an answer. "Two." Another square, this one twice as big as each of the first.

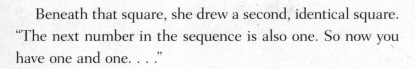

"Two plus one is three. Three plus two is five. Five plus three is eight. . . ." Sloane kept drawing squares, moving counterclockwise as she drew, until she ran out of space.

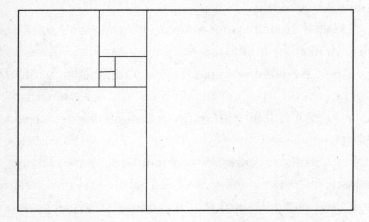

"Now imagine I kept going," she said, shooting Judd a very pointed look that I interpreted to mean that she thought he'd erred in forbidding her to draw on the wall. "And imagine I did *this*. . . ." She started drawing arcs through the diagonal of each square.

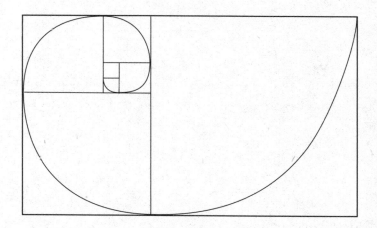

"If I kept going," she said, "and added two more squares, it would look exactly"—she turned to the spiral on the window—"like that."

I looked from Sloane's drawing to the layout of Vegas she'd drawn onto the window. She was right. Starting with the Apex, the killer was spiraling in. And if Sloane's calculations were correct—and I had no reason to doubt that they were—our UNSUB was doing so in a precise and predictable fashion.

Sloane began scrawling the numbers of the Fibonacci sequence across the margins of the page, and I remembered that the first time she'd told us about the sequence, she'd said that it was everywhere. She'd said that it was beautiful.

She'd said that it was *perfection*.

You see that same thing when you look at this pattern. I addressed the UNSUB. *Its beauty. Its perfection. Inked into Alexandra Ruiz's wrist. Burned into the magician's. Written on the old man's skin. Carved into Camille's flesh.*

You're not just sending a message. You're creating something. Something beautiful.

Something holy.

"Where's the next location?" Dean asked. "The next kill-point on the spiral—where is it?"

Sloane turned back to the window and tapped her finger just below the fifth X she'd drawn. "It's here," she said. "At the Majesty. All of the remaining kill-points are. The closer you get to the heart of the spiral, the closer they get to each other."

"Where at the Majesty?" Dean asked Sloane.

If the UNSUB continued killing a person a day, we might be minutes away from the next murder—and no more than hours.

"The Grand Ballroom," Sloane murmured, staring at the pattern inked onto the window, lost in what she saw. "That's where it has to be."

YOU

The knife is next.

Water. Fire. Impaling the old man on an arrow. Strangling Camille. Then comes the knife. That's the way this is done. That is how it must be.

You sit on the floor, your back to the wall, the blade carefully balanced on one knee.

Water.

Fire.

Impaling.

Strangling.

One, two, three, four . . .

Knife will make five. You breathe in the weapon's numbers: the exact weight of the blade, the speed with which you will slice it across your next target's throat.

You breathe out.

Water. Fire. Impaling. Strangling. The knife is next. And then—and then—

You know how this will end. You are the bard telling this tale. You are the alchemist, pulling the pattern apart.

But for now, all that matters is the blade and the steady rise and fall of your chest and the knowledge that everything you've worked for will come to pass.

Starting with number five.

CHAPTER 25

The FBI staked out the Grand Ballroom. For those of us who *weren't* licensed to participate in stakeouts, the day quickly devolved into a waiting game. The afternoon bled slowly into evening. The darker it got, the brighter the lights outside our marked-red window seemed to grow, and the harder my heart beat in my chest.

January first. January second. January third. January fourth. I kept thinking, over and over again, that today was the fifth. *Four bodies in four days. Next comes number five. That's how you think of them, isn't it? Not as people. As numbers. Things to be quantified. A part of your equation.*

My mind went to the photo I'd seen in my mother's file of a skeleton wrapped carefully in a royal blue shawl. Dean had read remorse into the way the body had been buried. I couldn't help seeing the contrast.

You don't feel remorse. I made myself focus on the Vegas killer. That, I could handle. That, I could do. *Why would you? There are billions of people in the world, and you've killed such a very small percentage of them. One, two, three, four—*

"Okay, that's it." Lia exited her bedroom, took one look at the rest of us, and flounced into the kitchen. I heard her bang open the freezer. A few seconds later, she was back. She tossed something at Michael. "Frozen washcloth," she told him. "Put it on your eye and stop with the brooding, because I think we all know that Dean has that market cornered."

Lia didn't wait to see if Michael followed her instructions before she turned to her next target. "Dean," she said, her voice wavering slightly. "I'm pregnant."

Dean's eyelid twitched. "No, you're not."

"Who's to say, really?" Lia countered. "The point is that sitting here waiting for the phone to ring and mentally going over worst-case scenarios isn't helping anybody."

"So what do you suggest we do?" I asked.

Lia hit a switch and a blackout screen slowly covered the wall of windows—and Sloane's writing. Sloane let out an indignant squeak, but Lia preempted any actual complaint.

"What I suggest," Lia said, "is that we spend the next three hours and twenty-seven minutes doing our best impressions of *actual* teenagers." She flopped down on the couch between Dean and me. "Who wants to play Two Truths and a Lie?"

"I have been kicked out of no fewer than four boarding schools." Michael wiggled his eyebrows, his tone giving no hint whatsoever as to whether or not what he was saying was true. "My favorite movie is *Homeward Bound*."

Isn't that the one with the lost pets trying to find their way home? I thought.

"And," Michael finished elaborately, "I'm thoroughly considering going into Redding's room tonight while he's sleeping and shaving my initials into his head."

Three statements. Two of them were true. One was a lie.

"Number three," Dean said darkly. "The lie is number three."

Michael couldn't quite manage a roguish smile with a fat lip, but he made his best attempt.

Lia, who was sprawled on her stomach on the carpet, propped herself up on her elbows. "How many boarding schools *have* you gotten kicked out of?" she asked.

Michael gave Dean a moment to process the fact that the deception detector had zeroed in on his first statement as the lie. "Three," he told Lia.

"Slacker," she opined.

"It's not my fault Sterling and Briggs haven't kicked me out yet." Michael ran a thumb along the edge of his split lip, an odd sheen in his eyes. "Clearly, I'm a liability. They're smart people. Expulsion number four is only a matter of time."

Better to make someone reject you, I thought, understanding more than I wanted to, *than to let them do it on their own.*

"*Homeward Bound?*" Dean gave Michael a look. "Really?"

"What can I say?" Michael replied. "I'm a sucker for warmhearted puppies and kitties."

"That seems statistically unlikely," Sloane said. She stared at Michael for several seconds, then shrugged. "My turn."

She caught her bottom lip between her teeth. "The average litter size for a beagle is seven puppies." Sloane paused, then offered up a second statement. "The word *spatula* is derived from the Greek word *spathe*, meaning broad, flat blade."

Sloane didn't quite grasp the intricacies of the game, but she knew that she was supposed to say two true statements and one false one. She twisted one hand into the other in her lap. Even if her truths hadn't been obvious, it was clear she was preparing to lie. "The man who owns this casino," she said, the words coming out in a rush, "is not my father."

Sloane had spent her entire life keeping this secret. She'd told me. She couldn't bring herself to tell the others—but she could lie. Badly, obviously, in a game devoted to spotting lies.

I could feel the others brimming with questions, but no one said a single word.

"You have to guess." Sloane swallowed, then looked up from her lap. "You *have* to. Those are the rules."

Michael poked Sloane's foot with his. "Is it the one about the beagles?"

"No," Sloane said. "No, it is not."

"We know." Dean's voice was as gentle as I'd ever heard it. "We know which one the lie is, Sloane."

Sloane let out a long breath. "Based on my calculations, now would be an appropriate time for someone to hug me."

Beside her, Dean opened his arms, and Sloane melted into them.

"Raise your hand if you didn't realize Dean was a hugger," Michael said, raising his own hand. Lia snorted.

"This hug is now completed." Sloane pulled back from Dean. "Two Truths and a Lie. Someone else go," she said fiercely.

I obliged. "I've never been hypnotized." *True.* "I'm double-jointed." *Lie.* I thought of Sloane, baring her heart. "The authorities found a body they think is my mother."

Sloane had come clean with the others. I owed them the same—even if Dean and Lia already knew.

"I've never seen any physical indication that you possess hypermobility," Sloane said. Her hands stilled in her lap. "Oh." The realization that I'd been telling the truth about the body washed over her, and she hesitated. "Based on my calculations . . ." she started to say, and then she just launched herself at me.

We might as well start calling this game Two Truths, a Lie, and a Hug, I thought, but something about the physical contact threatened the wall I'd put up in my mind, the one that stood between me and the dark place.

"My turn again." Michael met my eyes. I waited for him to say something—something true, something real. "I'm sorry about your mother," he told me. *True.* He turned to Sloane. "I'd be happy to punch your father, should the occasion arise." *True.* Then he leaned back on the heels of his hands. "And I've magnanimously decided against shaving my initials into Dean's head."

Dean glowered at Michael. "I swear to God, Townsend, if you—"

"Your turn, Lia," I cut in. Given Lia's uncanny ability to

make anything sound true, her rounds were by far the most challenging.

Lia tapped her fingertips along the edge of the coffee table, thinking. The steady rhythm of her tapping had my eyes drifting back toward the clock on the wall. We'd been playing for hours. Midnight was drawing closer and closer.

"I killed a man when I was nine years old." Lia did what she did best—provided a distraction. "I'm currently considering shaving *Michael's* head while he sleeps. And," she finished, her tone never changing, "I grew up in a cult."

Two truths and a lie. Lia's distraction took hold. By the age of thirteen, just before she'd come to the program, Lia had been on the streets. I knew that the ability to lie tended to be honed in certain kinds of environments—and none of them good.

I killed a man when I was nine years old.

I grew up in a cult.

Judd came into the room. I was so caught up in what Lia had just said—and trying to figure out which of those statements was true—that it took me several seconds to process the grim look on Judd's face.

I looked at the clock—a minute past midnight. *January sixth.*

Sterling called, I thought. My heart beat in my throat, my palms suddenly sticky with sweat.

"What have we got?" Dean asked the older man quietly.

Judd cut a brief glance at Sloane, then answered Dean's question. "Nothing."

CHAPTER 26

The FBI continued to monitor the Majesty's Grand Ballroom. Nothing on January sixth. Nothing on January seventh. On the eighth, Agent Sterling was in our suite when I woke up. She and Dean were sitting in the kitchen talking softly. Judd was at the stove making pancakes. For a moment, I felt like I was back at our house in Quantico.

"Cassie," Agent Sterling said when she saw me hovering in the doorway. "Good. Have a seat."

Glancing from Sterling to Dean, I did as I was told. Part of me expected news, but the rest of me took in the way Agent Sterling had greeted me, her posture, the fact that Judd slid a plate of pancakes in front of her, as well as Dean and me.

You didn't come here because you have news. You came here because you don't.

"Still nothing?" I said. "I don't get it. Even if Sloane was wrong about the location, there still should have been . . ."

Another body. Possibly *multiple* bodies.

"Maybe I saw the FBI and pulled back," Dean said, easing himself into the UNSUB's perspective. "Or maybe I've just taken to hiding the bodies."

"No." My gut reply came before I'd thought through the reasons. "You're not hiding the results of your work. You wanted the police to see the numbers. You wanted them to know those accidents weren't accidents."

You wanted us to see the beauty in what you're doing. The pattern. The elegance.

"This isn't just murder," Dean murmured. "This is a performance. This is art."

I thought of Alexandra Ruiz, her hair spread out around her on the pavement; of the stage magician, burned beyond all recognition; of the old man with an arrow through his heart. I thought of Camille Holt, her skin gray, her bloodshot eyes impossibly wide.

"Based on the nature of the crimes"—Agent Sterling's voice broke through my thoughts—"it's fairly clear we're dealing with an organized killer. These attacks were planned. Meticulously, down to the avoidance of surveillance cameras. We have no witnesses. The physical evidence is going nowhere. All we have is the story these bodies are telling about the person who killed them—and how that story is evolving over time."

She laid four pictures on the table.

"Tell me what you see," she said. I took her words to mean that class was in session.

I looked at the first picture. Alexandra Ruiz was a pretty girl, not that much older than me. *You thought she was pretty, too. You watched her drown, but you didn't hold her under. You didn't leave any marks on her skin.*

"It's not about violence," Dean said. "I never laid a hand on her. I never had to."

I picked up where Dean left off. "It's about power."

"The power to predict what she would do," he continued.

I concentrated. "The power to influence her. To knock over the first domino and watch the rest fall."

"To do the math," Dean filled in.

"What about the second victim?" Sterling asked. "Was it just math with him, too?"

I turned my attention to the second picture, the body burned beyond all recognition.

"I didn't kill him," Dean murmured. "I made it happen, but I didn't strike the match. I watched."

You spend a lot of time watching, I thought. *You know how people operate, and you despise them for it. For thinking, even for a second, that they're your equals.*

"It's not about overpowering people," I said out loud, my eyes locking onto Dean's. "It's about outsmarting them."

Dean bowed his head slightly, his eyes fixed on something none of us could see. "No one knows what I really am. They think they do, but they don't."

"It's important," I countered, "to show them. The numbers, the pattern, the planning—you want them to see."

"Who?" Agent Sterling prompted. "Whose attention is the UNSUB trying to get?" I could tell by the tone in her voice that she'd asked herself that question. The fact that she was also asking us told me something about the answer.

"Not just the FBI," I said slowly. "Not just the police."

Sterling tilted her head to the side. "Are you telling me what you think I want to hear, or are you telling me what your gut is saying?"

The numbers mattered to the UNSUB. *They matter to you, because they matter to someone else.* I'd thought that the UNSUB was performing. *For who?*

I answered Sterling's question. "Both."

Sterling gave a brief nod and then tapped her fingers against the third photo.

"The arrow," Dean said. "No more dominoes. I pulled the trigger myself."

"Why?" Sterling pushed us. "Power, influence, manipulation—and then blunt force? How does a killer make that transition? *Why* does a killer make that transition?"

I stared at the picture, willing myself to see the UNSUB's logic. "The message on the arrow," I said. "*Tertium.* For the third time. In your mind, they're all the same—drowning and watching someone burn alive and shooting the old man with an arrow, they're the same thing to you."

But they're not. That was what I couldn't shake. The

manner in which an UNSUB killed told a story about motivations and underlying psychological needs.

What story are you telling me?

"Camille Holt was strangled with her own necklace." Dean moved on to the final picture. "Organized killers typically bring their own weapons to the scene."

"Yes," Agent Sterling replied, "they do."

Strangling was personal. It was physical, far more about dominance than manipulation.

"You carved the numbers into her skin," I said out loud. "To punish her. To punish yourself for falling short of perfection."

You have a plan. Failure is not an option.

"What's the trajectory here?" Agent Sterling prompted.

"More violent with each kill," Dean said. "And more personal. He's escalating."

Agent Sterling gave a brief nod. "Escalation," she said, falling into lecture mode, "happens as a killer begins needing more with each kill. It can manifest in any number of ways. A killer who starts by stabbing victims once and then switches to stabbing them over and over is escalating. A killer who starts by killing once a week and then kills two victims in the same day is escalating. A killer who starts out targeting people who are easy to pick off and graduates to harder and harder targets is escalating."

"And," Dean added, "a killer who moves on to progressively more violent means with each subsequent kill is escalating."

I saw the logic inherent in what they were saying. "Diminished returns," I said. "Like a junkie shooting up and needing progressively stronger doses to get the same high each time."

"Sometimes," Agent Sterling agreed. "Other times, escalation can reflect a loss of control, brought on by some kind of external stressor. Or it might reflect a killer's growing belief that he's invulnerable. As the UNSUB becomes more grandiose, so do the kills."

You're escalating. I meditated on that for a moment. *Why?*

I spoke the next question to cross my mind out loud. "If the UNSUB is escalating," I said, "why would he stop?"

"He couldn't." Dean's voice was flat.

Four bodies in four days, and then nothing.

"Most serial killers don't just stop," Agent Sterling said. "Not unless someone or something stops them."

The way she said those words told me she was thinking about another case—about a particular killer she'd hunted once who *had* stopped. *The one who got away.*

"The most likely explanation for the sudden and permanent cessation of serial murder," Agent Sterling continued, "is that the UNSUB has been arrested on an unrelated crime or died."

I glanced at Judd. His daughter had been Agent Sterling's best friend. *Is your daughter's killer dead, Judd? Avoiding detection? Was he arrested on an unrelated crime?* I didn't need to know much about the case to know that those were questions that haunted both Sterling and Judd.

"What's next?" I asked Agent Sterling, tamping down on the urge to go further into her psyche.

"We have to figure out two things," my mentor replied. "Why our UNSUB escalated, and why he or she stopped."

"No one stopped."

Dean, Agent Sterling, and I all whipped our heads to the doorway. Sloane stood there, her hair still tousled with sleep.

"He can't just *stop*," Sloane said stubbornly. "It's not done yet. The Grand Ballroom is next."

I could hear it in Sloane's voice—she needed to be right. She needed to have done this one thing right.

"Sloane," Agent Sterling said gently, "there's a chance—a good one—that we inadvertently tipped off the killer. We disrupted the pattern."

Sloane shook her head. "If you start at the origin of the spiral and work your way out, you can stop at any time. But if you start at the outside and work your way in, there's a start, and there's a finish. The pattern is set."

"Can you continue monitoring the Grand Ballroom?" Dean asked Sterling. He knew Sloane as well as I did. He knew what this meant to her—and he knew that when it came to numbers, her instincts were better than anyone's.

Agent Sterling's reply was measured. "The casino's owner accommodated us when we said the Grand Ballroom might be at risk, but the management's good will is quickly running thin." The fact that Agent Sterling refused to refer to Sloane's father by name told me that she knew *exactly* who he was to Sloane.

151

"'Tell him it has to stay closed,'" Sloane said fiercely. "Tell him the pattern isn't complete yet. Make him listen."

He never listens to you. He's never really seen you.

"I'll do what I can," Agent Sterling said.

Sloane swallowed. "I'll figure it out. I'll do better. I'll find the answer, I promise, you just have to tell him."

"You don't have to do better," Agent Sterling said. "You've done everything we've asked of you. You've done everything right, Sloane."

Sloane shook her head and retreated to the living room. She pressed the button to lift the blackout curtain and stared at the calculations on the window. "I'll find it," she said again. "I promise."

CHAPTER 27

"What next?" I asked Agent Sterling quietly. She, Dean, and I had retreated to the hallway outside the suite.

"We can keep the Grand Ballroom closed for another day," Agent Sterling said. "Maybe two. But the FBI and local police can't afford to spare more than a couple of teams to monitor it. We have other leads to follow up on."

"Leads like Tory Howard?" I asked.

Agent Sterling just arched an eyebrow. "I take it in the midst of Michael's brawl you managed to overhear that part of our interview with Thomas Wesley?"

I nodded. For Dean's benefit, I filled in the blanks. "Wesley claimed that Tory was particularly gifted at hypnosis."

"Our attention has been focused on the numbers and the ballroom," Sterling replied. She lowered her voice to keep Sloane from hearing her. "But it might be time to start pursuing other leads."

How had our UNSUB gotten Alexandra Ruiz to tattoo the number on her arm? How had she come to be facedown in that pool with no signs of a struggle?

Manipulation. Influence.

"Hypnosis," Dean repeated. I could practically see him thinking that Tory Howard had lied to the police. She was hiding something.

"I should go," Agent Sterling said. "I told Briggs I wouldn't be gone long. Dean, keep working on the profile. Why the UNSUB escalated, why the UNSUB stopped, anything else that jumps out at you."

"And me?" I asked.

Sterling glanced back toward the living room. "I want you to get Sloane out of the suite and away from the case for a couple of hours. She has obsessive tendencies under the best of circumstances."

It went unsaid that these weren't the best of circumstances.

"Where should I take her?" I asked.

Agent Sterling's lips tilted slightly upward in a way that made me think I wouldn't like her answer. "I believe Lia said something about wanting to go shopping?"

"Is it me, or is it me?" Lia held up a top the color of a black opal. Even on the hanger, the cut was striking, with an asymmetrical neck and gathers at the waist. Before I could answer, Lia had picked up a second shirt: a dainty white peasant top. A skirt joined the shirts a moment later: brown, tan, and fitted.

Each item she picked up looked like it belonged on a different person—and that was the point. Lia didn't just try on clothing. She tried on personas.

I killed a man when I was nine.

I grew up in a cult.

I had no way of knowing which of those statements was true. And that was just the way Lia liked it.

"See anything you like, Sloane?" I asked our other companion. Sloane hadn't wanted to leave the suite. Ultimately, I'd lured her with the promise of espresso.

In response to my question, Sloane shook her head, but I noticed her running a hand lightly over a white top marked with a trio of artistic purple blotches.

"Try it on," Judd suggested gruffly. Logically, a sixty-year-old retired marine shouldn't have been able to fade into the background in a high-end boutique, but Judd had been standing still enough that I'd almost forgotten he was there. Agent Sterling had drafted him to accompany us, for safety.

I truly did not want to think what might come of Michael and Dean being left in the suite alone.

"Only seventy-one percent of visitors to Las Vegas play the odds while they're here," Sloane said, drawing her hand back from the light, silky fabric of the shirt. "More and more, people are coming for the shopping."

Lia picked up the top Sloane was looking at. "You're trying it on," she informed her. "Or I'm reneging on Cassie's offer of espresso."

Sloane frowned. "Can she do that?"

It quickly became apparent that, yes, Lia could. After Lia dragged Sloane to the dressing room, Judd turned to me. "You don't see anything you like?" he asked.

"Not yet," I said. In truth, I wasn't feeling much like shopping. I'd agreed with Agent Sterling when she'd said we needed to get Sloane out of the suite. I wanted to be there for my roommate, but no matter how hard I tried, I couldn't keep from wondering what the UNSUB was doing right now.

Why did you escalate? Why did you stop?

I forced myself to pick a dress up off a nearby rack. It was simple: an A-line cut in a brilliant, royal blue. It wasn't until I'd joined Lia and Sloane in the dressing room and tried it on that I realized it was the exact same shade as the shawl that had been wrapped around what were, in all likelihood, my mother's remains.

"Dance it off." *My mom is wrapped in a royal blue scarf, her red hair damp from cold and snow as she flips the car radio on and turns it up.*

This time, I couldn't fight the memory. I wasn't sure I wanted to.

"You can do better than that," she tells me, glancing over from the driver's seat, where she's dancing up a storm.

I'm six or seven, and it's so early in the morning that I can barely keep my eyes open. Part of me doesn't want to dance it off this time.

"I know," my mom says over the music. "You liked the town and the house and our little front yard. But home isn't a place, Cassie. Home is the people who love you most." She pulls over

to the side of the highway. "Forever and ever," she murmurs, brushing the hair away from my face. "No matter what."

"No matter what," I whisper, and she smiles, one of those slow-spreading, mysterious smiles that make me smile, too. The next thing I know, she's turned the music up as loud as it can go, and the two of us are out of the car, and we're dancing, right there on the side of the highway, in the snow.

"Cassie?" Lia's voice snapped me back to the present. For once, her voice was gentle.

We don't know the body is her, I thought, *not for a fact.* But staring at myself in the mirror, I didn't believe that. My eyes popped against the blue of the dress. My hair looked a deeper, almost jewel-toned auburn.

"That really is your color," Lia told me.

It was my mother's color, too, I thought. If a person had known my mother, had loved her, had thought she was beautiful—this was the color they would have buried her in.

Her necklace. Her color. An odd numbness descended over my body, my limbs heavy and my tongue thick in my mouth. I took the dress off and made my way back to the front of the store. Across the promenade, there was an old-fashioned candy shop. I fell back on the habits of my childhood, people-watching and telling myself stories about the customers.

The woman buying herself lemon drops just broke up with her boyfriend. The boys looking at candy cigarettes hope their mother doesn't realize they've tried the real thing. The little girl staring at a lollipop as big as her head missed her nap this afternoon.

My phone rang. I answered, still watching the little girl

across the way. She didn't reach for the lollipop. She just stared at it, solemn-eyed and still.

"Hello?"

"Cassie."

It took me longer to recognize my father's voice than it would have taken me to recognize Sterling's or Briggs's.

"Hey, Dad," I said, my throat closing in around the words, my mind awash in all the things I'd been trying to forget. "Now really isn't a good time."

Across the way, the solemn-eyed little girl eyeing the lollipop was joined by her father. He held out his hand. She took it. *Simple. Easy.*

"I was just calling to see how you're doing."

My father was trying. I could see that—but I could also see the ease with which the man across the way hoisted his little daughter onto his shoulders. She was three, maybe four years old. Her hair was red, brighter than mine, but it was easy enough to picture myself at that age.

I hadn't even known I had a father.

"I'm okay," I said, turning my back on the scene across the way. I didn't need to know whether or not the father would surprise his daughter with the lollipop. I didn't need to see the way she looked at him.

"I got a call from the police this morning." My father had a naturally deep voice.

So you weren't just calling to see if I was okay.

"Cassie?"

"I'm here."

"The forensics team was able to extract traces of blood from the shawl in which the skeleton was wrapped."

My mind took that information and ran with it. *If her blood was on the shawl, you must have wrapped her in it at some point before you—before you—*

"Preliminary analysis suggests it's the same blood type as your mother's." My father's voice was so controlled that I wondered if he'd written this down, if he was just reading a script. "They're running a DNA analysis. They're not sure the sample will be big enough, but if it is, we should have answers in the next few days." He wavered, just for a moment. "If they have to try to do a DNA analysis of the bones . . ." His voice broke. "That would take longer."

"Answers," I said, fixating on that one word. It came out like an accusation. *Her necklace. Her color.* "I don't just want to know if it's her. I want to know who did this."

"Cassie." That was all my father could say. His script had run out.

I turned back toward the candy store. The little red-haired girl and her father were long gone. "I have to go."

I hung up the phone just in time for Lia to pounce.

"I know," I said, my voice taut. "It's not my turn to have issues."

"Exhibit C as to why that's the case?" Lia grabbed my arm and began pulling me toward the back of the store. "Sloane just made a beeline out the employees-only exit," she said, her voice low. "And so did about five hundred dollars' worth of merchandise."

CHAPTER 28

Who takes a stressed-out kleptomaniac shopping? I thought in self-recrimination as we slipped out the back exit. *Seriously, who does that?* The door closed behind us. Sloane was standing a few feet away, the silk shirt clutched in one hand and some kind of bracelet in the other.

"Sloane," I said, "we have to go back inside."

"It's not just four bodies in four days," Sloane said. "That's what we missed. What I missed. January first, January second—those aren't just days. They're dates. 1/1. 1/2."

"I understand," Lia said, so convincingly that I could almost believe she did. "You can tell us all about it *after* we get back inside before either Judd or the sales girl notices we're gone."

"One, one, two." Sloane continued on as if Lia had never spoken. "That's the way the sequence starts. 1/1. 1/2. Do you see? The pattern hasn't been broken, because a body every day *was never the pattern*." Sloane's voice practically vibrated with intensity. "January first, second, third, and fourth—they're all Fibonacci dates. Thirteen, 1/3. One hundred and forty-four, 1/4." The words poured out of her mouth, faster and faster. "I just have to figure out the exact parameters he's using. . . ."

At the end of the alleyway, another door opened. Lia thought fast, pulling Sloane and me back against the wall. She needn't have bothered. The two people who exited were fully caught up in their own conversation.

I couldn't hear what either of them was saying, but I didn't need Michael there to tell me that emotions were running high.

Aaron Shaw. I registered Sloane's brother's presence a moment before I identified his companion. *And Tory Howard.*

Aaron said something, pleading with her. She pulled back, then went back into the building, slamming the door. Aaron cursed—loud enough that I could make out the words—then kicked the metal door.

"That's my favorite curse word, too," Sloane whispered.

"Somebody," Lia murmured, "has a temper."

The metal door banged open behind me, and I jumped. Judd stepped into the alleyway, scanning the perimeter for threats. I knew the exact second his eyes landed on Aaron Shaw.

"Girls," he said, "go back inside."

We did as we were told. The door closed behind us, leaving Judd in the alley.

"Excuse me." A man in a dark suit appeared in front of us. *Security.* He eyed the merchandise in Sloane's hand and the direction from which we'd come. "I'm going to have to ask you girls to come with me."

Security had caught Sloane on camera leaving the store. The fact that she'd also returned of her own volition didn't seem to negate their opinion that she'd shoplifted. I tried to trust that when Judd came back in from the alleyway and found us missing, he'd also find his way to the security office, where the three of us had been deposited in front of a man I recognized all too well.

You're the one who came to get Sloane's father the night Camille was murdered, I thought as the man stared back at us. He was of medium height, with unremarkable features and a poker face that would have done any professional proud. Something in the way he sat and moved screamed power and authority, maybe even a hint of danger.

"Do you know how much shoplifting costs this casino every year?" he asked us, his tone carefully controlled.

"Thirteen billion dollars' worth of merchandise is shoplifted annually." Sloane couldn't help herself. "I'd estimate your share of that to be less than point-zero-zero-zero-one percent."

Clearly, the man hadn't expected an actual answer.

"She wasn't shoplifting." Lia made it sound like the very idea of Sloane stealing anything was worthy of an eye roll. "She had a panic attack. She went outside for air. She came back in. End of story."

Lia's lie skated close enough to the truth that even with security footage, they would have trouble arguing her interpretation. Sloane had been agitated from the moment we'd entered the store. Sloane had gone outside. Sloane had come back in. *All true.*

"Victor."

The head of security looked up. The rest of us turned toward the door of his office. Aaron Shaw stood there, looking every bit as self-possessed and in control as he had the day we met him.

"Aaron," Victor greeted him.

Not Mr. Shaw, I noted. When it came to the hierarchy at the Majesty, it wasn't entirely clear which one of them came out on top.

"Can this wait?" Victor's tone made that sound more like an order than a question.

"I was just checking in on some of our VIP guests," Aaron replied. "These girls are staying with Mr. Townsend in the Renoir Suite."

The words *Renoir Suite* had Victor stiffening. *Big spenders, leave them be,* Aaron might as well have said.

"Let me do my job," Victor told Aaron.

"Your job is harassing teenagers with anxiety issues?"

Lia asked, arching an eyebrow at him. "I'm sure a variety of news outlets would find that fascinating."

Once Lia had given life to a creative interpretation of the truth, she was fully committed to it.

"Why don't we hear from the girl in question?" Victor said, narrowing his eyes at Sloane. "Were you, as your friend claims, having a panic attack?"

Sloane stared at the front corner of the man's desk. "Patients with panic disorders are more than ten times more likely to be double-jointed than controls," she said clearly.

"Victor." Aaron's voice held a note of steel. "I'll take care of this. You can go."

After a tense moment of silence, the head of security walked out of the room without a word. Clearly, Aaron held the upper hand here. I might have breathed a sigh of relief, but when Aaron closed the door behind the man, he turned back to us.

"Let's chat."

CHAPTER 29

Aaron took a seat on the edge of Victor's desk instead of behind it. "What's your name?" he asked Sloane quietly.

Beside me, Sloane opened her mouth, then closed it again.

"Her name is Sloane." Lia's chin jutted out as she answered on Sloane's behalf.

"What's your last name, Sloane?" Aaron's voice was gentle. I thought of the way he'd responded to Sloane's statistics with a smile the day we met him. And then I thought about the brief, heated exchange we'd seen between him and Tory.

"Tavish," Sloane whispered. She forced her gaze up, her blue eyes wide. "I meant to steal that shirt."

I groaned internally. Sloane had no capacity for deception whatsoever. *Then again*, I thought, *she's sitting here across from her father's son, not saying a word.*

"I'm going to pretend I didn't hear that," Aaron told us,

a smile tugging at the edges of his lips. It was hard to reconcile the man in front of us with the one we'd seen in the alleyway.

You know Tory. She knows you. Emotions were running high— I was struck, suddenly, by a possibility. *Maybe you really know Tory. Maybe Camille wasn't the one you were looking at that night at the sushi restaurant. Attraction, affection, tension—maybe you were watching Tory.*

What if Tory had chosen the Majesty for drinks that night because she wanted to see him? She'd lied to Briggs and Sterling about choosing the restaurant.

What if she's not afraid of Aaron? What if she's afraid he'll leave her? Or afraid someone will find out they're involved?

Someone, I thought, *like Aaron's father.*

"Tavish." Aaron repeated Sloane's last name back to her, then paused, like his mouth had gone dry. "My father had a friend once," he continued softly. "Her name was Margot Tavish."

"I have to go." Sloane bolted to her feet. She was trembling. "I have to go *now.*"

"Please," Aaron said. "Sloane. Don't go."

"I have to," Sloane whispered. "I'm not supposed to be here. I'm not supposed to tell."

She wanted him to like her. Even panicked, even trying to get away from him, she wanted him to like her so badly that I could feel it.

"We have the same eyes," Aaron told her. "They call them Shaw blue, did you know that?"

"A chameleon's tongue is longer than its body! And a blue whale's weighs two-point-seven tons!"

"I'm sorry," Aaron said, holding up his hands and taking a step back. "I didn't mean to scare you or to spring this on you or to put you on the spot. It's just that I found out about your mother right after I graduated high school. I went to see her. She said there was a child, but by the time I'd confronted my father, your mother had overdosed and you were gone."

Gone. It took me a second to do the math. Aaron would have graduated high school around the same time that Sloane was recruited to the Naturals program.

"You can't know about me," Sloane told Aaron softly. "That's the rule."

"It's not my rule." Aaron stood up and walked around to her side of the desk. "I'm not like my father. If I'd known about you sooner, I promise I would have—"

"You would have what?" Lia cut in protectively. Sloane was our family, more than she would ever be his, and right now, she was vulnerable and raw and bleeding. Lia didn't trust strangers, and she especially didn't trust this stranger—who we'd seen fighting with Tory Howard—with Sloane.

Before Aaron could reply, the door to the office opened. Judd was standing there. And so was Aaron's father.

CHAPTER 30

"Aaron," Mr. Shaw said. "If you could be so kind as to give us a moment."

Aaron didn't seem inclined to leave Sloane in a room with his father, and that told me volumes about them both.

"Aaron," Mr. Shaw said again, his voice perfectly pleasant. The older man had a powerful aura. I knew, before Aaron did, that he would give in to his father's demand.

You can't fight him, I thought, watching Aaron go. *No one can.*

Once Aaron was gone, Mr. Shaw turned the full force of his presence on the rest of us. "I'd like a moment with Sloane alone," he said.

"And I'd like a dress made of rainbows and a bed full of puppies who never grow old," Lia shot back. "Not happening."

"Lia," Judd said mildly. "Don't antagonize the casino mogul."

I took Judd's tone to mean that he wasn't planning on leaving Sloane alone with her father, either.

"Mr. Hawkins." The mogul in question surprised me by knowing Judd's last name. "If I wish to speak to my daughter, I will speak to my daughter."

Sloane's expression was painfully transparent when he said the word *daughter*. He meant it as an expression of ownership. She couldn't help hoping—desperately hoping—that it might be one of care.

"Sloane," Judd said, ignoring Shaw's display of dominance, "would you like to go back to the room?"

"She'd like," Shaw said, his words very precise, "to speak with me. And unless *you* would like me to let it slip to interested parties that your agent friends have been visiting teenagers in the Renoir Suite, you'll let Sloane do as she pleases."

We should have set our base of operations up off the Strip, I realized. *Off the radar, out of the way—*

"Cassie and Lia stay." Sloane's voice came out tiny. She cleared her throat and tried again. "You can go," she told Judd, her chin held high. "But I want Cassie and Lia to stay."

For the first time since he'd entered the room, Sloane's father actually looked at his daughter. "The redhead can stay," he said finally. "The lie detector goes."

I realized then—*Sloane's father knows what Lia can do. He doesn't just know that there's a connection between us and the FBI. He knows everything. How could he possibly know everything?*

"Sloane." Judd's voice was as calm as if he were sitting at the kitchen table, doing his morning crossword. "You don't have to do anything you don't want to do."

"It's fine," Sloane said, her fingers tapping nervously against her thigh. "I'll be fine. Just go."

Sloane's father waited until the door was closed before turning his attention back to his daughter—and to me. Clearly, I hadn't rated as a threat. Or maybe he'd just realized that Judd was never going to leave Sloane in here alone, and I was the lesser evil.

The fact that he'd kicked Lia out made me wonder what lies he was planning to tell.

"You look well, Sloane." Shaw took a seat behind the desk.

"I'm twelve percent taller than I was the last time you came to see me."

Shaw frowned. "Had I known you were going to be in Vegas, I would have made alternative arrangements for your little . . . group."

Alternative arrangements as in *farther away from him and his.*

I replied so that Sloane didn't have to. "You know what our group does. How?"

"I have friends in the FBI. I'm the one who suggested Sloane for your Agent Briggs's little program."

Sloane blinked rapidly, like he'd just tossed a bucket of water in her face. Michael's father had traded him to the FBI for immunity on white-collar crimes. Sloane's, apparently, had just wanted her out of town and away from his son.

"You need to stay away from my family." Shaw's voice was deceptively gentle as he refocused on Sloane. He sounded like Aaron had, his voice calm and soothing, but there was no mistaking his words. "I have Aaron's mother to think about."

"And the little girl." The words escaped Sloane's mouth.

"Yes," Shaw said. "We have to think about Cara. She's just a child. None of this is her fault, is it?" he asked, his tone still so gentle, I wanted to hit him as hard as Michael had punched the man at the pool.

None of this is Sloane's fault, either.

"Tell me you understand, Sloane."

Sloane nodded.

"I need to hear you say it."

"I understand," Sloane whispered.

Shaw stood. "You'll stay away from Aaron," he reiterated. "It would behoove you to encourage your FBI friends to do the same."

"This is a serial murder investigation," I said, breaking my silence. "You don't get to dictate who the investigators do and do not talk to."

Shaw turned his eyes—the same blue as Aaron's, the same blue as Sloane's—on me. "My son knows nothing that could be of use. The FBI is wasting their time with him as much as they're wasting their time on this ridiculous idea that a killer who's managed to evade arrest thus far would hog-tie himself to committing his next murder in the Majesty's Grand Ballroom, come hell or high water."

"It's not a ridiculous idea." Sloane stood up. Her voice trembled. "You just can't see it. You don't understand it. But just because you don't understand something doesn't mean you get to ignore it. You can't just pretend the pattern doesn't exist and hope it goes away."

The way he pretends you don't exist, my brain translated. *The way he ignores you.*

"That's enough, Sloane."

"It's not ridiculous." Sloane swallowed and turned toward the door. "You'll see."

YOU

Waiting is harder than you'd anticipated.

Every night, you sit with the knife balanced on one knee. Every night, you run through each iteration, each possibility, each second leading up to the moment when you will step up behind your target and use the knife to slit their throat.

Just another calculation. Another number. Another step closer to what you will become.

You want it. So badly you can taste it. You want it now.

But you are at the mercy of the numbers, and the numbers say to wait. So you wait, and you watch, and you listen.

You're told the FBI suspects that the next murder will take place in the Grand Ballroom. You're told they're watching it. Waiting, just like you. You take that to mean that someone has seen the pattern—just a fraction of it, just a piece. In your quietest moments, when you're staring at the blade, you wonder who at the FBI figured it out.

You wonder if that person truly appreciates what you have done, what you are doing, what you will become. But how could they? Whoever they are, whatever they think they know, it's only a fraction of the truth.

They know only what you've allowed them to know. You set them on the path to discovery.

It's not their attention you want.

Slowly, contemplatively, you take off your shirt. You pick up the knife. You turn to face the mirror, and you press the tip *of the blade to your skin and begin to draw. Blood beads up. You welcome the pain. Soon, you won't even feel it.*

Let the FBI come at you. Let them do their worst. And as for the rest of it, perhaps it's time to send a message. You are at the mercy of the numbers.

Let the world be at their mercy, too.

CHAPTER 31

When we got back to the suite, there were two packages waiting for us. The first contained footage of Sterling and Briggs's most recent interview with Tory Howard. The second was from Aaron Shaw.

Sloane wordlessly opened the second package. Inside were six tickets to tonight's performance of *Tory Howard's Imagine*. The advertisement included with them promised a "bewitching evening of mind-warping entertainment." On the bottom, Aaron had written, in a slanted, cursive scrawl, *On the house.* He'd signed his name.

"I have to go do something that isn't cry now," Sloane said. "And I'd like to do it alone." She bolted before any of us could say anything.

Lia and I exchanged a look. When Michael and Dean joined us, we brought them up to speed. Lia flipped her hair over her shoulder and did her best impression of someone who wasn't concerned about Sloane—or anyone other than herself.

"So," she said, picking up the footage the FBI had sent, "who wants to watch Sterling and Briggs cross-examine Aaron Shaw's girlfriend?"

On-screen, Agent Briggs, Agent Sterling, and Tory were in what appeared to be some kind of interrogation room, as was a man I assumed to be Tory's lawyer.

"Thank you for agreeing to meet with us again." Briggs sat across from Tory. Sterling was to his left. Tory's lawyer sat beside her.

"My client was glad to come down and clear up any lack of clarity that may exist in her prior statements." The lawyer's voice was smooth and baritone. Even from a distance, his watch looked expensive.

Tory didn't hire him. I didn't second-guess the intuition. Tory was tough, she was a straight talker, and she was a survivor. At one point in time, she'd been in the foster system. She'd fought for everything she had. She would unquestionably hire the best lawyer she could afford to keep the FBI from strong-arming her—but her preference would lean toward someone more aggressive, with less of a fondness for designer suits.

"Ms. Howard, when we last spoke to you, you indicated that Camille Holt was the one who chose the Majesty's restaurant as your destination that night."

"Did I?" Tory didn't bat an eye. "That's not right. I was the one who suggested we go there."

I flashed back to seeing Tory in the alleyway with Aaron. Had they been discussing this interview? Had he told her what to say?

"Were you aware that the location of Camille's murder was set in advance?" Agent Briggs asked.

"No," Michael answered on her behalf. "She wasn't. Look at that." He gestured in the direction of the screen, though I couldn't tell what part of Tory's expression had tipped him off. "She's gut-punched."

Agent Sterling took advantage of the moment. "What is your relationship with Aaron Shaw?"

Tory was still absorbed enough in the revelation about Camille's murder that she might have actually answered, but her lawyer leaned forward. "My client will not be answering any questions about Aaron Shaw."

"Check out the nostril flare on the lawyer on that one," Michael said. "Closest thing to emotion the guy's shown so far."

In other words: "He's more concerned with protecting Aaron than protecting Tory," I said. *She didn't hire him,* I thought again. *The Shaws did.*

On-screen, Sterling and Briggs exchanged a meaningful glance. Clearly, they'd picked up on that, too.

"Understood," Agent Briggs told the lawyer. "Moving along, Ms. Howard, we were hoping you could lend us your expertise on hypnosis."

Tory glanced at the lawyer. No objections.

"What do you want to know?"

"Can you describe the process through which you hypnotize someone?" Briggs asked. He was keeping the questions general.

Treat her like an expert, not a suspect, I thought. *Smart.*

"I generally start with having volunteers count backward from one hundred. If I want a bigger impact, I might use a technique that gets a quicker result."

"Such as?"

"It's possible to shock someone into a hypnotic state," Tory said. "Or you can start some kind of automatic sequence—like a handshake—and then interrupt it."

"And once someone is under," Briggs said, "you can implant certain suggestions, cause them to act in certain ways?"

Tory was many things, but naïve wasn't one of them. "If you have something specific in mind, Agent Briggs," she said, "just ask."

Sterling leaned forward. "Could you hypnotize someone into getting a tattoo?"

"That would depend," Tory replied evenly, "on whether or not the person you were hypnotizing was open to getting a tattoo in the first place." I thought she might leave it there, but she didn't. "Hypnosis isn't mind control, Agent Sterling. It's suggestion. You can't alter someone's personality. You can't make them do something they truly do not want to do. The hypnotized person isn't a blank slate. They're merely . . . open."

"But if someone were open to getting a tattoo—"

"Then, yes," Tory said. "I might be able to implant that suggestion. But seeing as how I value my job and not getting sued by angry audience members, I try to stick to things that are a little less permanent."

Alexandra Ruiz's tattoo was made of henna, I thought. *Less common than a regular tattoo—and less permanent.*

"Can anyone be hypnotized?" The questioning bounced back to Agent Briggs.

"You can't force someone under who doesn't want to go." Tory leaned back in her seat. "And some people are more easily hypnotizable than others. Daydreamers. People who had imaginary friends as children."

Beside Tory, the lawyer looked at his watch.

"How quickly could someone learn to do what you do?" Briggs asked Tory.

"To do it as well as I do it?" Tory asked. "Years. To be able to hypnotize someone, period? I know people who claim they can teach it in under ten minutes."

I saw the next question coming.

"Have you taught anyone?"

Tory's eyes darted toward the lawyer. "I believe," he said, standing up and gesturing for Tory to do the same, "that my client has indulged your interest long enough."

Aaron, I thought. *She taught Aaron.*

The footage cut to static. After a moment's silence, Lia spoke up. "Every single word out of her mouth was true."

The real question, I thought, *is what she wasn't saying.*

"I want to go."

I looked up to see Sloane standing in the doorway.

"Go where?" Michael asked her.

"To *Tory Howard's Imagine*," Sloane said. "Aaron sent us complimentary tickets. I want to go."

I thought back to the way he'd rescued Sloane from the head of security, the way he'd ignored the shoplifting, the way he'd sworn that if he had known about her, things would have been different.

I thought of Sloane's father telling her to stay away from his son.

A knock sounded at the door. "Delivery," someone called. "For Ms. Tavish."

Dean was the one who opened the door. He accepted the box, his expression guarded. I wondered if he was thinking of the gifts I'd been sent once upon a time—boxes with human hair in them, boxes that marked me as the object of a killer's fascination.

We waited for Judd to open the box. There, against a backdrop of sedately striped tissue paper, was the shirt Sloane had tried to steal.

There was a card inside. I recognized the handwriting as Aaron's. The message said simply, *I'm not like my father.*

Sloane stroked her hand lightly over the silk shirt, an expression halfway between heartbreak and awe settling over her features.

"I don't care what anyone says," she said softly. "Not Briggs. Not Sterling. Not Grayson Shaw." She gingerly lifted the shirt out of the box. "I'm going."

CHAPTER 32

All six of us went. Judd seemed to believe that was the lesser of two evils—the greater of those evils being the possibility that Sloane might find a way to go alone.

As we found our seats, I scanned the auditorium. My gaze landed on Aaron Shaw a moment before he registered Sloane's presence. In an instant, his entire demeanor changed, from perfectly polished—every inch his father's heir apparent—to the person I'd caught a glimpse of back in the security office. *The person who cares about Sloane.*

He made his way through the crowd toward us. "You came," he said, zeroing in on Sloane. He smiled, then hesitated. "I'm sorry," he said. "About earlier."

For a moment, in that hesitation, he looked like Sloane.

Beside me, our numbers expert cleared her throat. "A substantial portion of apologies are issued by people who have nothing to apologize for." That was Sloane's way of telling him that it was okay, that she didn't blame him for giving in to their father, for leaving her with him.

Before Aaron could reply, a girl about his age appeared beside him. She wore dark jeans and a fashionably loose shirt. Everything about her—accessories, haircut, posture, clothes—said *money*.

Old money, I thought. *Understated*.

After a moment's hesitation, Aaron greeted her with a kiss to the cheek.

A friend? I wondered. Or more than that? And if so, then what is Tory?

"Ladies and gentlemen." A deep voice came over the auditorium speakers. "Welcome to *Tory Howard's Imagine*. As you prepare to be swept into a world where the impossible becomes possible and you find yourself questioning the very depths of the human mind and experience, we ask that you set your cell phones to silent. Flash photography is strictly forbidden during the show. Break the rules, and we may be forced to make you . . . disappear."

The moment he said the word *disappear*, a spotlight highlighted the center of the stage. A light fog rose off the ground. One second the spotlight was empty, and the next, Tory was standing there, clothed in tight black pants and a floor-length leather duster. She whipped her arm out to one side and suddenly, without warning, she was holding a flaming torch. The spotlight dimmed. She brought the flame to the bottom of her jacket.

My mind went to the second victim. Within a heartbeat, Tory was wearing a coat of fire. With a stage presence far more magnetic than I would have ever imagined, she lifted the torch to her lips, blew out the flame, and disappeared.

"Good evening," she called from the back of the room. The audience turned to gape at her. The coat was burning blue now. "And welcome to . . . *Imagine*." She threw her arms out to the side, and suddenly, the back two rows were on fire, too. I heard someone scream, then laugh.

Tory smiled, a slow, sexy smile. The flames surged, then disappeared. She stepped through the smoke. "Let's get started," she said. "Shall we?"

When most people watch a magic show, they try to figure out how the magician does it. I wasn't interested in the magic. I was interested in the magician. She wasn't Tory, not the Tory I'd seen before. The persona she'd slipped into the moment she'd walked onto the stage had a mind and a will and a personality of its own.

"And now, ladies and gentlemen, I'm looking for volunteers. Specifically"—Stage-Tory raked her eyes over the audience, as if she could make out each of our faces and read each of our thoughts—"I'm looking for individuals who would like to participate in the portion of tonight's show devoted to hypnotism."

Hands shot up all over the crowd. Tory went through, calling people up—a handful of women, an eighty-five-year-old man who punched a fist into the air when he climbed up on stage. "And . . ." she said, drawing out the word once she had about a dozen volunteers pulled out, ". . . you."

For a second, I thought she was pointing at me. Then I realized she was pointing in front of me—at the girl sitting next to Aaron. Sloane's brother went ramrod stiff. The girl next to him stood up. A couple of seats down from me, so did Michael. When Tory realized Michael was acting like she'd called on him, she rolled with the punches. "Looks like I got two for the price of one. Both of you, come on up!"

"Michael," I said, reaching for him as he brushed past me.

"Come on, Colorado," he told me. "Live a little."

Up on stage, Michael gave a courtly bow to the audience and took his seat. Tory faced her volunteers and spoke to them for a moment. None of us could hear what she said. After two or three seconds, she turned back to the crowd and the volume came back up on her microphone.

"I'm going to count backward from one hundred," she said, pacing the row in front of her volunteers. "One hundred, ninety-nine, ninety-eight. I want you to picture yourself lying on a raft, next to an island. Ninety-seven, ninety-six, ninety-five. You're drifting. Ninety-four, ninety-three. The further I count, the farther you go. Ninety-two, ninety-one . . ."

As she counted, Tory went by each of the volunteers. She took their heads in her hands and rolled them back and forth.

The further I count, the farther you go. She kept saying those words.

"Your body is heavy. Your head, your neck, your legs, your arms . . ." Up and down the row she went. She tapped a couple of participants on the shoulder and sent them back to their seats, then began to describe a light, floating sensation. "Your body is heavy, but your right arm is weightless. It floats up . . . up . . . seven, six . . . The further I count, the farther you go. Five, four, three, two . . ."

By the time she hit one, the nine volunteers remaining on the stage were slumped in their chairs, their right arms creeping upward. I turned toward Lia.

Is Michael faking it? I raised an eyebrow at Lia, hoping to get an answer, but her concentration was fixed on the stage.

"You're on the beach," Tory told her hypnotized subjects. "You're sunbathing. Feel the sun on your skin. Feel the warmth."

Their faces instantly relaxed, smiles crossing their lips.

"Don't forget to put on sunscreen." Tory's voice was light and silky now.

I couldn't help snorting as Michael began rhythmically rubbing pretend sunscreen all over his biceps. He flexed for the crowd.

"Now," Tory said, walking up and down the length of the stage. "Whenever you hear me say the word *mango*, you will come to believe that you have just passed gas. Loudly. In a crowded room."

It was five minutes before Tory said the word *mango*. Immediately, all of the hypnotized subjects started looking distinctly uncomfortable, except for Michael, who gave an elaborate shrug, and the girl who'd been sitting with Aaron, who took a step forward. And then another. And another.

She walked straight to the edge of the stage, her head bowed. Just when I thought she might walk off the front, she came to a sudden halt.

"Miss, I'm going to need you to take a step back," Tory called.

The girl lifted her head. Her light brown hair fell away from her face. She stared at the audience, her gaze piercing. "*Tertium*," she said.

One of the stage lights shattered and popped.

"*Tertium*," the girl repeated, her voice louder, more piercing.

Tory was trying to get her to back up, trying to wake her up, but she couldn't.

"*Tertium*." The girl was screaming now. Behind her, the rest of the hypnotized subjects stood perfectly still. Michael broke away from the others, his eyes cogent and clear.

The girl raised her hands to the side, palms out. Her voice lowered itself to a coarse but powerful whisper that hit me like spiders crawling down my spine. "I need nine."

CHAPTER 33

The girl's eyes rolled back in her head. She collapsed. Tory leapt forward. In the row in front of us, Aaron pushed his way to the aisle.

The curtain came down. An uneasy murmur spread through the audience. The people around us had no idea what had just happened. They had no idea what it meant.

You.

Need.

Nine.

The thought came to me in pieces. I forced air into my lungs.

"Nine." Sloane's voice somehow managed to reach my ears through the dull roar of the crowd. "*Tertium. Tertium. Tertium.* Three. Three times three—"

"Please remain in your seats," a deep voice commanded over the loudspeaker. "The show will resume momentarily."

Judd took one look at the potential for chaos and jerked his head toward the nearest exit.

"What about Townsend?" Dean said as we pushed our way through the crowd. "He's still onstage."

Judd deposited us safely in the hallway. "I'll go get Michael," he told Dean. "You stay here and watch the girls."

That got a substantial eyebrow raise out of Lia. "I do hope my dowry is large enough to attract a virile man," she told me wistfully. "I'm so very helpless on my own."

Dean was wise enough not to reply.

Once Judd was out of earshot, Lia lowered her voice. "So are we all thinking that either Aaron's little girlfriend is our killer and she just had a psychotic break, or that our killer somehow hypnotized her into delivering that message?"

I nodded. After a second or two, Dean agreed. "Yes."

"*Tertium* again," Lia commented. "You think our guy considers that his name?"

Tertium, I thought. *Meaning the third time.*

The third time. The third time. The third time.

I need nine.

"It's not a name," I told Lia. "It's a promise." I turned to look at Sloane, to get her read on the numbers—but she wasn't beside me. I whirled, doing a three-sixty.

No Sloane.

Lia cursed, then slammed back into the theater. An instant later, Dean and I were on her heels. Sloane was usually easy to spot, but in a crowd this large, the best I could do was follow Lia and think, *Sloane came here to see Aaron. And the last time I saw her, she was talking about the numbers.*

That meant that she was either trailing after Aaron or she'd gone straight to the source of the numbers. *The girl.* Either way, she was probably—

"Backstage," I yelled to Lia, struggling to keep up with her as she pushed her way to the front of the auditorium. Two bouncer-types were positioned on either side of the stage. Lia leaned forward and whispered something in one of their ears. The man paled and stepped aside, allowing us to pass.

I truly did not want to know what Lia had told him, but I had to admit that her particular skill set *definitely* had its uses.

Backstage, I spotted Michael crouched near the girl, who was sitting up now. Judd stood behind Michael. Sloane wasn't with them. That left one likely option.

"Find Aaron," I said, "and we'll find Sloane."

"You son of a bitch."

I turned, just in time to see Beau Donovan slam Aaron Shaw up against a wall. Aaron had three or four inches and a good thirty pounds on Beau, but Beau came at him like he was completely unaware of that fact.

"I found Aaron," Lia said.

Aaron threw Beau off him. Beau skidded backward on his heels, then came at Aaron again. This time, a small blond blur stepped in front of Aaron.

Sloane.

Dean lunged forward. He hated violence. He avoided it at all costs because he could never be sure that he wouldn't wake up one day and like it too much. But if anyone laid so much as a finger on Sloane . . .

Aaron stepped in front of Sloane a second before Beau collided with her. Dean latched a protective arm around Sloane's waist and pulled her back. Beau shoved Aaron again, and Aaron snapped and surged forward. They both went down. Within seconds, Aaron was on top and unquestionably in control. Beau's gaze locked onto Aaron's face with intense hatred.

"What is your problem?" Sloane's brother spat.

In answer, Beau resumed his struggle for the upper hand. Aaron held him in place, the way a wolf might pin a pup.

"My problem?" Beau said. "My problem is *you*. You bring your little high-class, never-worked-a-day-in-her-life girlfriend *here*? To my sister's show?" Beau didn't give Aaron time to respond. "You think that you can treat people like they're nothing—"

Beau surged again, and this time, he ended up on top just long enough to land a solid punch to Aaron's jaw before security swarmed them. The guards pulled Beau off of Aaron—a little harder than necessary—and then looked to Aaron for instruction.

"Allison is not my girlfriend," Aaron said calmly. "She's just a family friend, and I was as surprised to see her here as you were."

"I doubt that."

Aaron and Beau turned in unison to look at Tory. She was still dressed in her costume from the show, but she was fully herself again. *No muss. No fuss.*

Nothing can hurt you unless you let it.

"You're the one who called her up on stage," Aaron told Tory. "What the hell were you thinking, Tory?" He paused. "What did you do to her?"

"She didn't *do* anything!" Beau struggled beneath the security guard's hold. "You probably set the whole thing up, you sick son of a—"

"Enough!" Tory shouted. Beau stilled. Tory dragged her gaze from him to Aaron, and her eyes hardened. "I want you both out of here. Now."

The *now* seemed to be directed at the security guards.

"Sir," one of them told Aaron, visibly uncomfortable with the words exiting his mouth. "I'm going to have to ask you to leave."

Aaron's eyes never left Tory's face. "Tory, let me explain."

"You don't need to explain." Tory's voice was emotionless, but there was steel underneath. "Our relationship is strictly professional." She looked around at the audience they'd gathered—including Sloane, Lia, Dean, and me—and her voice hardened. "It always has been."

"You heard her," Beau told Aaron, his eyes hard.

"Don't." Tory rounded on Beau, her voice cracking whip-loud through the air. "I didn't ask you to do this, Beau, and I am done cleaning up your messes." She swallowed, and I got the sense that sending Beau away was even harder for her than ending things with Aaron. "Leave," she said, her voice lower. "Now."

Without waiting for a response, Tory turned back to the stage and started yelling out directions for the stagehands. "Get a doctor up here for Ms. Lawrence. Then call the head of security and inform him that we have a situation. I want this show back up and running in five minutes."

"I'm afraid that won't be possible." Agent Briggs knew how to make an entrance—in this case, with his badge held high for everyone to see. "Special Agent Briggs, FBI," he said, his voice carrying. "I'm going to need to ask you all some questions."

YOU

Could you be any clearer? The numbers. The spiral. The dates. It's an act of contrition. An act of devotion.

An act of revenge.

You've waited so long. You've waited, and you've planned, and now that you're this close, you can feel it. The old anger, creeping back into your veins. The power.

The fear.

You will finish it. Three times three times three. You will be worthy.

This time, you will not fail.

CHAPTER 34

The dream started the way it always did. I was walking through a narrow hallway. The floor was tiled. The walls were white. Fluorescent lights flickered overhead. On the ground, my shadow flickered, too.

At the end of the hallway, there was a metal door. I walked toward it. *Don't. Don't open the door. Don't go in there.* The warning came from my conscious mind, which knew all too well what lay down that road.

But I couldn't stop. I opened the door. I stepped into the darkness. I reached for the light switch on the wall. I felt something warm and sticky on my hands.

Blood.

I flipped the switch. Everything went white. All I could do was blink until the scene settled in front of me.

A spotlight.

A crowd.

I was onstage, wearing the royal blue dress I'd tried on

in the store. My gaze traveled over the audience, picking out the ones I'd marked in advance for readings. The woman in the white vest, clutching her purse like it might sprout legs and run away. The teenager whose eyes were already tearing up. The older gentleman in the pale blue suit, sitting dead center in the front row.

This isn't right, I thought frantically. *I don't want to do this.* I turned, and in the wings, I saw myself. Younger. Watching. Waiting.

I woke with a start. My hands were wound tightly in the sheets. My chest heaved up and down. I was alone in the room. *No Sloane.* Processing that, I rolled over to look at the clock and froze.

The walls were completely covered. Sheet after sheet of paper, marked in red. *This must have taken Sloane all night,* I thought. She hadn't said a word when we'd gotten back to the room—not about the message from our killer, not about Aaron and the accusations Beau had flung at him.

Rolling out of bed, I went to examine Sloane's work more closely. Twelve sheets of printer paper had been affixed to the wall in four rows of three.

January, February, March . . .

I was looking at a handwritten calendar. Dates had been circled at seemingly random intervals. *Six in January, three in February, four in March.* I scanned the next row. *A handful in April, only two in May.*

"Nothing in June or July," I murmured out loud. My hand lifted. I pressed my fingers to the day that would always jump out at me in any calendar. *June 21st.* That was the day my mother had disappeared. Like the rest of the days in June, it was unmarked on Sloane's calendar.

I scanned the remainder of the months, then moved on to the rest of the walls in our room. More calendars. More dates. Taking a step back, I took in the full scope of what Sloane had done. There were years' worth of calendars on these walls, with the same dates marked on every one.

"Sloane?" I called toward the bathroom. The door was closed, but a moment later, I got a reply.

"I'm not naked!"

In Sloane-speak, that was as good as an invitation to come in. "Did you sleep at all last night?" I asked as I opened the door.

"Negative," Sloane replied. She was wrapped in a towel and staring at the mirror. Her hair was wet. On the mirror's surface she'd drawn a Fibonacci spiral. It covered her face in the reflection.

Sloane stared at herself through the spiral. "My mother was a dancer," she said suddenly. "A showgirl. She was very beautiful."

That was the first time I'd ever heard Sloane mention her mother. I knew, then, that she'd been awake all night for a reason beyond the papers on the walls.

"My biological father likes beautiful things." Sloane turned to look at me. "Tory is aesthetically appealing, don't you think? And the other girl with Aaron was very symmetrical."

You're wondering if Aaron takes after your father. You're wondering if Tory is his secret, the way your mother was his father's.

"Sloane—" I started to say, but she cut me off.

"It doesn't matter," Sloane said, in the tone of someone to whom it mattered very much. "January twelfth," she said fiercely. "That's what matters. Today's the ninth. We have three days."

"Three days?" I repeated.

Sloane nodded. "Until he kills again."

"Tertium. Tertium. Tertium." Sloane stood in the middle of our suite, gesturing to the paper-covered walls. "Three times three is nine."

I need nine.

"And three times three times three," Sloane continued, "is twenty-seven."

Tertium. Tertium. Tertium. Three times three times three.

"Remember what I said yesterday about the dates and how I think they're derived from the Fibonacci sequence?" Sloane said. "I spent all night going through the different possible methods of derivation. But this one"—she pointed to the first wall I'd investigated—"is the only version where, if you end the sequence twenty-seven dates in, you also end up with exactly three repetitions within the sequence."

Three. Three times three times three.

"It was just a theory," Sloane said. "But then I hacked the FBI's server."

"You *what?*"

"I did a search over the past fifteen years," Sloane clarified helpfully. "For murders committed on January first."

"You hacked the FBI?" I said incredulously.

"And Interpol," Sloane replied brightly. "And you'll never guess what I found."

Security holes that the world's most elite crime-solving agencies seriously need to patch?

"Eleven years ago there was a serial killer in upstate New York." Sloane walked over to the next wall, years' worth of calendars papering it from ceiling to floor. She knelt and pressed her fingers to one of the calendar pages.

"The first victim—a prostitute—turned up dead on August first of that year." She moved her hand down the page. "Second victim on August ninth, third victim on August thirteenth." She moved on to the next page. "September first, September fourteenth." She bypassed October. "November second, November twenty-third." She slowed as she brought her hand to rest on the date marked in December. "December third."

She looked up at me, and I did the mental count. *Eight,* I thought. *That's eight.*

I looked for the next date. *January first.*

"It's the same pattern," Sloane said. "Just with a different start date." She turned to the last wall. There was a single piece of paper on it. The first thirteen numbers of the Fibonacci sequence.

1, 1, 2, 3, 5, 8, 13, 21, 34, 55, 89, 144, 233

"1/1," Sloane said, "January first. In the first iteration I tried, the second date generated was 1/2. But that method limits you to dates in the first third of the month. Hardly efficient. Instead . . ." She drew a square around the second *1* and the 2 that followed it. "Voila. 1/12. Split in a different spot, that's 11/2, so we add both of those dates to the list. Tack on the next digit in the sequence, and you've got 11/23. Once we've made all the dates we possibly can including the first integer in the sequence, we move on to the second. That gives us 1/2 and 1/23. And if you split 1/23 after the two instead of the one, that gives us 12/3. Then on to the third integer, 2/3. February only has twenty-eight days, so 2/35 is just filler. We go on to 3/5, then 5/8, 8/1, 8/13, 1/3, 3/2, 3/21, 2/1, 2/13, 1/3—you see how January third just repeated?"

My brain raced as I tried to keep up.

"If you end the sequence after it's produced twenty-seven dates—*three times three times three*—you've generated exactly three repeated dates: January third, February third, and May eighth."

I tried to parse what Sloane was saying. If you generated a total of twenty-seven dates based on the Fibonacci sequence, you ended up with a pattern that was consistent not only with our killer's pattern, but also with a series of nine murders committed over a decade ago.

I need nine.

"The case from eleven years ago," I said, commanding Sloane's attention. "Did they ever catch the killer?"

Sloane tilted her head to the side. "I'm not sure. I was just looking at the dates. Give me a second." Sloane's eidetic memory meant that she automatically memorized anything she read. After going back over the files in her head, she answered the question. "The case is still open. The killer was never caught."

Most serial killers don't just stop, I thought, Agent Sterling's words echoing in my mind. *Not unless someone stops them.*

"Sloane," I said, trying to keep my mind from racing too fast. "The killer who ended his run on January first—how did he kill his victims?"

This time, it took Sloane a fraction of a second to pull the information to the front of her mind. "He slit their throats," she said. "With a knife."

CHAPTER 35

I tried Sterling's cell, then Briggs's. Neither of them answered. *They were probably up all night,* I thought, *talking to witnesses, trying to figure out who, if anyone, hypnotized Aaron's "friend" to deliver that message.*

"I'm going to talk to Dean," I told Sloane. "Catch him up on what you just told me." I took in the dark circles under Sloane's eyes. "You should try getting some sleep."

Sloane frowned. "Giraffes only sleep four and a half hours a day."

Knowing a losing battle when I saw one, I let her be. Making my way quietly across the suite, I stopped outside Dean's room. The door was cracked open. I placed my hand flat on the wood.

"Dean?" I called. When he didn't respond, I knocked lightly. The door drifted inward, and I caught sight of Dean sleeping. He'd pushed his bed to one side of the room and slept with his back to the wall. His blond hair fell gently into his eyes. His face was free of tension.

He looked peaceful.

I began backing out of the doorway. The floor creaked, and Dean bolted up in bed, his eyes unseeing, his hand thrust out in front of him. His fingers were curved, like he'd caught a ghost by the neck.

"It's me," I said quickly. When he still didn't register my presence, I turned on the light. "It's me, Dean." I stepped toward the bed. *It's just me.*

Dean's head swiveled. He stared through me. And then a moment later, he was back. His eyes focused on mine. "Cassie." He said my name the way another person might rattle off a prayer.

"Sorry," I told him, coming closer. "For waking you up."

"Don't be sorry," Dean said, his voice rough.

I crawled onto the bed beside him. His hands found their way to the ends of my hair, his touch soft. He closed his eyes for a moment, taking in the warmth of my body. When he opened them, they were calmer, clear.

"Something's wrong," Dean said, observant as always. I wondered if he could see the tension in my shoulders. I wondered if he could feel it with his featherlight touch.

"Sloane found something." I let his touch steady me, even as it steadied him. "She derived a series of twenty-seven dates from the Fibonacci sequence. Then she did a search on the FBI's database for serial murders where one or more of the killings happened on New Year's Day."

"Briggs and Sterling gave her that kind of access?"

My facial expression must have answered that question for me.

"She hacked the FBI." Dean paused. "Of course she did. She's Sloane."

"She found a decade-old case that fits the same pattern," I told him. "Nine victims, killed on Fibonacci dates."

"MO?" Dean asked.

"Killer used a knife. He attacked from behind and slit his victims' throats. The first victim was a prostitute. I don't have information on any of the others."

"Nine bodies," Dean repeated. "On dates derived from the Fibonacci sequence."

I shifted my body, leaning into his. "Last night, the message was 'I need nine.' *Need,* Dean, not 'want,' not 'I'm going to kill nine.' *Need.*"

The number of victims mattered, the same way the numbers on the wrists did, the same way the dates did.

"The case Sloane found is still open," I told Dean. "It was never closed. Sterling said that serial killers don't just stop killing."

Dean heard the question I hadn't yet put into words. *Could we be dealing with the same killer?*

"Eleven years is a long time for a killer to deny himself," Dean said. I saw the shift in Dean before his words confirmed it. "Each time I kill, I need more. To go without, for so long . . ."

"Is it even possible?" I asked Dean. "Can an UNSUB kill nine people and then just . . . wait?"

"Our UNSUB just killed four people in four days," Dean replied. "And now he's waiting. Smaller scale, same concept."

The numbers matter. The numbers told the UNSUB where to kill, when to kill, how long to wait. But making sure a portion of the sequence appeared on each victim's wrist?

From the beginning, we'd read that as a message. What if the message was *I've done this before?*

Suddenly, my throat tightened. *Tertium,* I thought.

"Dean." My lips felt numb. "What if the word on the arrow didn't just refer to Eugene Lockhart being the UNSUB's third victim this time around?"

Tertium. Tertium. Tertium. I could hear the girl saying the word. I could see her gaze staring out into the crowd.

"The third time." Dean slid to the end of the bed. He sat there for a moment in silence, and I knew he was putting himself in the killer's shoes, walking through the logic without ever saying it out loud. Finally, he stood. "We need to call Briggs."

CHAPTER 36

Dean made the call.

Pick up, I thought. *Pick up, Briggs.*

If this *was* the killer's third time going through this pattern—nine bodies, killed on Fibonacci dates—we weren't dealing with a novice. We were dealing with an expert. *The level of planning. The lack of evidence left behind.*

It fit.

A second realization followed on the heels of the first. *If our killer was slitting throats more than a decade ago, we're looking for someone no younger than their late twenties.* And if the New York murders had been the second set and not the first . . .

"Briggs." Dean's voice was terse, but calm. I turned toward him as he began bringing Briggs up to speed. "We have reason to believe this might not be our UNSUB's first rodeo."

Dean fell silent as Agent Briggs replied. I closed the space between Dean and me and put a hand on his arm. "Tell him that Sloane broke the code," I said. "The UNSUB is going to kill again—in the Grand Ballroom—on January twelfth."

Dean hung up the call without saying another word.

"What?" I asked him. "Why did you hang up?"

Dean's grip tightened over his phone.

"Dean?"

"Briggs and Sterling got a call at three in the morning."

There was only one reason to call the FBI at three in the morning. *It's too soon,* I thought. *Sloane said the next murder would be on the twelfth. The pattern—*

"The Majesty's head of security was attacked," Dean continued. "Blunt-force trauma."

I thought of the man who'd pulled us into the security office. The one who had come to get Sloane's father the night Camille was murdered.

"It fits the MO," Dean continued. "New method. Numbers on his wrist."

"Weapon?" I asked.

"A brick."

You bashed his head in with a brick. You took a brick and wrapped your fingers around it, and rage exploded inside of you, and you—

"Cassie." Dean cut my thought off. "There's something else you should know."

Did you get tired of waiting? I asked the UNSUB silently. *Did something set you off? Did you get a rush out of watching this man go down? Did you savor the sound of his skull cracking?* I couldn't stop. *Each time, you feel more invincible, less fallible, less human.*

"Cassie," Dean said again. "The victim was still alive when they found him. He's in a medically induced coma now, but he's not dead."

Dean's words snapped me out of it.

You made a mistake, I thought. This was a killer who didn't *make* mistakes. Having left a victim alive would gnaw at him from the inside out.

"We need more information," I said. "Pictures of the crime scene, defensive wounds on the victim, anything that might help us walk through it."

"They don't need us to walk through anything," Dean said.

"Explain how that sentence could possibly be true."

I turned in the direction of the voice that had spoken those words and saw Lia. I wondered how long she'd been standing there, watching the interplay between Dean and me.

"They don't need us to profile it, because there was a witness." Dean looked from Lia to me. "They've already apprehended the suspect."

On-screen, Beau Donovan sat in an interrogation room. His hands were cuffed behind his back. He was staring straight ahead—not *at* Sterling and Briggs, but *through* them.

"This isn't right," Sloane said, plopping down on the floor beside the coffee table. A moment later, she popped back up, pacing. "It was supposed to happen on the twelfth. It doesn't add up."

She didn't say that she *needed* it to add up. She didn't say that she needed this one thing to make sense.

"Mr. Donovan, a witness puts you at the crime scene, crouched over the victim, writing on his wrist." Briggs was playing bad cop. It wasn't so much in the words he said as in the way he said them, like each part of that statement was a nail in Beau Donovan's coffin.

A muscle in Beau's cheek twitched.

"Fear," Michael said. "With a heaping side of anger, and underneath that . . ." Michael searched the lines of Beau's face. "Playing around the corners of the lips—*satisfaction*."

Satisfaction. That was more damning than either anger or fear. Innocent people weren't *satisfied* when they were arrested for attempted murder.

"Beau." Agent Sterling wasn't a natural fit for good cop, but based on what we knew of Beau, she must have suspected he'd be more likely—though still *not* likely—to trust a female. "If you don't talk to us, we can't help you."

Beau slumped in his seat, as much as he could with both hands cuffed behind his back.

"You were found with *this* in the pocket of your sweatshirt." Briggs threw down an evidence bag. Inside was a permanent marker. Black. I registered the color, but didn't dwell on it. "What do you think the chances are that forensics shows us your pen is a match for *this*?" Briggs laid a photo beside the evidence bag. *The head of security's wrist.*

Written on it was a four-digit number.

"Nine-zero-nine-five," Sloane read. She walked forward

until she was almost blocking the screen. "It's the wrong number. *Seven-seven-six-one.*" She punctuated each number by tapping the middle finger on her right hand against her thumb. "That's what's next. That number"—she gestured toward the screen—"doesn't appear anywhere in the first hundred digits of the Fibonacci sequence."

On-screen, Agent Briggs wielded silence like a weapon. He was waiting for Beau to crack.

"I don't have to say anything to you."

Michael raised an eyebrow at Beau's tone, but this time, I didn't need a translation. *Bravado.* The kind born of being kicked too hard for too long.

Agent Sterling walked around to Beau's side of the table. For a moment, I thought he might lunge at her, but instead, he stiffened as she moved to unlock his cuffs.

"You don't have to say anything," she agreed. "But I think you want to. I think there's something you want us to know."

Michael took in Beau's nonverbal response, then made a finger-gunning motion at the screen. "Point to the lady," he said.

"You told us that Camille Holt was nice to you." Agent Sterling retreated back to her side of the table, never breaking eye contact with Beau. "Right now, it's looking an awful lot like you killed her."

"Even if I told you I didn't," Beau grunted, "you wouldn't believe me."

"Try me."

For a moment, I actually thought he might. Instead, he

settled back in his seat again. "I don't feel much like talking," he said.

"During our last interview, you told us you were with Tory Howard when Camille was murdered." Agent Briggs leaned forward. "But we've recently come to believe that Tory was with Aaron Shaw that night."

"Maybe I was trying to protect her," Beau spat. "From you assholes."

"Or maybe," Briggs suggested, "you were really trying to protect yourself. Tory and Aaron have been keeping things on the down low. She didn't want to give his name as her alibi. She must have thought she was pretty lucky when you volunteered yourself for that role." He leaned forward. "She just didn't realize that when she allowed you to do so, she became *your* alibi for that night, too."

Smart, I thought. Looking at Beau on paper, it was easy to underestimate him. High school dropout. Working a crappy job. He made no effort whatsoever to give the impression that he was anything more—but his success at the poker tournament told a very different story.

He's used to being dismissed and ignored, but has a very high IQ, I thought.

"Tory lied to us." Briggs lowered his voice. "Maybe we should be looking at charging her as an accessory."

"Briggs," Sterling said sharply—good cop until the end.

Agent Briggs leaned across the table, getting in Beau's face and going in for the kill. "Tell me, Beau, has Tory ever taught you how to hypnotize someone?"

CHAPTER 37

Briggs and Sterling kept at it, but Beau didn't say a word. Eventually, they left him to stew and put in a call to us.

"Thoughts?" Briggs asked on speaker.

"It's not him." Sloane was practically vibrating with intensity. "You have to see that. The numbers? *Wrong.* The location? *Wrong.* The timing?" Sloane turned her back on the phone. *"It's all wrong."*

Silence descended. Dean filled the void. "He's got the potential for violence." The way Dean phrased that observation made me wonder if he saw any of himself in Beau. "He's been living at the bottom of a hierarchy that favors those with money and power, and he has neither. Given the opportunity, he'd enjoy playing a game where he came out on top." Dean leaned on the counter, his head bowed. "He's angry, and I'm guessing he's spent a lot of his life being tossed aside like garbage. If the Majesty's head of security does die, Beau won't feel bad about it. Given the choice, he'd probably pick up that brick again."

"But—" Sloane started to say.

"But," Dean said, "Sloane's right. The numbers on the victims' wrists aren't just a part of this UNSUB's MO. They're a part of his signature. He *needs* to mark his victims. And I'm not convinced we're dealing with an UNSUB who, after four meticulously planned kills, gets caught *writing* numbers onto the wrist of the fifth before the man is even dead."

"The *wrong* numbers," Sloane put in emphatically.

Sterling cleared her throat. "I tend to agree with Sloane and Dean. Our UNSUB's MO has changed with each kill. And so has the method with which the victims were marked. Until now."

Eugene Lockhart had numbers written on his wrist in a permanent marker, too, I realized.

"Say you'd killed someone." Lia instantly had the room's attention. "Or, in Beau's case, say that you thought the person you'd hit with a brick was about to die." She leaned back on the heels of her hands, and my mind went back to Two Truths and a Lie.

I killed a man when I was nine.

"Maybe you had a choice. Maybe you didn't. And afterward," Lia continued, her voice light and airy, "say you didn't want to get caught. What do you do?"

Seconds ticked by in silence. Dean was the one who provided the answer. He knew Lia better than any of us. "You lie."

"You lie," Lia repeated. "You cover it up. And if you happened to know there was a serial killer out there . . ." Lia shrugged.

"Maybe Beau heard about the numbers," I said, picking up where Lia had left off. "Not what the pattern was, exactly, just that there *were* numbers on all of the victims' wrists."

Sterling picked up where I left off. "He grabs that brick. He hits the victim. Panics, and to cover, he tries to make it look like the work of our UNSUB."

Anger. Fear. Satisfaction. Everything Michael had said Beau had been feeling fit with this interpretation of events.

Beau wasn't our UNSUB. He was mimicking our UNSUB.

"That means the pattern's not broken," Sloane whispered. "The pattern isn't wrong."

You are not broken, I translated. *You are not wrong.*

"Grand Ballroom. January twelfth." Sloane held out first one finger, then another, like she was counting. "The pattern says the next murder is going to happen in the Grand Ballroom on January twelfth."

Three days. If Sloane was right about the Fibonacci dates, that wasn't our only problem.

"Speaking of the pattern," I told Sterling and Briggs, dread seeping back over my body, "there's something else you should know."

CHAPTER 38

"Sloane hacked the FBI's files. Based on what she found, you think our UNSUB might have done this before." Agent Sterling let her summation of what I'd just said hang in the air for several seconds before she added, "Twice."

"It's just a theory," I replied before either of the agents could decide that now was a good time to lecture Sloane on the virtues of *not* hacking the FBI. "But the case Sloane found was never solved, and it fits the pattern."

"With respect to location as well?" Briggs asked. I could practically *hear* him rubbing his temples. "Was that killer working in a spiral?"

"A Fibonacci spiral," Sloane corrected. "And no, he wasn't."

"Numbers on the wrists?" Sterling asked.

"No," Sloane said again.

No numbers on the wrist. No spiral. If we were dealing with the same killer, then that killer had changed. That wasn't unheard of, but we typically saw changes in an UNSUB's MO—the necessary elements of a crime. Writing numbers on the victims' wrists wasn't *necessary*. Killing them in a spiral was a *choice*. A killer's MO might change, but typically, the signature stayed the same.

"The numbers were always there." Sloane's voice was insistent. "Even if he didn't write them on someone's wrist, or kill in the right locations, they were there."

In the dates, I finished silently. Maybe the signature, the deep-seated psychological *need* being manifested in the UNSUB's behavior, was that the kills *needed* to be driven by the numbers. Viewed from that perspective, the additional elements of the Vegas crimes weren't a departure in signature.

They were an escalation. *More numbers, more rules.*

"I'm older now," Dean said, testing out the possibility. "Wiser, better. I've waited for so long, planned so long. . . ." His voice was lower when he profiled, deeper. "Once upon a time, I was an amateur. Now, I'm an artist. Invincible. Unstoppable."

"And this time," I said slowly, "you want credit."

That's why you wrote the numbers on your victims' wrists, I thought. *You wanted us to crack the code. You wanted us to see the full extent of what you'd done.*

"We'll have a hard enough time convincing the local PD

that Beau Donovan isn't our serial killer *without* bringing up a decade-old case that, on the surface, looks completely unrelated." Briggs's voice broke into my thoughts. "The powers that be in this city want this case solved. Now. If we push the theory that this last attack isn't the work of our UNSUB, we can expect the cooperation we've seen up to this point to dry up pretty quickly."

"Meaning," Lia said, "that you might lose your complimentary suite at the Desert Rose. I hear there are some *lovely* establishments just off the Strip."

"Meaning," Agent Briggs countered, "that if we want a list of hotel guests to compare to witnesses and persons of interest in the New York case, those same powers that be are probably going to refuse to hand anything over without a warrant."

"And," Agent Sterling added soberly, "Grayson Shaw will almost certainly insist on opening back up the Grand Ballroom at the Majesty."

My fingers curled themselves inward, my nails lightly scratching the surface of my palms. *Three days.* That was how long we had until the next murder. That was how long we had to convince Sloane's father that reopening the ballroom was a mistake.

"What do you want us to do?" Dean was nothing if not focused.

"For now," Agent Briggs said, "we just need you to stay put. Stay in the room and stay out of trouble. We're on it."

— — —

Whether or not Sterling and Briggs were "on it," none of us had any intention of sitting around and twiddling our thumbs until they came up with our next assignment.

I grabbed a pen and the Majesty notepad by the phone and wrote down the names of everyone we'd talked to so far on this case, then crossed off two: the head of security and Camille Holt. He was in a coma; she was dead. Neither were suspects.

"The New York murders were committed eleven years ago," I said. "By virtue of their ages, that rules out not just Beau Donovan, but also Aaron Shaw and Tory Howard."

Children could be made to do horrible things—Dean was proof enough of that. But slitting someone's throat from behind? That wasn't the MO of a child with limited reach.

I went through the rest of the names on my list. Thomas Wesley was thirty-nine, which put him at twenty-seven and serving as the CEO of his first company at the time of the New York murders. The professor was thirty-two, and a quick internet search informed me that he'd done his undergraduate degree at NYU. I hesitated slightly, then added a final name to the list.

Grayson Shaw.

Sloane's father was in his early fifties. He was clearly a man who thrived on power and being in control. The way he'd treated Sloane told me that he had tendencies toward seeing people as possessions and behaving callously and unemotionally toward them.

I would have bet Michael's car that, as the owner of the

Majesty corporation, Grayson Shaw made frequent trips to New York.

"Far be it from me to suggest that Sloane hack the FBI again," Michael said, preventing Sloane from dwelling on her father's name, "but I think Sloane should hack the FBI again."

Judd appeared in the doorway a moment later. He eyed Michael, eyed the rest of us, and then went to make himself some coffee.

"You missed out on a lot of action this morning," Lia called after him.

He didn't so much as turn around. "I don't miss out on much."

In other words: Judd knew quite well what we'd spent our morning doing. He just hadn't interfered—and he wasn't going to interfere now. Judd's priority wasn't solving cases, or making sure the FBI *didn't* get hacked. His job was keeping us safe and fed.

No matter what.

As far as he was concerned, most everything else came out in the wash.

"If *tertium* doesn't just mean that our killer has a fixation on the number three, if it really *does* mean that this is the third time our killer has pulled this routine," Lia was saying beside me, warming up to Michael's suggestion, "it only makes sense to see if we can dig up the case we're missing."

Only Lia could make hacking the FBI sound *reasonable*.

"I can set up a program," Sloane volunteered. "Not just

for the FBI, but for Interpol, local police databases, anything I already have a back door into. I'll have it search any available records that fit our parameters. Last time, I did a manual search for a single Fibonacci date. This will take a little more time up front, but the results will be more comprehensive."

"In the meantime." Judd came to stand at the edge of the kitchen. "The rest of you miscreants can eat."

Michael opened his mouth to object, but Judd quelled him with a look.

"Room service?" Michael suggested smoothly.

"Only if you want to rack up a two-hundred-dollar bill," Judd replied.

Michael made his way over to the nearest phone. He'd been remarkably low-key since the fight at the pool, but I knew before he even started to place his order that he'd try his best to rack up a *three*-hundred-dollar breakfast bill.

The only thing Judd vetoed was the champagne.

While we waited for the food, I retreated to take a shower. I'd been going a million miles an hour since Sloane had explained the dates to me that morning. A shower would be good for me. Even better, it might quiet my mind enough that I could really think.

When I'd first joined the program, we'd been restricted to cold cases, fed no more than the occasional scrap about whatever case our handlers were currently working. In the three months since the rules had changed, we'd worked a half-dozen active cases. The first one we'd solved in less than three days. The second, even faster than that. The third had taken almost a week, but this one . . .

So many details. The longer the case dragged on, the more information my brain had to juggle. The UNSUB's profile evolved with each kill, and now that it looked like we might be dealing with a repeat offender, my brain had kicked into hyperdrive. The files I'd read. The interviews I'd watched. My own first impressions.

I was learning that the hardest thing about being a profiler was figuring out what information to discard. Did it matter that Beau and Tory had both spent time in foster homes? What about the way Aaron both resented and bowed down to his father? The slightly clingy vibe I'd gotten from Thomas Wesley's assistant? The drink the professor had ordered, but only pretended to drink?

Even now that our suspicions were targeted at suspects over the age of thirty, I couldn't turn off the part of my brain that arranged and rearranged what I knew about everyone involved, continually looking for meaning.

I couldn't shake the feeling that I was missing something. Then again, being a profiler meant that I always felt like I was missing something, right up until the case was closed. Until the killing *stopped*—and not just for a day or two days or three.

For good.

The sound of the shower spray beating against the tub was rhythmic and soothing. I let it drown out my thoughts as I stepped into the shower and under the spray. *Breathe in.*

Breathe out. I turned, arching my neck and letting the water soak my hair and dribble down the front of my face.

For a few, blissful minutes my mind was quiet—but it never stayed quiet for long.

June twenty-first. That was where my brain went when I wasn't trying to force it to think about one thing or another. *My mother's dressing room. Blood on my hands. Blood on the walls.*

"Dance it off, Cassie."

I could compartmentalize. I could distract myself. I could focus on the current case to the exclusion of everything else—but still, the memories and the fears and the sinking certainty about the skeleton in that dirt-road grave were there, waiting for me, just below the surface.

My dreams were proof enough of that.

June twenty-first, I thought again. I remembered standing in front of the calendars Sloane had drawn, pressing my fingers to the date. *No Fibonacci dates in June.*

And still, my mind cycled back. *June twenty-first.*

Why was I thinking about this? Not about my mother—I didn't need my expertise in the human psyche to figure that one out—but about the date? I pictured myself standing in front of the calendar, going through it month by month. *A handful in April, only two in May. None in June.*

A breath caught in my throat. My hand lashed out of its own accord, turning the shower off. I stepped out, barely remembering to wrap a towel around my torso on my way back into the bedroom.

I walked over to the wall with the colored objects sitting—large to small—on the glass shelf. I looked past the sheets Sloane had put up for January, for February, for March, for April.

Two dates in May.

"May fifth," I said out loud, my entire body tensing. "And May eighth."

Six years, this May, Judd had told me. But that wasn't all he'd told me. He'd told me the date on which Scarlett was murdered. *May eighth.*

I didn't remember walking to the kitchen, but the next thing I knew, I was there, towel and all, dripping on the floor.

Michael's gaze went to my face. Dean went very still. Even Lia seemed to sense that now wasn't the moment to make a comment about my state of undress.

"Judd," I said.

"Everything okay there, Cassie?" He was standing at the counter, doing a crossword.

All I could think was that the answer had to be *no.* When I asked, Judd had to say *no.*

"The UNSUB who killed Scarlett," I said. "Nightshade. How many people did he kill?" I realized, distantly, that the question I'd asked couldn't be answered with a *yes* or a *no.*

Judd's expression wavered, just for an instant. I thought he would refuse to answer, but he didn't.

"As far as we know," he said, his voice hoarse, "he killed nine."

YOU

Everything can be counted. Everything but true infinity has its end.

Without the knife in hand, all you can do is lightly trace the pattern on the surface of your shirt. You can feel the cuts underneath, feel the promise you etched into your own skin.

Around. Up and down. Left and right.

Seven plus two is nine.

Nine is the number. And Nine is what you were always meant to be.

CHAPTER 39

Serial killers don't just stop. Agent Sterling had been the one to tell me that. I'd realized at the time that she had been thinking about the UNSUB who had killed Scarlett Hawkins.

I just hadn't realized that Scarlett was Nightshade's ninth.

As Judd stood there, staring at and through me, my brain regurgitated everything I'd ever overheard about his daughter's death. Briggs and Sterling had been assigned to the Nightshade case shortly after they'd arrested Dean's father. They'd gone after the killer hard. And in retaliation, he'd come after them.

He'd killed their friend, a member of their team—one who was never supposed to be on the front lines—in her own lab.

They never caught him. I couldn't stop the words from cycling through my mind, over and over again. *And serial killers don't just stop.*

New York, eleven years ago.

D.C., five and a half.

And now Vegas.

Dean came to stand beside Judd. Neither of them was much for words. I could see, in the way they stood, echoes of the man who'd lost his daughter and the twelve-year-old boy he'd put aside his grief to save.

"We need to look up the dates of the rest of Nightshade's kills." When Dean spoke, it wasn't to offer comfort. Judd wasn't the type you comforted.

You don't want comfort. You never have. You want the man who killed your daughter, and you want him dead.

I understood that, better than most.

"We don't need to look up anything." Judd's voice was hard. "I know the dates." His chin wavered slightly, his lips curving inward toward his teeth. "March fourth. March fifth. March twenty-first." I could hear the marine in his tone as he spoke, like he was reading a list of fallen comrades. "April second. April fourth."

"Stop." Sloane came over and grabbed his hand. "Judd," she said, her heart in her eyes, "you can stop now."

But he couldn't. "April fifth. April twenty-third. May fifth." He swallowed, and even as his face tightened, I could see the sheen of tears in his eyes. "May eighth."

The muscles in Judd's arms tensed. For a moment, I thought he was going to push Sloane away, but instead, his fingers curved around hers. "The dates match?" he asked her.

Sloane nodded, and once she started, she couldn't stop nodding. "I wish they didn't," she said fiercely. "I wish I'd never seen it. I wish—"

"Don't," Judd told her sharply. "Don't you ever apologize for being what you are."

He gently returned her hand to her side. Then he looked around at each of us, one by one. "I should be the one to tell Ronnie and Briggs," he said. "And I should do it in person."

"You go." Lia beat me to responding. "We'll be fine." Lia rarely spoke in sentences that short. The look on her face reminded me that Judd had been taking care of Lia since she was thirteen years old.

"I don't want you poking around in the Nightshade file." Judd stared at Lia as he issued that order, but it was clear he was talking to all of us. "I know how you all work. I know the second I walk out the door, you'll be wanting to have Sloane pull up the details so you can dive in headfirst, but I'm pulling rank." Judd leveled a hard stare at each of us in turn. "You go near that file without my say-so, and I'll have you on the next plane back to Quantico, this case be damned."

There wasn't a person in the room who thought Judd made idle threats.

Room service arrived fifteen minutes after Judd left. None of us touched the food.

"Judd was right," Michael said, breaking the silence that had descended in Judd's wake. "It's too early in the day for champagne." He walked over to the bar and pulled out a bottle of whiskey. He got down five glasses.

"You really think this is the appropriate time to drink?" Dean asked him.

Michael stared at him. "Redding, I think this is the very definition of 'an appropriate time to drink.'" He turned to the rest of us. I shook my head. Lia held up two fingers.

"Sloane?" Michael asked. It was indicative of his personality that he rationed her caffeine intake, but didn't bat an eye at the thought of offering her hard liquor.

"In Alaska, you can be criminally prosecuted for feeding alcohol to a moose."

"I'm going to take that as a no," Michael said.

"In America," Dean pointed out, "you can be criminally prosecuted for underage drinking." Lia and Michael ignored him. I knew Dean well enough to know that his mind wasn't really on the bottle of whiskey. It was on Judd.

So was mine.

Without details, I could only sketch out the barest bones of a profile of the UNSUB who'd killed Judd's daughter. *The FBI came after you hard. You went after them personally.* That told me we were dealing with someone with no fear, who lived to put fear into others. Someone who saw killing as a game. Someone who liked to win. More likely male than female, even though the name *Nightshade* strongly suggested the killer's weapon of choice had been poison, which was more typically associated with women.

Unable to get further than that, I took a step back and

viewed this from the other side of the equation. I knew very little about Nightshade, but I knew a few things about Judd's daughter. Months ago, Agent Sterling had told me a story. We'd been held captive at the time, and she'd told me that as a kid, her best friend, Scarlett, was continually coming up with ridiculously dire scenarios and brainstorming how to get out of them. *You've been buried alive in a glass coffin with a sleeping cobra on your chest,* she would say. *What do you do?*

On another occasion, Judd had indicated that a school-aged Scarlett had once convinced a young Veronica Sterling to accompany her on a "scientific expedition" that involved some minor (or possibly not-so-minor) cliff-scaling.

You were fearless and funny and too stubborn to be talked out of anything once your mind was set, I thought, reading between the lines of what I knew. Scarlett had grown up to work in the FBI labs. *Were you working the Nightshade case?* I asked her silently. *Is that why you were in the lab that night?* I thought of Sloane getting a puzzle on the brain and refusing to let go until the numbers made sense. *Was that what you were like?*

Without reading the file, there was no way for me to know. *Did you see your killer, Scarlett? Did he watch you die?* The questions kept coming, one after another. *Was it fast, or was it slow? Did you call for help? Did you think about cobras and glass coffins? About Sterling and Briggs and Judd?*

A knock at the door pulled me from my thoughts. I shivered. Like a kid saying Bloody Mary into a mirror, part of me felt like I might have pulled the dark thing toward me, just by thinking his name.

Dean stood and walked toward the door, Michael and Lia on his heels. Dean stared through the peephole. "What do you want?" Whoever was on the other side, Dean wasn't feeling friendly.

"I have something for you."

The voice was muffled slightly by the door, but I recognized it anyway.

"Aaron?" Sloane came to stand beside Dean. For a split second, her face lit up. I saw the exact moment she remembered that her half brother might not be all that different from the father they shared.

"Sloane." Aaron spoke to her now, instead of Dean. "I know what you do for the FBI. My father told me."

I didn't trust Sloane's father—and that made it very hard to trust Aaron.

"I don't like it," Aaron continued. "This isn't the kind of life I want for you. This isn't the conversation I want us to be having. But I need to get something to the FBI."

Dean's eyes darted to Lia. She nodded. Aaron was telling the truth.

"Then give it to the police," Dean barked back, still not inclined to open the door.

"My father owns the police." Aaron pitched his voice lower. I struggled to hear him. "And he wants Beau Donovan in jail."

At the mention of Beau's name, I took a step forward.

What Aaron was saying fit with what Agent Briggs had said about the powers that be wanting a neat resolution to their little serial killer problem.

"Please," Aaron said. "The longer I stand in the hallway, the better the chances someone catches me on a security feed, and then we'll have bigger problems than the fact that you don't trust me."

Dean walked into the kitchen. He opened one drawer, then another. A moment later, he went back to the front door.

Carrying a butcher's knife.

CHAPTER 40

Dean opened the door. Aaron stepped in, eyed Dean's knife, and let the door shut behind him.

"I appreciate that someone's watching out for Sloane," Aaron told Dean. "But I also feel compelled to point out that a knife like that wouldn't do much good if the person on the other side of this door had a gun."

All that glitters is not gold, I thought, taking in the warning embedded in Aaron's words. *You're used to the people around you being armed. The world you grew up in is a dangerous, glittering place.*

Dean gave Sloane's brother a dead-eyed stare. "You might be surprised."

Aaron must have seen something there that sent a chill down his spine. "I'm not armed," he assured Dean, "and I'm not here to hurt anyone. You can trust me."

"Not an incredibly trusting fellow, Dean," Michael said lightly. "Must come from being raised by a psychotic serial killer with a fondness for knives." He gave Aaron a steely smile. "Do come in."

Aaron's eyes sought out Lia. "You're the one who can detect lies?" he asked.

"Who?" Lia said. "Me?"

"I'm not armed," Aaron said again, staring her straight in the eye. "And I'm not here to hurt anyone."

Without another word, he took a seat in the living room. Dean sat opposite him. I stayed standing.

"As you are doubtlessly aware," Aaron started, "Beau Donovan and I got into an altercation last night."

The debacle backstage at Tory's show seemed like a lifetime ago—and given what we'd learned since then, almost painfully insignificant.

"You brought another girl to Tory's show." Sloane didn't look at Aaron as she spoke. She stared at the window behind him—at her map and her calculations and the Fibonacci spiral. "Beau considers Tory his sister. I suspect a nontrivial percentage of his demographic would have reacted similarly, under such circumstances." Then, as if that weren't clear enough, Sloane elaborated. "According to my calculations, there was a ninety-seven-point-six percent chance you deserved to be punched in the nose."

Aaron's lips tilted upward slightly. "I heard you were good with numbers."

I couldn't detect even a hint of criticism in Aaron's tone. From Michael's expression, I didn't think he caught any, either. My mind went to Sloane saying that she wanted Aaron to like her.

I studied Aaron. *You do like her. You want to know her.*

"How about we focus on this mythical *thing* you need us to give to the FBI?" Lia came and sat on the arm of Dean's chair. She didn't like strangers, and she didn't trust them—especially not with Sloane.

Aaron reached into his jacket pocket and pulled out a clear case. Inside, there was a DVD. "Security footage," he said. "Taken from a pawn shop across the street from where Victor McKinney was attacked."

Lia's silence seemed to confirm that the DVD was what Aaron had said it was.

"Victor was our head of security," Aaron continued. "From his perspective—and my father's—Beau Donovan was a security risk."

Beau had attacked Aaron. He hadn't done any damage, but to a man like Grayson Shaw, I doubted that mattered. If Sloane's father viewed Sloane as little more than an inconvenient possession, his legitimate son would be viewed not just as property, but as an extension of himself.

I'd seen that dynamic before—with Dean's father.

"If you'll play the footage, you'll see that Victor was the one who followed Beau, not the other way around. Victor was the one who slammed Beau against a wall. And Victor," Aaron made himself finish, "is the one who pulled a gun and put it to the side of Beau's head."

Dean absorbed that information in a heartbeat. "Your head of security never had any intention of pulling the trigger."

Aaron leaned forward. "Beau didn't know that."

Sloane's father liked issuing orders and ultimatums. It was a small hop to threats. Beau wasn't a person who would take well to being threatened. He had a temper. The moment the gun came out, he would have fought back.

"He grabbed a loose brick," Aaron said.

Blunt-force trauma.

"Self-defense," I said out loud. If Victor McKinney had drawn a gun on Beau, it was a clear case of self-defense. And if Aaron had seen the connection between Beau's arrest and what the Majesty's head of security had been sent to do, Grayson Shaw almost certainly had as well.

"How could your father let Beau take the fall for the first four murders?" I asked. "Doesn't he care that there's a serial killer still out there?"

"My guess?" Aaron replied. "My father thinks he and the FBI have scared the original killer away. He's not one to look a gift horse in the mouth. As it stands, Beau Donovan will never lay hands on me again, and no one is questioning why the Majesty's head of security went after Beau."

"Why bring this to us?" Lia asked. "Daddy Dearest isn't going to be very happy with you."

"He rarely is." Aaron stood, shrugging off the words like they meant nothing—which, of course, told me they meant more than he would ever admit.

You're the golden boy. The first-born son. The heir.

I stared at him for a moment, my mind assembling the pieces of the puzzle. *You don't go against your father without a reason.* "Tory," I said. "You did this for Tory."

Aaron didn't reply, but Michael translated his expression. "Yeah," he said, sounding gut-punched at the depth of emotion he saw on Aaron's face. "He did."

I read between the lines of Michael's words, my gaze locked on Aaron's. *You love her.* The realization took hold in the pit of my stomach.

Aaron's phone buzzed. He looked down, saved from confirming that he'd risked his father's wrath to save Beau because Beau was Tory's brother.

"Do we want to know what that text says?" Sloane asked.

Aaron looked up, meeting his sister's gaze. "That would depend on how you feel about the man Beau put in a coma waking up."

CHAPTER 41

Aaron left. It didn't take long to confirm what he'd told us. Victor McKinney—the Majesty's head of security and our latest victim—was awake. Briggs and Sterling were on their way to the hospital to interview him, armed with Aaron's accusations. We played the video, which was exactly what Aaron had said it was, and forwarded the footage to Sterling and Briggs. When they did talk to the Majesty's head of security, they'd have some very pointed questions for him.

Half an hour later, my phone rang. I almost answered out of reflex, expecting it to be Sterling or Briggs, but at the last second, I saw the caller ID.

My father.

Just like that, I was twelve years old again, walking down the hallway toward my mother's dressing room door. *Don't open it. Don't go there.*

I knew what he was calling to say.

I knew that once that door was open, nothing could ever be the same.

I declined the call.

"That's not a happy Cassie face," Michael prodded me.

"Drink your whiskey," I told him.

Sloane raised her hand, like a student waiting to be called on in class. "I think I would like some whiskey now," she said.

"First," Michael told her seriously, "I need to verify that you have no plans to feed this whiskey to a moose."

"He's kidding," Dean said, before Sloane could tell us the exact likelihood of stumbling over a moose in a Las Vegas casino. "And nobody's drinking any more whiskey."

Dean walked over to the counter and picked up the notepad I'd been making notes on earlier. He stared at the three remaining names.

The professor. Thomas Wesley. Sloane's father.

I approached Dean and looked over his shoulder at the list. *Focus on this, Cassie. These names, this case.*

Not the phone call. Not an answer I already knew.

"Eleven years ago," I said, addressing the UNSUB out loud and forcing everything else from my mind, "you slit the throats of nine people in a four-month period ranging from August to January."

"Five years ago," Dean responded, "I did it again. Poison, this time."

The changing method had always been one of the more perplexing aspects of the Vegas murders. Most killers had a single preferred method of killing—or, if not a method or weapon of choice, at least an *emotional* kill type. Poison meant killing without physical contact—not dissimilar from orchestrating an accident in which a young woman drowns. Slitting someone's throat, on the other hand, was closer to putting an arrow through an old man's chest. Neither was as painful as, say, burning alive.

"The last time we had an UNSUB who fluctuated this much from kill to kill," I said slowly, thinking back to the case we'd worked involving Dean's father, "we were dealing with multiple UNSUBs."

Dean's jaw clenched, but when I laid a hand on his shoulder, he relaxed under my touch.

" 'I need nine,' " Dean said after a moment. "*I*, not *we*."

As different as the four murders we were dealing with in Vegas were, *something* about them felt the same. Not just the numbers on the wrists, not just the locations or the dates, but the meticulousness of the method, the compulsive desire to send a message with each kill.

That didn't strike me as the work of multiple UNSUBs—not unless one of them was the architect behind it all.

You want to be recognized. You want to be heard.

It was there on every wrist, there in the message the UNSUB had carved into the arrow, there in the message a bystander had been hypnotized to deliver. *You don't want to be stopped. But you do want—very much—to be seen. You want to be larger-than-life,* I thought. *You want the world to know what you have done. You want to be a god among men. And for that,* I thought, *you need nine.*

"Why nine?" I asked. "What happens after the ninth?"

Dean echoed the most significant part of that question. "Why stop?"

Why stop eleven years ago? Why stop after killing Scarlett Hawkins?

"I need to see the file," I told Dean.

"You know we can't."

"Not Scarlett's. The other case Sloane found. The one in New York."

Sloane was sitting in front of the coffee table, holding the DVD Aaron had given us. She'd put it back in the case and was staring at it. I knew, instinctively, that she was thinking about Tory and what Aaron had done for her.

She was thinking—painfully *hoping*—that maybe Aaron wasn't like their father after all.

"Sloane," I said, "can you hack the FBI database and pull up the New York file?"

Having a flawless memory herself, Sloane didn't quite grasp the utility of rehacking a file she'd already read, but she did as I asked and set the DVD aside. Her fingers flew across the keyboard. After several seconds, she paused, then hit a few keys, then paused again.

"What's wrong?" I asked.

"The program I wrote earlier," Sloane said, "it finished its search."

"Let me guess," Lia put in. "It returned the Nightshade case, which we, under threat of exile, cannot so much as breathe on."

"Yes," Sloane said. "It did."

Lia tilted her head to one side. "Why doesn't that sound entirely true?"

"Because," Sloane said, turning the computer around so the rest of us could see, "that's not the only case it returned."

CHAPTER 42

Sloane's search hadn't yielded one case. Or two. Or three.

"How many are there?" I asked, my throat dry.

"Going back to the 1950s," Sloane replied, "almost a dozen. All serial murder, all unsolved."

I leaned back against the counter, my hands gripping the edge. "Nine kills each time?"

"I set the search to return anything over six," Sloane said. "With the thought that some victims may not have been discovered or linked to the same UNSUB."

"But all of the victims in each case were killed on one of the twenty-seven Fibonacci dates you identified," Dean said.

Sloane nodded. Without waiting for another question, she began skimming the files. "All over the country," she reported. "Three in Europe. Stabbings, beatings, poison, arson—it's all over the map."

"I need pictures," I said. "Anything you can get, from any

file that's not Nightshade's." Judd had forbidden us to go anywhere near the Nightshade case. But the others . . .

All of those victims. All of those families . . .

I had to do something. Nothing I did could possibly be enough. "This many cases," I told Dean, "going back that far . . ."

"I know." He met my eyes. Dean's father was one of the most prolific serial killers of our time. But this was so far beyond even him.

All over the world, going back sixty years—the chances that we were dealing with a single UNSUB were dwindling by the second.

"How good is this program?" Lia asked Sloane.

"It's only returning files that fit the parameters." Sloane sounded mildly insulted.

"No," Lia said. "What's the return rate?" Every muscle in her face was tight. "How many is it missing?"

The numbers lie, I realized, following Lia's train of thought. *Oh, God.*

Sloane closed her eyes, her lips moving rapidly as she went over the numbers. "When you take into account the number of databases I don't have access to, the likelihood of old records being digitalized, the role the FBI has played in the investigation of serial murders over the years . . ." She rocked slightly in her chair. "Half," she said. "At best, I might have gotten about half of the cases from 1950 until now."

Almost a dozen had been unfathomable. Twice that? *Not possible.*

"How many?" I said. "Total victims, how many are we talking?"

"At minimum?" Sloane whispered. "One hundred and eighty-nine."

One hundred and eighty-nine dead bodies. One hundred and eighty-nine lives snuffed out. One hundred and eighty-nine families who had lost what I'd lost. Lost *like* I'd lost.

One hundred and eighty-nine families who had never gotten answers.

Dean called Agent Sterling. I couldn't stop thinking about the look on Judd's face when he'd talked about Scarlett's murder. I couldn't stop thinking about my mother and the blood on her dressing room walls and the nights I'd spent waiting for the police to call. They never did. I waited, and they never called—and when they finally did, it wasn't any better. The days since they'd found the body—they weren't any better.

One hundred and eighty-nine.

It was too much.

I can't do this.

I did it anyway, because that was what I'd signed up for. That was what profilers did. We lived through horror. We submerged ourselves in it again and again and again. The same part of me that let me compartmentalize my mother's case would let me do this, and the same part of me that couldn't always fight the memories meant I would pay for it.

Profiling came with a cost.

But I would pay it again and again and again to make it so that even just one child never came home to blood on the walls.

Our in-suite printer nearly ran out of ink printing off the pictures of the bodies—and that was only for the case files Sloane had managed to fully access.

Mapping out the progression over time, several things became clear. *Old and young, male and female.* The victims ran the gamut. The only group not represented was children.

No kids. I wanted to cling to that, but I couldn't.

The next thing that became clear, to my profiler's eye, was that some sets of victims were more homogeneous than others. One case might involve only female victims with long blond hair; another might show clear signs that the murders had been those of opportunity, with no patterning to the victim choice at all.

"Multiple killers." Dean hadn't looked at the spread for more than thirty seconds when he said the words. "And it's not just a shift over time. Even back-to-back cases have totally different signatures."

To some of you, choosing the victims is paramount. To others, the target is beside the point.

Eleven cases. Eleven different killers. *Nightshade didn't kill those people in New York.* Viewed in the context of the larger pattern, it was easier to see. *Nine victims, killed on Fibonacci dates.* Everything else—everything that told us who the killer was—was different. It was like looking at eleven people writing the same sentence, over and over again. *Different handwriting, same words.*

So where did that leave our Vegas killer?

"Seven different methods of murder." Sloane's voice broke into my thoughts. Like her, I counted. One set of victims had been strangled. The New York killer had slit his victims' throats; another had also used a knife but showed a preference for stabbing. Two sets of victims had been impaled through the heart—one with metal bolts and another with whatever happened to be on hand at the scene. Two sets had been beaten to death. A case in Paris featured victims who were burned alive.

The most recent case—only two and a half years old—was the work of an UNSUB who broke into homes and drowned the inhabitants in their own bathtubs.

And then there were the ones who'd been poisoned.

Sloane stood, staring down at the pictures. "The closest cases are three years apart." Sloane squatted and began pulling out photos—one from each case for which we had them. With the same efficiency with which she'd organized the glass objects on the shelf in our room, she began ordering them, spacing some closer together than others. She waved for paper, and Michael supplied it.

What does Michael see when he looks at these pictures? The thought struck me suddenly and violently. *Is there any emotion on a dead person's face?*

Beside me, Sloane scribbled on sheets of paper, making

notes about the cases we didn't have pictures for. She integrated those in with the others on the floor.

There's a pattern. I didn't need her to tell me that. To these killers—however many of them there were, whatever they were doing—the pattern was everything.

Sloane kept tearing pages off the notepad. The sound of her ripping sheet after sheet off was the only one in the room. She placed the blank pages in open gaps.

"Assume a three-year interval between each case and the one that follows," Sloane murmured, "and you can extrapolate where we're missing data."

Three years, I thought. *Three is the number.*

"It repeats." Sloane jerked back, like she was afraid the papers might infect her, like she was afraid they already had. "Every twenty-one years, the pattern repeats. Impaled, strangled, knifed, beaten, poisoned, drowned, burned alive." She made her way down the row, filling in methods for the blank pages. When she started over, her voice went up an octave. "Impaled, strangled, knifed, beaten, poisoned, drowned, burned alive. Impaled—"

Her voice broke. Michael caught her and held her still, his arms wrapping around her and pulling her back to his chest. "I've got you," he said.

He didn't tell her it was okay. We all knew it wasn't.

Dean crouched over the pattern Sloane had pulled out. "Cassie," he said.

I knelt. Dean tapped one of the photos. *Drowning.*

Starting there, I realized why Dean had called me over and not Sloane. *Drowning, burning alive, impaled through the heart—*

Alexandra Ruiz.
Sylvester Wilde.
Eugene Lockhart.
Our UNSUB was going in order.

CHAPTER 43

You need nine, because that's the way this is done. Those are the rules. My understanding of the Vegas UNSUB shifted. *There is an order. You're following it.*

But being a follower isn't enough.

The numbers on the wrists, the Fibonacci spiral—none of that was present in any of the other cases Sloane had pulled. Each of the cases in front of us had employed one of seven methods.

You're going to do it all.

"Where are we in the cycle?" I asked. "Is our current UNSUB part of it, or does he break it?"

"Last case was two and a half years ago," Sloane said. "Three years before that, we have the Nightshade case."

Six years in May, I thought.

"So the UNSUB is early," I said. "Unless you go based on calendar year, and then—technically—it fits the pattern."

Alexandra Ruiz had died after midnight on New Year's Eve. *January first. A date for beginnings. A date for resolutions.*

"If we assume the UNSUB started at the beginning of the established cycle," Dean said, "then that cycle starts with drowning."

The most recent set of nine victims had been drowned.

"This isn't a culmination," I translated. "It's not a grand finale. If it were, it would have happened before they started the cycle over."

They. The word settled over me and refused to leave. "Who's doing this?" I asked, looking down at the pictures. "Why?"

Hundreds of victims killed over decades. Different killers. Different methods.

"They're doing it because someone told them to." Lia managed to sound utterly bored, but she couldn't look away from the pictures splayed out on the floor. "They're doing it because they believe this is how it has to be done."

When I was nine years old, I killed a man.

I grew up in a cult.

Lia's statements from Two Truths and a Lie came back to me, and suddenly, it occurred to me that—per the rules of the game—both of those statements could be true, so long as what she'd said about considering shaving Michael's head was not.

It would be just like Lia to tell outrageous truths and a joking, mundane lie.

Once upon a time, your name was Sadie. Now wasn't the

time to profile Lia, but I couldn't stop it, any more than Sloane could have stopped looking for the Fibonacci dates. *Someone used to give you gifts for being a good girl. You were on the streets by the time you were thirteen. Sometime before that, you learned not to trust anyone. You learned to lie.*

Dean's brown eyes settled on Lia. Their history was palpable in the air. For a moment, it was like no one else was in the room.

"You think we're dealing with some kind of cult," Dean said.

"You're the profiler, Dean," Lia responded, never looking away from his face. "You tell me."

A string of victims every three years, killed in prescriptive ways on dates dictated by the Fibonacci sequence.

There was an unquestionable element of ritual to that.

"Say we are dealing with a cult," Michael said, keeping his voice casual, never looking at Lia. "Does that make our guy a member?"

I turned the question over in my head. Lia answered it.

"Cult 101," she said. "You don't talk to outsiders." Her voice was strangely flat. "You don't tell them what they're not blessed enough to know."

The numbers on the wrists. The Fibonacci spiral. If there was some kind of group operating behind the scenes, they'd managed to avoid detection for more than six decades—until someone had turned Sloane onto the code.

Lia didn't need experience with *this* cult to see meaning in that. "I'm going to go play some poker." She stood up, shedding her previous affect as easily as someone stepping out of a dress. "If you try to stop me," she said with a smile that looked so real, I almost believed it, "if you try to come with me, I will make you regret it." She flounced to the door. Dean started to stand, and she gave him a look. A silent conversation passed between them.

She loved him, but right now, she didn't want him. She didn't want anyone.

Lia rarely showed us her true self. But what we'd just seen was more than that. The flat voice, the words she'd said—that wasn't just the real Lia. That was the girl she'd spent years running from.

That was *Sadie*.

"Parting gift," Lia said on her way out, twirling a finger through her jet-black hair, no sign of that girl in her now, "for those of you who might be a little slow on the uptake. Whoever our killer is, I'd bet a lot of money that he's not a part of this group. If he were, the cult would be monitoring him. And if they were monitoring him and they found out that he'd shared even one of their secrets?" Lia shrugged, the very picture of careless indifference. "He wouldn't be our problem. He'd already be dead."

YOU

You step out into the fresh air. Inside, you're smiling. Outside, you show a different face to the world. People have their expectations, after all, and you would hate to disappoint.

Drowning, fire, the old man impaled on the arrow, strangling Camille.

The knife is next.

Then beating a man to death with your bare hands.

Poison will be easy. Eloquent.

And then the last two—dealer's choice. There should be nine ways. If you were in charge, there would be.

Three times three times three.

Nine is the number of victims. Three is the number of years between.

Nine seats at the table.

You pause at the doors to the Desert Rose. Not your preferred hunting grounds, of course. But a fine place to visit. A fine place to look at what you have made.

A fine place to anoint number five.

Everything is going according to plan. Word of your kills is spreading. You know they monitor others with similar proclivities. Looking for talent. For threats.

The Masters will finally see you for what you really are.

What you have become.

CHAPTER 44

Michael announced he was going after Lia less than a minute after she left.

"She doesn't want you there, Townsend," Dean said tersely. Lia didn't want *Dean* there, either. It was killing him not to go after her, but as protective as he was, Dean would only push Lia so far.

"Luckily for us," Michael replied airily, "I've never met a bad idea I did not immediately embrace like the dearest of friends." He went into his room, and when he came out, he was putting on a casual blazer, looking every inch the trust-fund kid. "I believe Lia when she says that she will make me regret going after her," he told Dean. "But it just so happens regrets are a specialty of mine."

Michael buttoned the top button on his jacket and waltzed out the door.

"Michael and Lia have been physically involved no fewer

than seven times." Sloane seemed to think volunteering that information might prove helpful.

Dean's jaw tightened slightly.

"Don't," I told him. "She's safer with him than she is alone."

Whatever Lia had been feeling when she walked out the door, Michael would have seen it. And my gut was telling me that he'd felt it, too. Of all of us, Michael and Lia were the most similar to each other. It was why they'd been drawn together when he'd first come to the program, and why, as a couple, they'd never worked long-term.

"Would you feel better if you knew where they were going?" Sloane asked. Dean didn't reply, but Sloane texted Lia anyway. I wasn't surprised when she got a reply. Lia was the one who'd told me we were at issue capacity. She wouldn't ignore Sloane—not in a city where Sloane had spent most of her life being ignored by her own flesh and blood.

"So?" Dean said. "Where are they going?"

Sloane walked over to the window and stared out—through the spiral. "The Desert Rose."

It was forty-five minutes between the time Michael walked out the door and the time Judd walked in. Agent Sterling followed. Briggs entered last. He came to stand in the middle of the suite, staring at the papers covering the floor.

"Explain." Briggs resorting to one-word commands was never a good thing.

"Based on Sloane's projections, we're looking at nine victims every three years for a period of at least sixty years, with a different signature underlying each set." Dean kept it brief, his voice remarkably dispassionate, given the content of what he was saying. "The cases are spread out geographically, no repeating jurisdictions. The methods of killing go in a predictable order, and that order mirrors our UNSUB's first four kills. We believe we're dealing with a fairly large group, most likely one with a cult-like mentality."

"Our UNSUB isn't a part of the cult," I continued. "This isn't a group that advertises its existence, and that's exactly what the additional elements of our UNSUB's signature—the numbers on the wrists, the fact that the Fibonacci sequence determines not only the dates on which he kills but also the exact location—effectively do."

"He's better than they are." Sloane wasn't profiling. She was stating what was, to her mind, a fact. "Anyone can kill on certain dates. This . . ." She gestured to the papers carefully arranged on the floor. "It's simplistic. That?" She turned toward the map on the window, the spiral. "The calculations, the planning, making sure the right thing happens in the right place at the right time." Sloane sounded almost apologetic as she continued, "That's perfection."

You're better than they are. That's the point.

"We knew the numbers written on the victims' wrists were a message," I said. "We knew they mattered. We knew it wasn't just our attention he wanted."

It's theirs.

"That's it." Judd's voice was rough. "You're done." He couldn't order Agent Sterling off this case. That was outside of his purview. But the rest of us weren't. He was the final word on our involvement in any investigation. "All of you," he addressed those words to Dean, Sloane, and me. "It's my decision. It's my call. And I say we're done."

"Judd—" Sterling's voice was calm, but I thought I could hear a note of desperation underneath.

"No, Ronnie." Judd turned his back on her, staring at Sloane's window, his entire body bow-string tight. "I want Nightshade. Always have. And if there's a larger group involved in what happened to Scarlett, I damn well want them, too. But I won't risk a single one of these kids." The idea of walking away was killing Judd, but he refused to waver. "You've got what you need from them," he told Sterling and Briggs. "You know where the UNSUB is going to strike. You know when. You know how. Hell, you even know why."

I could make out a hint of Judd's reflection in the window. Enough to see his Adam's apple bob as he swallowed.

"It's my call," Judd said again. "And I say that if you've got anything else you need a consult on, you can damn well ship it to Quantico. We're leaving. Today."

Before anyone could respond, the door to the suite opened. Lia stood there, looking supremely satisfied with herself. Michael stood behind her, soaked from head to toe in mud.

"What—" Briggs started to say. Then he corrected himself. "I don't want to know."

Lia strolled into the foyer. "We never left the suite," she announced, lying to their faces with disturbing conviction. "And I certainly didn't beat the pants off a bunch of professionals playing recreational poker at the Desert Rose. In related news: I have no idea why Michael's covered in mud."

A glop of mud fell from Michael's hair onto the tile floor.

"Get cleaned up," Judd told Michael. "And all of you, get packed." Judd didn't wait for a reply before turning to retreat to his own room. "Wheels up in one hour."

CHAPTER 45

"I do hope you found your stay to your liking." The concierge met us in the lobby. "Your departure is a bit abrupt."

His tone made that sound like a question. It was closer to a complaint.

"It's my leg," Michael told him in a complete deadpan. "I walk with a limp. I'm sure you understand."

As far as explanations went, that one held little to no explanatory power, but the concierge was flustered enough that he didn't question it. "Yes, yes, of course," he said hurriedly. "We just have a few things for you to sign, Mr. Townsend."

While Michael dealt with the paperwork, I turned to look back at the lobby. At the front desk, dozens of people stood in line, waiting to check in. I tried not to think about the fact that in three days, any one of them—the elderly man, the guy wearing the Duke sweatshirt, the mother with three small children—could be dead.

The knife is next. I knew—personally, viscerally—how much damage could be done with a knife. *We're not finished,* I thought vehemently. *This isn't done.*

Leaving felt like running away. It felt like admitting failure. It felt the way I had at twelve, each time the police had asked me a question I couldn't answer.

"Excuse me," a voice said. "Sloane?"

I turned to see Tory Howard, dressed in her standard uniform of dark jeans and a tank. She seemed hesitant—something she'd never struck me as before. "We didn't get a chance to meet the other night," she told Sloane. "I'm Tory."

The hesitation, the softness in her voice, the fact that she knew Sloane's name, the fact that she'd lied to the FBI to keep her relationship with Aaron a secret—*you love him, too,* I realized. *You can't un-love him, no matter what you do.*

"You're leaving?" Tory asked Sloane.

"There is a ninety-eight-point-seven percent chance that statement is accurate."

"I'm sorry you can't stay." Tory hesitated again, and she said, softly, "Aaron really did want to get to know you."

"Aaron told you about me?" Sloane's voice wavered slightly.

"I knew he had a half sister he'd never met," Tory replied. "He wondered about you, you know. When you stepped in front of him that night at the show, and I saw your eyes . . ." She paused. "I did the math."

"Strictly speaking, that wasn't a mathematical calculation."

"You matter to him," Tory said. I knew, in the pit of my stomach, that it cost her to say the words, because there was a part of her that couldn't be sure that *she* mattered to Aaron. "You mattered to him before he even knew who you were."

Sloane absorbed that statement. She pressed her lips together and then blurted out, "I have gathered that there is an overwhelmingly large chance that your relationship with Aaron is intimate and/or sexual in nature."

Tory didn't flinch. She wasn't the type to let you see her hurting.

"When I was three . . ." Sloane trailed off, averting her eyes so that she wasn't looking straight at Tory. "Grayson Shaw came to my mother's apartment to meet me." The words were costing Sloane to say—but they were even harder for Tory to hear. "My mother dressed me up in a white dress and left me in the bedroom and told me that if I was a good girl, my daddy would want us."

The white dress, I thought, my stomach twisting and my heart aching for Sloane. I knew how this story ended.

"He didn't want me." Sloane didn't go into the particulars of what had happened that afternoon. "And he didn't want my mother so much after that."

"Trust me, kid," Tory replied, steel in her voice, "I've learned my lesson about getting in bed with Shaws."

"No," Sloane said fiercely. "That's not what I meant. I'm not good at this. I'm not good at talking to people, but . . ."

She sucked in a breath of air. "Aaron brought the FBI evidence that Beau acted in self-defense—evidence they never would have seen otherwise. I'm told there's a very high probability he did that for you. I thought that Aaron was like his father. I thought . . ."

She'd thought Tory was like her mother. Like her.

"Aaron fights for you," Sloane said fiercely. "You say I matter to him, but you matter, too."

"Beau was cleared of all charges this morning," Tory said finally, her voice rough. "That was Aaron?"

Sloane nodded.

Before Tory could reply, my phone rang in my bag. I considered ignoring it or declining the call again, but what was the point? Now that we'd been pulled off the case, there was nothing left to distract me. Nowhere else to run.

"Hello." I turned away from the group as I answered.

"Cassie."

My father had a way of saying my name, like it was a word in a foreign language, one he could get by in, but would never fluently speak.

"They got the test results back." I said it so that he wouldn't have to. "The blood they found. It's hers, isn't it?" He didn't reply. "The body they found," I pressed on. "It's her."

On the other end of the phone line, I heard a sharp intake of breath. I heard him jaggedly let it out.

While I waited for my father to find his voice and tell me what I already knew, I walked toward the exit. I stepped out into the sunshine and a light January chill. There was a fountain out front—massive and the color of onyx. I came to stand at the edge of it and looked down. My reflection flickered over the surface, dark and shadowed.

"It's her."

I realized, when my father said the words, that he was crying. *For a woman you barely knew?* I wondered. *Or for the daughter you don't know any better?*

"Nonna wants you to come home," my father said. "I can get an extended leave. We'll take care of the funeral, bury her here—"

"No," I said. I heard the pitter-patter of small feet as a child ran up to the fountain next to me. A little girl—the same one I'd seen that day at the candy shop. Today she was wearing a purple dress and had a white origami flower tucked behind one ear.

"No," I said again, the word ripping its way out of my throat. "I'll take care of it. She's *my* mother."

Mine. The necklace and the shroud she'd been wrapped in and the blood-spattered walls, the memories, the good and the bad—this was *my* tragedy, the great unanswered question of *my* life.

My mother and I had never had a home, never stayed anywhere very long. But I thought she'd like being laid to rest near me.

My father didn't argue with me. He never did. I hung up the phone. Beside me, the little girl solemnly considered the penny in her hand. Her bright hair caught in the sun.

"Are you making a wish?" I asked.

She stared at me for a moment. "I don't believe in wishes."

"Laurel!" A woman in her mid-twenties appeared at the little girl's side. She had strawberry blond hair pulled back into a loose ponytail. She eyed me warily, then pulled her daughter close. "Did you make your wish?" she asked.

I didn't hear the girl's reply. I stopped hearing anything, stopped registering any sound other than the running water in the fountain.

My mother was dead. For five years, she'd *been* dead. I was supposed to feel something. I was supposed to mourn her and grieve and move on.

"Hey." Dean came up beside me. He wove his hand into mine. Michael took one look at my face and put a hand on my shoulder.

He hadn't touched me—not once—since I'd chosen Dean.

"You're crying." Sloane stopped short in front of us. "Don't cry, Cassie."

I'm not. My face was wet, but I didn't feel like I was crying. I didn't feel anything.

"You're an ugly crier," Lia said. She brushed my hair lightly out of my face. "Hideous."

I let out a choked laugh.

My mother's dead. She's dust, and she's bones, and the person who took her away from me buried her. He buried her in her best color.

He took that away from me, too.

I let myself be bundled away. I let myself retreat into Dean and Michael, Lia and Sloane. But as the valets pulled our cars around, I couldn't help glancing back over my shoulder.

At the little red-haired girl and her mother. At the man who joined them and tossed his own coin into the fountain before lifting the girl onto his shoulders once more.

CHAPTER 46

The private airstrip was clear, but for the jet. It sat on the runway, ready to spirit us to safety. *This isn't over. It isn't done.* The objection was just a whisper in my head this time, drowned out by a dull roar in my ears and the numbness that had settled over my whole body.

The agony of not knowing what had happened to my mother—of never being able to silence that last sliver of *maybe*—had been with me so long, it felt like a flesh-and-blood part of me. And now, that part of me was gone. Now, I knew. Not just in my gut. Not just as a matter of deduction.

I *knew*.

I felt hollow, empty inside where the uncertainty had been. *She loved me more than anything.* I tried to summon up the memory of her arms around me, what she smelled like. But all I could think was that one day, Lorelai Hobbes had been my mother and a mentalist and the most beautiful woman I'd ever seen, and the next, she was just a body.

And now, just bones.

"Come on," Michael said. "Last one on the plane gets their initials shaved into Dean's head."

Every time I felt myself going under, they pulled me back up.

Dean was the last one on the plane. I went in front of him, trying to fight through the fog with each step. I was better than this—better than giving in to the numbness and going hollow inside because I'd found out something I already knew.

I knew. I made myself think the words. *I always knew. If she'd survived, she would have come back for me. Somehow, some way. If she'd survived, she wouldn't have left me alone.*

By the time I turned down the aisle, Lia, Michael, and Sloane had already claimed seats near the back. On the first seat to my left, there was an envelope with Judd's name on it, written in careful cursive scrawl. I paused.

Somewhere, beneath the numbness and under the fog, I felt something.

This isn't over, I thought. *This isn't done.*

I picked the envelope up. "Where's Judd?" I said. My voice was rough against my throat.

Dean eyed the envelope in my hand. "He's talking to the pilot."

My heart beat once in the time it took Dean to turn around and go for the cockpit.

This wasn't Agent Sterling's handwriting. It wasn't Agent

Briggs's. I'd learned, months ago, to stop telling myself *it's nothing, it's probably nothing* when the hairs on the back of my neck stood up.

"Judd." Dean's voice reached me a second before I turned toward the cockpit myself.

"Just a little electrical trouble," Judd assured Dean. "We're taking care of it."

This isn't over. This isn't done.

I held the envelope wordlessly out to Judd. My hand didn't shake. I didn't say a word. Judd eyed it for a moment, then looked at me.

"It was on the seat." Dean was my voice when I had none.

Judd took the envelope. He turned his back on us to open it. Fifteen seconds later, he turned back around.

"Get off the plane." Judd's voice was gruff, no-nonsense, calm.

Michael responded like Judd had shouted. He grabbed his bag and Sloane's. He pushed Sloane lightly in front of him and turned to Lia. He didn't say anything—whatever she saw in his face was enough.

Off the plane. Into Judd's rental car. Michael didn't say a word about leaving his own car behind.

"The envelope," Dean said as we pulled away from the runway. "Who was it from?"

Judd gritted his teeth. "He signed it 'an old friend.'"

I froze, unable to exhale, a breath turning stale in my lungs.

"The man who killed your daughter." Lia was the only one with balls enough to say it out loud. "Nightshade. What did he want?"

I forced myself to start breathing again.

"To warn us," I answered without meaning to. "Threaten us. Those electrical problems with the plane. They weren't an accident, were they?"

Judd was already on the phone with Sterling and Briggs.

Nightshade's here in Vegas, I thought. *And he doesn't want us to leave.*

I'd feared that thinking about Scarlett's killer might conjure him up like a ghost in the mirror. I'd known that our UNSUB was attempting to attract the attention of Nightshade and the others like him. I hadn't thought about what it would mean if the UNSUB succeeded. *The organization—group—cult—*

They're here.

Five minutes later, Judd was at the airport ticket counter, attempting to book us on the next commercial flight *anywhere*. But the moment the woman behind the counter typed his name into the computer, her brow knit.

"I already have tickets reserved under your name," she said. "Six of them."

I knew before I'd even fully processed what she was saying that this was Nightshade's doing, too. *You chose Scarlett for your ninth*, I thought, unable to stop myself. *You chose her because she mattered to Sterling and Briggs and they dared to think they might stop you. You chose her because she was a challenge.*

Of all of Nightshade's victims, Scarlett was his greatest feat. She would be the one he went back to. The one he re-lived. *You've watched Judd, haven't you? Every now and again, you like to remind yourself of what you took from him—from all of them.*

I wanted that guess to be off the mark. I wanted to be wrong. But the fact that Nightshade wanted us to stay in Vegas—the fact that Nightshade even knew there *was* an "us"...

Six tickets. The woman behind the counter printed them off and handed them to Judd. I knew before I looked that they would have our names on them.

First names. Last names.

The flight was to D.C.

You know who we are. You know where we live. The implications were chilling. Nightshade had been watching—quite possibly since he'd killed Scarlett Hawkins and Judd had moved in with Dean.

Killers don't just stop, I thought, but in this group, they did. *Nine and done.* Those were the rules. *Some killers take trophies,* I thought. *To re-live what they've done, to get some portion of that rush.*

If Nightshade had been watching off and on, whenever he needed a fix—if he was in Vegas—then he knew what was happening here.

You've never killed Judd—never killed us, because the rules say you stop at nine. But an organization like yours—a cult like yours—would have a way of dealing with threats.

Lia had said it herself: if the Vegas UNSUB had been a part of this group, he would be dead. And if the cult realized that we'd made the connection, if they saw *us* as a threat . . .

Nightshade would probably love for the kids Judd was caring for to be the exception to the rules.

Judd slammed the tickets down onto the counter. He turned and was on his phone again in an instant. "I'm going to need transport, a security detail, and a safe house."

CHAPTER 47

The safe house was sixty-five miles northeast of Las Vegas. I knew this because Sloane felt compelled to share the calculation—as well as at least half a dozen others.

We were all on edge.

That night, in a strange bed with armed federal agents in the adjacent room, I stared up at the ceiling, not even trying to sleep. Briggs and Sterling were still in Vegas, working against a ticking clock to stop the UNSUB before he killed again. Another team had been assigned to take Judd's statement about his communications with Nightshade. That statement hadn't included any information about a cult of serial killers that had gone undetected for more than sixty years.

That information had been declared need-to-know.

Outside of our team, only two people had been read

in—Agent Sterling's father, FBI Director Sterling, and the director of National Intelligence.

Two days, I thought as the clock ticked past midnight. Two days until our UNSUB killed again—unless Nightshade killed him first.

You're here to clean up a mess. I could feel my heart pounding in my throat, but I forced myself to go deeper into Nightshade's psyche. *Your work is neat. Clean. Poison is an efficient enough means of removing pests.*

I tried not to wonder if Nightshade was the only one whose attention our UNSUB had caught.

I tried not to wonder if the other members of the cult knew about us, too.

You could have killed this UNSUB, I thought, focusing on Nightshade, the evil I could name. *As soon as you got here, you could have killed this imposter making a mockery of something he does not understand. Throwing it in your faces. Attempting to fashion himself into something more.*

So why wait? Had Nightshade not made any more progress than we had at identifying the UNSUB? Or was he biding his time?

That was the question that dogged me the first night in the safe house. The second night, my thoughts shifted toward the way Nightshade had signed his message to Judd.

An old friend.

It feels true to you, doesn't it? I thought. *That killing Scarlett linked you and Judd. You chose her for what she was—a challenge, a slap in the face to Sterling and Briggs. But after . . .*

When he'd stopped—when he'd completed his ninth and disappeared from the FBI's radar—he'd have needed something to fill that void.

There were days when I couldn't draw the line between profiling and guessing. Hovering on the verge of sleep, I wondered how much of my understanding of Nightshade was intuition and how much was imagination, making mountains of molehills, because molehills were all that I had.

Even now, even after everything, Judd still wouldn't let us touch the Nightshade file.

Exhaustion wore at me, like the elements biting at a body as it decomposed. I hadn't slept in nearly forty-eight hours. In that time, I'd received confirmation of my mother's death and been made aware of the fact that the man who'd killed Judd's daughter was watching us all.

I fell asleep like a drowning man making a conscious decision to stop coming up for air.

This time, the dream started on the stage. I was wearing the royal blue dress. My mother's necklace sat like a shackle around my throat. The auditorium was empty, but I could feel them out there—eyes, thousands of eyes, watching me.

My skin crawled with it.

I whirled toward the sound of footsteps. It was faint, but I could hear the footsteps getting louder. *Closer.* I started backing away, slowly at first, and then faster.

The footsteps came faster, too.

I turned to run. One second, I was onstage, and the next, I was running through the forest, my feet bare and bleeding.

Webber. Daniel Redding's apprentice. Hunting me like a deer.

A twig snapped behind me, and I whirled. I felt a ghost of a whisper on the back of my neck and a hand trailing lightly over my arm.

I scrambled backward and went down hard. I hit the ground and kept falling—down, down into a hole in the ground. Up above, I saw Webber, standing at the edge of the hole and holding his hunting rifle. A second person stepped up beside him. *Agent Locke.*

Lacey Locke, née Hobbes, looked down at me, her red hair pulled high on her head, a pleasant smile on her face.

She was holding a knife. "I've got a present for you," she said.

No. No, no, no—

"You've been buried alive in a glass coffin." Those words came from my right. I turned. It was dark in the hole, but I could just barely make out the features of the girl next to me.

She looked like Sloane—but I knew, deep in the pit of my stomach, that she wasn't.

"There's a sleeping cobra on your chest," the girl wearing Sloane's body said. "What do you do?"

Scarlett. Scarlett Hawkins.

"What do you do?" she asked again.

Dirt hit me in the face. I looked up, but all I saw this time was the glint of a shovel.

"You've been buried alive," Scarlett whispered. "What do you do?"

The dirt was coming faster now. I couldn't see. I couldn't breathe.

"What do you do?"

"Wake up," I whispered. "I wake up."

CHAPTER 48

 woke up on the banks of the Potomac River. It took me a moment to realize that I was back in Quantico, and another after that to realize that I wasn't alone.

There was a thick, black binder open on my lap.

"Enjoying a bit of light reading?"

I looked up at the person who'd asked that question, but couldn't make out his face.

"Something like that," I said, realizing even as I did that I'd said these words before. *The river. The man.*

The world around me jumped, like a jarring film cut.

"You live at Judd's place, right?" the faceless man was saying. "He and I go way back."

Way back.

My eyes flew open. I sat up—in bed this time. My hands grappled with the sheet. I was tangled in it, shaking.

Awake.

My hands worked their way over my legs, my chest, my

arms, as if looking for assurance that I hadn't left part of myself back on the Potomac, in the dream.

The memory.

The stage, running, being buried alive—that was the work of my twisted subconscious. But the conversation on the riverbank? That was real. That had happened, right after I'd joined the program.

I'd never seen the man again.

I swallowed, thinking of the envelope Nightshade had left for Judd on the plane. I thought of the message he'd signed from "an old friend." Nightshade had known all of our names. He'd made the ticket arrangements, because he wanted Judd to know: *you could have gotten to any of us, at any time.*

If I was right about that—about why Nightshade had left the note, about his fixation on Scarlett as his crowning achievement and, through her, on Judd—it was all too easy to believe that Nightshade might have dropped by to say hello when a new person arrived in Judd's life.

The rules are specific. Nine victims killed on Fibonacci dates. Normal killers kept killing until they got caught—but this group was different. This group didn't get caught.

Because they stopped.

Judd was in the kitchen. So were two of the agents on our protection detail. "Can you give us a minute?" I asked them. I waited until they'd left to speak again. "I need to ask you something," I told Judd. "And you're not going to want to tell me the answer, but I need you to anyway."

Judd had a crossword in front of him. He laid down his pencil. That was as close to an invitation to continue as I was going to get.

"Given what you know about the Nightshade case, given what you know about Nightshade himself, given whatever was in that envelope on the plane—do you think he came here for our killer and just happened to spot you while he was here, or do you think . . ." My mouth went dry. I swallowed. "Do you think that he's been watching us all this time?"

Theories were just theories. My intuition was good, but it wasn't bulletproof, and I'd been given few enough details to work with that there was no way of knowing how far off the mark I might be.

"I don't want you working on Nightshade," Judd said.

"I know," I told him. "But I need you to answer the question."

Judd sat, stone-still and staring at me, for more than a minute. "Nightshade sent something to the people he killed," Judd said. "Before he killed them, he sent them a flower. A bloom, taken from a white nightshade plant."

"That's how he got the name," I said. "We assumed he'd used poison. . . ."

"Oh, he did," Judd said. "It wasn't nightshade, though. The poison he used was undetectable, incurable." A shadow flickered across Judd's eyes. "Painful."

You sent them something to let them know what was coming. You watched them. You chose them. You marked them.

"It never occurred to me he might still be watching." Judd's voice was harder now. "Best we could figure, the person who killed Scarlett was in jail or dead. But knowing what I know now?" Judd leaned back in his seat, his eyes never leaving mine. "I think the son of a bitch was watching. I think he'd have killed a dozen more if they'd have let him. But if he had to content himself with nine . . ."

He would have made the most of it.

I closed my eyes. "I think I met him," I said. "Last summer."

CHAPTER 49

 couldn't provide a description of the man. Michael, who'd been with me that day at the river, couldn't do much better.

Three minutes, six months ago. My brain stored all kinds of information about people—but even in a dream, I hadn't been able to make out the phantom's face.

Michael's voice broke into my thoughts. "Now strikes me as the appropriate time for a distraction."

I was sitting on the couch, staring at nothing. Michael took a seat on the other end, leaving space for Dean between him and me.

Whatever complications there were between us, this was so much bigger.

"Now," Michael said, determined to bring levity to a moment where there was none, "having recently been involuntarily drafted into a rather *violent* mud wrestling competition myself"—he shot a dirty look at Lia—"it occurs to me that perhaps we could—"

"No." Dean took the seat between Michael and me.

"Excellent," Michael replied with a smile. "That leaves Lia, Cassie, Sloane, and me for the wrestling. You can referee."

"Tomorrow's the twelfth." Sloane sat down on the floor in front of us, pulling her legs to her chest and wrapping her arms around them. "We keep talking about mud wrestling and . . . and Nightshade, and how he knew we were here, and what he's doing—but tomorrow's the twelfth."

Tomorrow, I filled in for her, *someone dies.*

Judd still hadn't let us look at the Nightshade case file—as if not knowing might protect us, when he knew as well as we did that ship had sailed. But Sloane was right—even bundled off to a safe house, with armed guards policing our every move, we didn't have to sit back and wait.

"We know where the Vegas UNSUB is going to strike," I said, looking from Sloane to the others. "We know he's going to use a knife." The word *knife* would always come rife with images for me. I let the sickening memories roll over me, and I pushed on. "We need more."

"Funny you should say that," Lia said. She reached for the TV control and turned the television on to ESPN. "Personally," she said, "I don't consider poker a sport."

On-screen, five individuals sat around a poker table. I only recognized two of them—the professor and Thomas Wesley.

"Beau Donovan is in the other bracket," Lia volunteered. "Assuming they let him back in after his recent brush with the law. The top two players from each bracket plus one wild card will face off tomorrow at noon."

"Where?" Sloane beat me to the question.

"The tournament has been hopping from one casino to the next," Lia said. "But the finals are at the Majesty."

"Where at the Majesty?" I asked.

Lia met my gaze. "Take a wild guess."

January twelfth. The Grand Ballroom.

"Open to the public?" Dean asked.

Lia nodded. "Got it in one."

Grayson Shaw must have gone against the FBI's wishes and resumed business as usual.

"My father should have listened to me." Sloane didn't sound small or sad this time. She sounded *angry*. "I'm not normal," she said. "I'm not the daughter he wanted, but I'm right, and *he should have listened.*"

Because he hadn't, someone would die.

No. I was sick of losing. A killer had taken my mother away from me. Now, the man who'd killed Judd's daughter had taken our home. He'd watched us, he'd threatened us, and there was nothing we could do about it.

I wasn't just going to sit here.

"No one dies tomorrow," I told the others. "No one."

I stared at the screen, looking for an answer, willing my mind to do what my genetic predispositions and my mother's early training had formed me to do.

"Who's happier about their hand?" Lia asked Michael. "Smirky or Intense?"

I barely registered Michael's reply. Wesley had dressed in keeping with his image. *Millionaire. Eccentric. Rake.* In contrast, the professor was self-contained, dressed to blend among businessmen, not to stand out at the table.

Precise. Single-minded. Contained.

We were looking for someone who planned ten steps ahead. *You need nine, and you have to know that with each one, the pressure will mount.* Someone who planned as meticulously as this killer—who was as grandiose as this killer, who prided himself on being better, being *more*—would have a plan to circumvent suspicion.

You have alibis, I thought, staring at Thomas Wesley. *You're the one who tipped the FBI about Tory's powers of hypnosis.*

On-screen, the professor won the hand. The slightest of smiles pulled at the edge of his lips. *You win because you deserve to,* I thought, slipping out of Wesley's perspective and into the professor's. *You win because you've mastered your emotions and decoded the odds.*

I could see bits and pieces of our UNSUB's profile in both of them, but I couldn't shake the feeling that there was something missing, some piece of the puzzle that would let me say, definitively, *yes* or *no*.

I closed my eyes, trying to concentrate and work my way through what that information might be.

"Sloane discovered the Fibonacci dates because she knew our UNSUB was obsessed with the Fibonacci sequence," I said finally. "So how did our UNSUB discover them?"

If the pattern was oblique enough that the authorities had never discovered it, never linked the cases we could now attribute to this group, how had our UNSUB?

I tried to push my way through to the answer. *You know what they do. You want their attention.* It was more than that, though. *You want what you're owed.* These murders weren't just attention-getters. Viewed from the perspective of a group that valued its invisibility, they were attacks.

"Tell Briggs and Sterling to look for a history of trauma," I said. "See if we can tie anyone from this case to a victim in one of the prior cases."

To find the pattern, you would have had to be obsessed. I knew that kind of obsession and knew it well. *Maybe they took something from you. Maybe this is you taking it back.*

"They'll want to look at family members of suspects as well." Dean knew obsession as well as I did, for different reasons. "It's possible we could be looking for a relative of a member—a child or sibling who was denied admission himself."

To do *this*, to put this much time and effort and calculation into getting this group's attention . . . *It's personal,* I thought. *It has to be.*

You want to be them, and you want to destroy them. You want power where you've had none.

You want it all.

"It's always personal," Dean said, his thoughts working in tune with mine. "Even when it's not."

"There are other cases," Sloane said quietly, her hands clasped in front of her body. "Other victims."

"The cases your program didn't find," I said.

There was a long pause.

"It is possible," Sloane mumbled, "that I got bored yesterday and wrote another program."

A chill settled on the surface of my skin and burrowed deep. Profiling the Vegas UNSUB was one thing, but the cult was another altogether. Nightshade's message to Judd—whatever the content—had conveyed one thing very clearly, through its existence alone.

No matter who you are, or where you go, no matter how well-protected you are, we'll find you.

Judd was right to try to pull us off the case. He was right to try to stop us before we were in too deep.

But it's too late, I thought. *We can't un-see what we've seen. We can't pretend. We can't stop looking, and even if we could . . .*

"What did your program find?" Lia asked Sloane.

"Instead of scanning law enforcement databases, I programmed it to scan newspapers." Sloane shifted to a cross-legged position. "Several of the larger ones have been working on digitizing their archives. Add in the databases of historical societies, library documents, and virtual depositories of non-fiction texts, and there's a wealth of information to search." She twisted her hands against each other. "I couldn't use the same parameters, so I just searched for murders on Fibonacci dates. I've been weeding through them by hand."

"And?" Dean prompted.

"I found a few of our missing cases," Sloane said. "Most weren't identified as serial murder, but the date, year, and method of killing match the pattern."

Some UNSUBs were better at hiding their work than others.

"We'll have to tell Sterling and Briggs about those cases," I said. "If we think the Vegas UNSUB might have a connection to one of them—"

"There's something else," Sloane cut in. "The pattern, it goes back a lot further than the 1950s. I've tracked at least one case as far back as the late 1800s."

More than a century.

Whatever this was, whoever these people were—they'd been doing this for a very long time.

Passed down, I thought. *Over decades and generations.*

Without warning, Lia slammed Michael back against the wall, pinning his hands over his head.

"Now really isn't the time or the place," Michael told her.

"What the hell is wrong with you?" Lia asked, her voice furious and low.

"Lia?" I said. She ignored me, and when Dean called her name, she ignored him, too.

"Where do you get off?" Lia asked Michael. She kept his right arm pinned with her left and brought her right hand up to the bottom of his sleeve. His eyes flashed, but before he could fight back, she'd pulled the sleeve roughly back.

"You just had to come with me," Lia spat. "You wouldn't let me walk out of that hotel room alone. I didn't need you there. I didn't *want* you there."

My eyes landed on the arm Lia had bared. Breath rushed out of my lungs like I'd been hit with a block of cement.

There, raised against Michael's skin like welts, were four numbers.

7761.

YOU

You plan for every contingency. You see ten moves ahead. This is not supposed to be happening.

Your target had a room booked through the end of the week. He was not supposed to leave.

Nine.

Nine.

Nine.

Your temples pound with it. Your heart races with it. You can feel your plan disintegrating, feel it falling apart. This is what you get for playing it safe. This is what you get for holding back. Are you what you claim to be, or aren't you?

"I am." You say the words. It takes everything in you not to scream them. "I am!"

A complication is just a complication. An opportunity. To take what you want. To do what you want. To be what you were always meant to be.

You press the tip of the knife to your stomach. Blood beads up on the surface.

Just a little complication.

Just a little blood.

Circle. Circle. Circle. Around. Up and down. Left and right.

Do it, *a voice whispers from your memory.* Please, God, just do it.

Everything but true infinity has its end. All mortal men must die. But you were never meant to be mortal. You were born for things such as these.

Tomorrow is the day, and the day will be perfect.

"So it has been decided," you murmur, "and so it shall be."

CHAPTER 50

"How long?" I asked Michael, my eyes locked on his wrist.

He knew exactly what I was asking. "It showed up this morning, itching like hell."

More than thirty-six hours after we'd left Vegas.

"Toxicodendrons." Sloane pulled her legs back to her chest, her hands worrying at the knees of her jeans. "Plants in the toxicodendron genus produce urushiol. It's a sticky oil, a powerful allergen. If Michael's been exposed before, the delay of onset for the rash the second time would be between twenty-four and forty-eight hours."

"Pretty sure I'd know if I'd been exposed before," Michael pointed out.

"Poison ivy and poison oak are toxicodendrons."

Michael did a one-eighty and nodded sagely. "I have been exposed before."

Lia's grip on his arm tightened painfully. "You think this

is funny?" She loosened her hold and pushed away from him. "You're scheduled to die tomorrow. Hilarious."

"Lia—" Michael started to say.

"I don't care," Lia told him. "I don't care that you probably got that coming after me. I don't care that you wore long sleeves to hide it from the rest of us. I don't care if you have some sick death wish—"

"I didn't ask for this," Michael cut in.

"So you're not planning to sneak off to Vegas tomorrow by yourself to try to lure this UNSUB out?" Lia folded her arms and tilted her head to one side, waiting.

Michael didn't respond.

Tomorrow. January twelfth. The Grand Ballroom.
The knife.

"That's what I thought," Lia said. Without another word, she turned and walked out of the room.

"So," Michael commented, "that went over well."

"You aren't going back there to play bait." Dean got up and went to stand toe to toe with Michael. "You aren't leaving this house."

"I'm touched, Redding," Michael said, bringing a hand to his heart. "You care."

"You aren't leaving this house," Dean repeated. There was a quiet intensity in his voice.

Michael leaned forward, his face in Dean's. "I don't take orders from you."

There was a beat, during which neither one of them backed down.

"I get it. You don't like running away." Dean's voice was quiet, his eyes never leaving Michael's. "You don't run. You don't hide. You don't cower. You don't beg."

Because none of those things ever work. Dean didn't say that. He didn't have to.

"Get out of my head." Michael's expression matched the one he'd worn before he'd plowed his fist into that father's face at the pool.

"Dean," I said. "Give us a minute."

With one last hard look at Michael, Dean did as I asked, leaving in the direction Lia had gone minutes before and taking Sloane with him.

Silence sat heavily between Michael and me.

"You should have told us," I said quietly.

Michael studied my expression, and I didn't even try to keep him from seeing what I felt. *I'm angry, and I'm terrified. I can't do this. I can't sit around and wait for them to identify your body, too.*

"You know me, Colorado," he said, his voice soft. "I've never been very good at *should*."

"Try harder," I told him fiercely.

"Look what trying gets you." Michael might not have meant to say those words, but he meant them. He was talking about me. And Dean. He'd spent the past few months pretending he'd never been interested in me. He'd flipped his emotions off, like I'd never mattered to him at all.

Look what trying gets you.

"You don't get to do that," I said, feeling like he'd kicked me in the teeth. "You don't get to make me the reason you do or don't do anything. I'm not a reason, Michael. I'm not something you *try* for." I took a step forward. "I'm your friend."

"You used to look at me and feel something," Michael said. "I know you did."

Michael was marked for death. A serial killer from Judd's past was stalking us all. But we were doing this—right here, right now.

"I never had friends," I said. "Growing up, it was just me and my mom. There was never anyone else. She never let there be anyone else."

For the first time since I'd gotten the call from my father, I *felt* something about my mother's death. *Anger*—and not just at the person who killed her. She'd gone away, and even if that hadn't been her choice, *she* was the reason there was no one else—no friends, no family, *nothing* until social services tracked down my dad.

"When I joined the program," I told Michael, "I didn't know how to really be with people. I couldn't . . ." The words wouldn't come. "I kept everyone at a distance, and there you were, smashing through every wall. I felt something," I told Michael. "You made me feel something, and I am grateful for that. Because you were the first, Michael."

There was a long silence.

"The first friend," Michael said finally, "that you ever had."

"That may not mean much to you." It hurt me to admit that. "To you, I might not be worth anything, if I'm with Dean. But it means something to me."

The silence that followed was twice as long as the first.

"I don't like running away." Michael brought his eyes from the floor to mine. "I don't run, I don't hide, I don't cower, I don't beg, Cassie, because running and hiding and begging—it doesn't work. It never works."

Michael was repeating the words Dean had said to him. He was admitting it out loud. To me.

I looked down at the angry red numbers on his arm. *7761. January twelfth. The Grand Ballroom. The knife.*

"It's not running," I told Michael, "if we catch him first."

CHAPTER 51

We had eleven hours and twenty-seven minutes until midnight.

First order of business was calling Sterling and Briggs. It took them two hours to extract themselves from the case and get to us. They questioned Michael and Lia about their little foray to the Desert Rose. What had they done there? Who had they seen?

"You don't remember anything out of the ordinary?" Briggs asked Michael. "Running into someone? Talking to someone?"

"Letting someone write a number on my arm in invisible, poison-ivy ink?" Michael suggested archly. "Shockingly, no. I remember dropping something. I remember bending down to pick it up." He closed his eyes. "I dropped something," he repeated. "I bent to pick it up. And then . . ."

Nothing.

"Pattern interruption," Sloane said. "It's the second-quickest method of inducing hypnosis."

To be hypnotized, you have to want to be hypnotized. Tory's words rang in my ears. Either she was lying, or Michael hadn't been on guard around the UNSUB.

Or both.

"You don't remember anything else?" Dean said.

"Well, when you phrase it like that, I remember exactly what happened. You have unmasked the killer, Redding. How do you do it, you profiling fiend?"

"You know who the killer is?" Sloane's eyes went comically wide.

"That was sarcasm," Dean told her, sparing a glare for Michael.

"What about the moments leading up to the gap in your memory?" Agent Sterling said, redirecting the conversation. "You said you were playing poker, Lia?"

"With a group that included Thomas Wesley," Lia filled in. "I trounced all of them. Michael was just my arm candy. After that, we split up. He went to cash in the chips, and I went to sign him up for mud wrestling against his will."

I tried to picture it in my mind—*Lia at a poker table, Michael beside her. Lia is winning. Her fingers play at the tips of her dark hair. Beside her, Michael fastens and unfastens the top button on his blazer.*

What had made our UNSUB stop and take notice? *Why Michael?*

"What happens if the intended victim isn't in the Grand

Ballroom on January twelfth?" Briggs posed the question to the room as a whole.

"Four variables." Sloane tapped the thumb on her right hand to each of her fingers as she rattled them off. "Date, location, method, and victim."

"If the equation changes, the UNSUB has to adapt." Sterling worked her way through the logic out loud. "The date and the method are necessary to achieve the UNSUB's primary objective. The location and making sure the number shows up on his victim's wrist—those are psychologically meaningful, symbols of mastery. To adapt, the UNSUB would have to give up some portion of the power and control that mastery represents."

"I'll want that back," Dean said. "The power. The control."

January twelfth. The knife. Those were the constants in this equation. If it came down to the location and the victim . . .

The spiral is your greatest work. A sign of rebellion. A sign of devotion. It's perfect.

"You would change victims rather than location," I said, sure enough of that.

"I'll adapt," Dean ruminated. "I'll choose someone new— and whoever I choose will pay for the fact that I had to."

I didn't want to think about the ways that a killer could go about reclaiming power and control with a knife.

"My father won't cancel tomorrow?" Sloane asked, her voice tight. "He won't even consider moving it to a different part of the casino?"

Briggs gave a shake of his head.

Power. Control. Sloane's father wouldn't let go of that any more than the UNSUB would.

"If I were to go to the tournament tomorrow," Michael spoke up, "then we wouldn't just know where this guy's going to be, or what he's planning to do. We'd know who the target is." He turned to Briggs. "You used Cassie for bait on the Locke case. You paraded her out for an UNSUB to see, because there was a life at stake, and you thought you could protect her. How is this any different?"

My gut twisted, because it wasn't.

"If I'm not there," Michael continued unflinchingly, "this guy just chooses someone else. Maybe you catch him, maybe you don't." He paused. "There's a good chance someone dies bloody."

I didn't want Michael to be right. But he was.

Someone dies tomorrow. At the appointed time. At the appointed place. By your knife.

"This UNSUB isn't the only one who'll be there tomorrow." Judd appeared in the doorway. "You go, Michael, and you'll be wearing more than one target on your back."

I didn't hear a trace of doubt in the old man's words. *He thinks Nightshade will be there.*

Agent Sterling met Judd's eyes. "I'd like to see the note he sent you."

Judd nodded to one of the agents on guard detail, and the man disappeared and returned a moment later with an evidence bag. Inside was the envelope from the plane.

Agent Sterling took a pair of gloves out of her pocket. She reached into the envelope. She pulled out a photo. After a moment, she flipped it over to read the back.

She looked over at Briggs. "Flower," she reported hoarsely. "White."

I remembered Judd telling me that Nightshade had sent each of his victims a flower—the bloom of a white nightshade—before they died. And now he'd sent Judd a photograph of the same.

"He sent you a flower?" I asked Judd, panic winding its way down my spine, my heart in my throat. *Not Judd. Not here, not now, not again.*

"He did," Judd allowed. I remembered what he'd said about Nightshade's poison of choice. *Undetectable. Incurable. Painful.* "Maybe it's too late for me," Judd continued, his voice hard, "and maybe it isn't, but I'm telling you, he'll be there tomorrow."

Nightshade hadn't wanted us leaving Las Vegas. He'd tampered with the plane. He'd made sure Judd knew we had nowhere to go.

Had he known that the UNSUB had marked Michael? Had Nightshade been watching? Was he watching us still?

Don't, I told myself. *Don't give him that kind of power. Don't let your mind make him into anything other than a man.*

"Nightshade chose all of his victims beforehand," I said, treating him as no more significant than any other UNSUB. "He sent them flowers."

A *warning.* A *gift.*

"Stalking behavior," Dean said shortly. "Not indicative of an opportunity killer. If I'm Nightshade, if I'm focused on Judd? If I've received permission from the cult to eliminate any and all problems, or finally reached the point where permission doesn't matter? I'd rather take something from Judd *here* than at the Majesty tomorrow."

Nightshade had gotten to Scarlett in the FBI labs. He had to know we'd been taken to a safe house. And to a man like that, us being in protection might just look like a challenge.

"It's settled, then," Michael said, even though it was anything but. "No place is safe, and I'm going."

CHAPTER 52

Michael going had been deemed a last resort.

By two in the morning, it was looking like the only option.

No matter how many times I went back over the profile, nothing changed. The ritualized elements of the crimes made it difficult to nail down even the most basic aspects of the UNSUB's demographic. *Drowning. Fire. Impaling. Strangling.* The methods told us nothing about the killer, other than the fact that he was going in a fixed order.

Young or old? Intelligent, definitely, but educated? It was difficult to say. If we were dealing with an UNSUB between the ages of twenty-one and thirty, I would say that person was filling a role similar to the role Webber had played to Dean's father. Apprentice. A younger UNSUB committing these murders was proving himself. He was grandstanding, looking for approval—yearning for it. Much older than that and the UNSUB wouldn't see himself as an apprentice at all. Viewed from that perspective, this became less about approval and more about proving himself dominant. An older UNSUB, executing this plan to perfection, would be setting himself above the cult—likely from a position of power himself.

You want power—either because you've already had a taste of it and want more, or because you've been made to feel powerless for too long.

I forced my mind back to the victims. In the prior Fibonacci cases, victimology had been one of the distinguishing features that allowed us to tell the killers apart. *There has to be something,* I kept thinking. *I have to be missing something.*

Drowning. Strangling. Those victims had been young, female. The gorier deaths had been reserved for males.

You don't like hurting women. I turned that over in my head. *You will, of course, to suit your goal. But given a choice, you'd prefer it to be neat.* That made me wonder about the UNSUB's other relationships. *A mother? A daughter? A love?*

My temples pounded. *What else?* I couldn't stop, I couldn't let myself stop. We had five hours before Michael left for the Majesty. No matter how heavily guarded he was, no matter how much we knew, that wasn't a risk I wanted to take.

January twelfth. The Grand Ballroom. The knife.

I had to keep going. I had to think. I had to see whatever it was that we were missing.

Think. We were looking for someone highly intelligent, organized, charming enough to put people at ease. *Alexandra*

Ruiz. The girl at Tory's show. Michael. The UNSUB had hypnotized at least three people.

"Cassie." Michael's voice broke into my thoughts. "Go to bed."

"I'm fine," I said.

"Liar." Lia was two-thirds asleep on the couch. She didn't even open her eyes to speak. She'd been going back over interviews, looking for anything she might have missed the first time.

Sloane had been staring at the pattern for hours.

"Briggs and Sterling are calling in the cavalry," Michael said. "There will be no fewer than a dozen agents, armed to the teeth, watching my every move. The moment they catch sight of a knife, the UNSUB goes down."

That was how this was supposed to go, but there was a reason this plan was a last resort.

Victimology, I thought. *Four victims.* I couldn't stop. I didn't. Not until the agents came the next morning to take Michael away.

CHAPTER 53

They put Michael in a bulletproof vest. They put a wire on him. Video, audio—whatever he saw, whatever he heard, Sterling and Briggs would, too. The other agents were also wired—video only—and those feeds would be accessible not only by Briggs as he coordinated the mission, but by the rest of us back at the safe house.

It only takes one detail, I thought. *One moment, one realization for everything to fall into place.*

I couldn't push down the part of me that was thinking that it only took one moment, one mistake, for this to go wrong, too.

Dean, Lia, Sloane, and I sat huddled on the couch as we waited. Lia refused to show any sign of nerves. Sloane, in contrast, was rocking back and forth.

Beside me, Dean shook his head. "I don't like this," he said. "Townsend's unpredictable. He has no regard for his own safety. He's constitutionally incapable of backing down from a fight."

"Tell you what, Dean," Lia replied. "When Michael gets back, we'll get the two of you a room. Obviously, there are *feelings* involved."

"We're all worried," I told Dean, ignoring Lia. "I don't like this any more than you do."

Sloane whispered something beside us. I couldn't make out what she said.

"Sloane?" I said.

"January twenty-third," she whispered. "February first, February third, February thirteenth."

It took me a second to register that she was rattling off the next four Fibonacci dates.

I need nine.

We'd been focused on the next kill—January twelfth. But if we didn't catch the UNSUB, this was what was next.

"The parking garage," Sloane said. "Then the buffet, then the day spa." The spiral was centered on the Majesty. It started out and spiraled in—and once it settled there, it kept going, closer and closer to the spiral's center.

"Where does it end?" I asked her. We'd been so focused on what the UNSUB had already done that I hadn't given much thought to the rest of the pattern. My heart pounded.

One detail. It only takes one detail.

Michael was still in transit. He wasn't there yet. It would be minutes yet before the plan was put in motion.

Please, I thought, not sure who or what I was begging—or even what, precisely, I was begging for.

"It ends in the theater," Sloane said, truly surprised the rest of us didn't know. "On February thirteenth."

"The poker tournament ends today." Lia pointed out the obvious. "It's going to be hard for most of the players to explain hanging around Vegas for long."

Wesley. The professor.

"I chose the Majesty for a reason," Dean said. "It was always going to end here. I knew, from the beginning, how this was going to end."

Why the Majesty? My eyes were so dry they hurt, my throat the same. My heart threatened to shatter my rib cage in my chest.

On the coffee table, the tablets Briggs had left for us jumped to life one by one, the screens going from black to active.

The video feeds were live.

The Grand Ballroom. January twelfth. Michael was there.

"The theater." I said the words out loud, my eyes on the screens, looking for anything, any hint of someone moving Michael's way. "It ends in the theater with victim number nine."

And that was when I saw it.

Alexandra Ruiz. Sylvester Wilde. Camille Holt.

What did they have in common?

"Victimology," I told Dean. "We don't have four victims. We have five."

Michael's not a victim. Not Michael. Not our Michael. I pressed back against the chorus in my head. The UNSUB had chosen him.

Why Michael?

"If you add Michael into the profile," I said, "then four out of the five victims are under the age of twenty-five."

Most killers had a type. If you set aside Eugene Lockhart as an outlier, our UNSUB's type was young. Beautiful. By some definition, *privileged*.

"A college girl celebrating the new year in Vegas. A stage magician with a show at the Wonderland. An actress who moonlighted playing professional poker." It hurt me to look at Michael on the screen. "A trust-fund boy."

"Average age of twenty-two," Sloane commented.

The spiral ends in the Majesty theater, I thought.

"Alexandra had long dark hair." The words tumbled out of my mouth, one after the other. "Who would she look like if you looked at her from behind?"

Dean answered first. "Tory," he said. "She'd look like Tory Howard." He turned to face me head-on. "Sylvester Wilde was a stage magician."

Like Tory.

Camille had died after going out for drinks with Tory that night. And Michael?

You saw him at the poker table next to Lia. She's got long, dark hair. Like Tory. And Michael? He fastens and unfastens the top button on his blazer, perfectly sure of his place in this world.

The pieces began falling into place in my head. I'd thought—multiple times—that we were looking for someone who planned ten steps ahead. *Someone who planned as meticulously as this killer,* my own thoughts played back on a loop, *who was as grandiose as this killer, who prided himself on being better, being more, would have a plan to circumvent suspicion.*

I'd asked myself about our UNSUB's relationships, about why he only chose to kill women when he could kill them cleanly.

The pattern ends in the Majesty theater. The final kill. The greatest sacrifice.

Nightshade's ninth kill had been Scarlett.

"Yours," I said out loud, "was always going to be Tory."

The Majesty. Tory. Planning ten steps ahead—

I knew who the killer was. My fingers scrambled for the phone. My hands shaking, I dialed Agent Sterling.

YOU

You make your way through the crowd toward the stage. Like you're supposed to be here. Like you own the place.

The knife is concealed by your sleeve.

There are cameras everywhere. Agents everywhere. They think you don't know. They think you can't see them, far more easily than they see you.

Your eyes land on your target. He's wearing a blazer. His fingers play at the top button.

Everything can be counted. The steps until you reach him. The number of seconds it will take your blade to cross his throat. And to think, this almost went differently.

To think, you almost settled for an imitation.

Three.

Three times three.

Three times three times three.

This is your inheritance. This is what you were always meant to be. A man bumps into you. Apologizes. You barely hear him.

1/1.

1/2.

1/3.

1/4.

1/12.

Nine seats at the table. Three seconds until it begins.

Three . . . two . . . and—the power goes off. Just like you planned. No lights. Chaos. Just like you planned.

You walk with purpose. You sidle up behind number five. You catch him in a chokehold and press the blade to his throat.

And then you start to slice.

CHAPTER 54

The screens went black. I had the phone pressed to my ear. *No answer. No answer. No—*

"Cassie." Agent Sterling came on. "It's fine. The UNSUB cut the power, but we have Michael secured."

Something gave inside of me, but I didn't have time for relief. The UNSUB's name was on the tip of my tongue. What came out was, "What if it's not Michael he's after?"

We'd been going off the assumption that if given a choice, the UNSUB would revert to the original plan, targeting Michael. But if he'd discovered his intended victim had left Las Vegas, if he'd changed the plan, if he'd already found a way of regaining power and control—

"Aaron," I told Agent Sterling.

Those words were met with silence.

"The UNSUB is Beau Donovan, and he's targeting Aaron Shaw," I plowed on. "Michael was only ever a stand-in. Beau saw him with Lia, and it was like looking at Aaron with Tory. If Beau thought, even briefly, that Michael wasn't an option, he'd compensate by going for the real thing."

"Briggs." I heard Sterling call out, even though she was keeping her voice low. "We're looking for Beau Donovan, targeting Aaron Shaw."

On-screen, the lights flickered back on. Over the phone, I heard a piercing scream. My eyes darted from one video feed to the next. Beside me, Sloane slipped off the sofa and to her knees in front of the coffee table, her hands on either side of one of the tablets.

The agent wearing the camera ran forward. The image shook. A crowd formed. The camera was jostled, and then the agent knelt.

Next to the body of Aaron Shaw.

A high-pitched wheezing sound filled the air. Lia sank to the floor and wrapped her arms around Sloane.

"I told him," Sloane whispered. "I told my father. January twelfth. The Grand Ballroom. I told him. *I told him. I told him.*"

He should have listened. But he hadn't, and now Aaron was pale and still and covered in blood. *Dead.*

"Cassie?" Agent Sterling's voice came back over the phone. I'd forgotten I was even holding it. "How sure are you about the UNSUB's identity?"

On one of the other screens, I saw Beau Donovan, standing near the stage. He didn't look like he'd just killed someone. Without Michael to read him, I couldn't tell if that was satisfaction on his face.

You don't have to say anything, Agent Sterling had told Beau during his interrogation. *But I think you want to. I think there's something you want us to know.*

Michael had indicated that Agent Sterling was right. There *was* something Beau wanted them to know, something he wouldn't say. *You wanted them to know how superior you are—better than the FBI, better than the group you're emulating.*

He's got the potential for violence, Dean had told us. The rest of Dean's assessment echoed in my head. *I'm guessing he's spent a lot of his life being tossed aside like garbage. Given the opportunity, he'd enjoy playing a game where he came out on top.*

We'd known the Vegas UNSUB was capable of arranging deaths that seemed like accidents. It wasn't much of a leap to think he might be able to plan an attack that looked like self-defense. *You picked a fight with Aaron. The Majesty's head of security came after you. You knew he would. You picked the fight with Aaron so that he would.* Beau had probably hypnotized that girl into joining Aaron at Tory's show, to give him an excuse to pick the fight. *You didn't kill Victor McKinney. You never meant to kill him—because he wasn't number five.*

He was your defense.

What better way to avoid suspicion than being arrested for the crimes and then exculpated and released?

You wrote the wrong number on his wrist. Misdirection.

"Cassie?" Agent Sterling said again.

On the floor, Sloane rocked back and forth, shuddering in Lia's arms.

I told Agent Sterling what she needed to hear. "I'm sure."

CHAPTER 55

The FBI took Beau Donovan into custody. He didn't evade arrest. He didn't resist.

He didn't have to.

You know we don't have proof. You've already constructed your defense.

You're going to enjoy this.

At the time of arrest, Beau had no weapon on him. Thanks to the blackout, no one could place him near the body. *You're better than that.* I'd spent enough time in our UNSUB's head to know that Beau would have had a plan for disposing of the weapon. *You didn't expect to be arrested, but what does it matter? They can't prove it. They can't touch you.*

Nothing can touch you now.

"Seventy-two hours." Sloane's voice was barely more than a whisper, rough and raw in her throat. The video feeds had been cut, but she was still staring at the blank screen, seeing Aaron's body the way I could close my eyes and see my mother's blood-spattered dressing room. "In most states, suspects can be held up to seventy-two hours before charges are filed," Sloane stammered on. "It's forty-eight in California. I'm . . . I'm . . . I'm not sure about Nevada." Her eyes welled with unshed tears. "I should be sure. *I should be.* I can't—"

I sank to the floor beside her. "It's okay."

She shook her head—shook it and shook it and shook it. "I told my father this was going to happen." She just kept staring at the blank screen. "January twelfth. The Grand Ballroom. I told him, and now—I'm not sure. Is it forty-eight hours in Nevada or seventy-two?" Sloane plucked at the air, her hands trembling. "Forty-eight or seventy-two? *Forty-eight or—*"

"Hey." Dean knelt in front of her and caught her hands in his. "Look at me."

Sloane just kept shaking her head. I glanced helplessly at Lia, who hadn't left Sloane's side.

"We're going to get him," Lia said, her voice as quiet as Sloane's, but deadly.

Somehow, the words permeated Sloane's brain enough that the younger girl stopped shaking her head.

"We are going to nail Beau Donovan to the wall," Lia continued, her voice low, "and he is going to spend the rest of his life in a box with the walls closing in on him. No hope. No way out. Nothing but the realization that he lost." Lia sold every word of that statement with 100 percent conviction. "If we have to do it in forty-eight hours, we'll do it in forty-eight hours, and if it's seventy-two, we'll do it in forty-eight anyway. Because we're that good, Sloane, and *we are going to get him.*"

Slowly, Sloane's breathing evened out. She finally met Dean's eyes, tears spilling out of her own. I watched them carve their way down her face.

"I was Aaron's sister," Sloane said simply. "And now I'm not. I'm not his sister anymore."

My throat tightened around the words I wanted to say. *You're still his sister, Sloane.* Before I could manage a verbal reply, I heard the front door open. A heartbeat later, Michael appeared at the threshold to the living room.

The full truth of the situation broadsided me with physical force. *It could have been Michael. If we'd never left Vegas, if Beau hadn't changed the plan, it could have been Michael.* I couldn't let myself think about it. I couldn't stop. *Michael's throat, slit with that knife. Michael, gone in an instant . . .*

Michael paused, his eyes on Sloane. He took in the tear tracks on her face, her rounded shoulders, a thousand and one cues I couldn't even see. Being a Natural meant Michael couldn't turn off his ability. He couldn't stop seeing what Sloane felt. He saw it, and he felt it, and I knew him well enough to know that he was thinking, *It should have been me.*

"Michael." Sloane choked out his name. For several seconds, she just stared at him. Her hands worked their way into fists by her side. "You're not allowed to go away again," she told him fiercely. "Michael. You're not allowed to leave me, too."

Michael hesitated just a moment longer, then he took one step forward and then another, collapsing to the ground beside us. Sloane latched her arms around him and held on for dear life. I could feel the heat from their bodies. I could feel their shoulders racked with sobs.

And all I could think, huddled on the floor with them, a mass of grief and anger and loss, was that Beau Donovan thought he'd won. He thought he could take and kill and tear lives apart and that nothing and no one could touch him.

You thought wrong.

CHAPTER 56

The clock was ticking. Instinct and theories weren't enough. Being *sure* wasn't enough.

We needed evidence.

You plan. You wait, and you plan, and you execute those plans with mathematical precision. I could see Beau in my mind, his lips upturned in something like a smile. Waiting for our time to run out. Waiting for the FBI to let him go.

Sloane sat in front of the television, a tablet plugged into the side. She wasn't crying now. She wasn't even blinking. She was just watching the moment her brother's corpse had been discovered, again and again.

"Sloane." Judd stood in the doorway. "Sweetheart, turn that off."

Sloane didn't even seem to hear him. She watched the camera footage shake as an agent ran toward Aaron's body.

"Cassie. Turn it off." Judd issued the order to me this time.

You want to protect us, I thought, knowing quite well where Judd's need to do that came from. *You want us to be safe and well and warm.*

But Judd couldn't protect Sloane from this.

"Dean." Judd turned his attention to my fellow profiler.

Before Dean could reply, Sloane spoke up. "Six cameras, but none of them are stationary. I can extrapolate Beau's position, but the margin of error in calculating his trajectory is bigger than I would like." She paused the footage over Aaron's corpse. For a moment, she lost herself to the image of her brother's blood-spattered body, her gaze hollow. "The killer was right-handed. Spatter is consistent with a single wound, left to right across the victim's neck. The blade was angled slightly upward. Killer's height is roughly seventy-point-five inches, plus or minus half an inch."

"Sloane," Judd said sharply.

She blinked, then turned away from the screen. *It's easier,* I thought, slipping from Judd's perspective into Sloane's, *when the body belongs to "the victim." Easier when you don't have to think Aaron's name.*

Sloane shut off the television. "I can't do this."

For a moment, Judd looked relieved. Then Sloane got out her laptop. "I need stationary footage. Higher resolution." Seconds later, her fingers were flying over the keys.

"Hypothetically speaking," Lia said to Judd, "if Sloane were hacking the Majesty's security feed, would you want to know?"

Judd looked at Sloane for several seconds. Then he walked over to her and pressed a kiss to the top of her head. *She won't stop. She can't. You know that.*

His mouth set into a firm line, Judd turned back to Lia. "No," he grunted. "If Sloane were illegally hacking her father's casino, I would not want to know." Then he glanced back at Dean and Michael and me. "But, hypothetically speaking, what can I do to help?"

You had less than a minute to do what needed to be done.

As Sloane watched the security footage she'd hacked, murmuring numbers under her breath, I slipped into Beau's perspective, trying to imagine what he'd been thinking and feeling in those moments.

You knew exactly where your target was standing. You knew Aaron wouldn't panic when the lights went off. Aaron Shaw was at the top of the food chain. You knew it would never occur to him that he might be your prey.

"Suspect was walking toward the stage at a rate of one-point-six meters per second. Victim was twenty-four meters away, at a forty-two-degree angle to suspect's last marked trajectory."

You knew exactly where you were going, exactly how to get there.

Sloane froze the footage and did a screen capture, the second before the lights went out. She repeated the process when the lights came back on. *Before. After. Before. After.*

Sloane toggled back and forth between the still images. "In fifty-nine seconds, the suspect moved forward six-point-two meters, still facing the stage."

"His pupils were dilated," Michael put in. "Before the lights went off, his pupils were already dilated—alertness, psychological arousal."

"If I can do this," Dean murmured, "I'm invincible. If I can do this, I'm worthy."

Aaron was the Majesty's golden son, the heir apparent. Killing him was an assertion of power. *This is your inheritance. This is what you are. This is what you deserve.*

"Beau's posture changes," Michael continued. "It's subtle, but it's there, beneath the poker face." Michael indicated first one image, then the other. "Anticipation before. And after: elation." He swung his eyes back to the first photo. "Look how he's holding his shoulders." He glanced at Sloane. "Play the footage."

Sloane brought up the video and let it play.

"Restricted motion," Michael said. "He's fighting tension in his shoulders. He's walking, but his arms are still by his sides."

"The knife," Dean murmured beside me, his eyes locked on the screen. "I had it on me. I could feel it. That's why my arms aren't moving. The knife is weighing me down." Dean swallowed, shifting his eyes to me. "I have the knife," he said, his voice pitched unnaturally low. "I am the knife."

On-screen, everything went black. Seconds ticked by in silence.

Adrenaline surged through your veins. I imagined being Beau. I imagined sidling up behind Aaron in the dark. *No hesitation. He's stronger than you are. Bigger. All you have is the element of surprise.*

All you have is a holiness of purpose.

I imagined sliding the blade across Aaron's throat. I imagined letting it drop to the floor. I imagined walking back, through the dark. I imagined knowing, with an unworldly, overwhelming certainty that death was power. *My power.*

On-screen, the lights came back on, jarring me from the brief instant when I'd stopped talking to Beau and let myself *be* him. I could feel the heat from Dean's body beside me—I could feel the dark place he'd been the moment before.

The place I'd gone, too.

"Look at his arms," Michael said, gesturing to Beau.

They swing slightly as you walk. You're lighter now. Balanced. Perfect.

"I've done what needed to be done." Dean looked down at his hands. "And I got rid of the knife."

"The knife was found less than a meter away from the body." Sloane spoke at a stilted, uneven pace. "Killer dropped it. He would have backed away. Couldn't risk stepping in Aaron's blood." There was something brittle in her voice, something fragile. "Aaron's blood," she repeated.

Sloane looked at crime scenes and saw numbers—spatter patterns and probability and signs of rigor mortis. But no matter how hard she tried, Aaron would never just be *number five* to her.

"The suspect's not wearing gloves." Lia was the one who made the observation. "I doubt he left fingerprints on the knife. So what gives?"

Sloane closed her eyes. I could feel her cataloging the possibilities, going through the physical evidence again and again, hurting and hurting and pushing through it—

"Plastic." Judd had never weighed in on one of our cases before. He wasn't FBI. He wasn't a Natural. But he was a former marine. "Something disposable. You wrap the knife in it, dispose of it separately."

That's it. My heart skipped a beat. *That's our smoking gun.*

"So where did I dispose of it?" Dean asked.

Not a trash can—the police might look there. I forced myself to back up, to walk through it step by step. *You make your way through the crowd—to Aaron. You come up behind him. You slice the knife across his neck—quick. No hesitation. No remorse. You peel the plastic off, drop the blade.*

Thirty seconds.

Forty seconds.

How long has it been? How long do you have to make your way back to where you were when the lights went out?

You push your way through the crowd.

"The crowd," I said out loud.

Dean understood before the others. "If I'm a killer who thinks of every contingency, I don't throw the evidence away. I let someone else do it for me. . . ."

"Preferably after they get home," I finished.

"He planted the evidence on someone," Lia translated. "If I'm his mark, and I get home and find a plastic bag in my pocket? I throw it away."

"Unless it has blood on it," Sloane said. "A drop, a smear..."

I saw the web of possibilities, the way this played out. "Depending on who you are, you might call the police." I considered a second possibility. "Or you might burn it."

There was a beat of saturated silence, brimming with the things none of us would say. *If we don't find it, if we don't find the person who has it . . .*

Our killer would win.

CHAPTER 57

"We need Beau's trajectory." Sloane tapped the pad of her thumb across each of her fingers, one after the other, again and again as she spoke. "Point A to point B to point C. How did he get there? Who did he pass?"

Before. After. Before. After. Sloane went back to switching from one still image to the next. "There are at least nine unique paths with a likelihood greater than seven percent. If I isolate the length and angle of the suspect's stride after the lights came back on . . ." Sloane stopped talking, lost to the numbers in her head.

The rest of us waited.

And waited.

Tears welled in Sloane's eyes. I knew her—I knew her brain was racing, and I knew that number after number, calculation after calculation, all she could see was Aaron's face. His empty eyes. The shirt he'd bought her.

I wanted him to like me, she'd told me.

"Don't look at Beau." Lia broke the silence in the room. She caught Sloane's gaze and held it. "When you're looking for a lie, sometimes you look at the liar, and sometimes you look at everyone else. The better the liar, the better the chance that your tell is going to come from someone else. When you're dealing with a group, you don't always watch the person speaking. You watch the worst liar in the room." Lia leaned back on the heels of her hands, the casual posture belied by the intensity in her voice. "Don't look at the suspect, Sloane."

Lia might have been trying to spare Sloane from looking—again and again—at Beau, knowing what he'd done to Aaron, but it was good advice. I could see the exact moment it took hold in Sloane's mind.

Don't look at the suspect. Look at everyone else.

"Crowds move," Sloane said, her voice going up in pitch as she gathered steam. "When someone works their way through a crowd, people move. If I can isolate the migration patterns during the blackout . . ." Her eyes darted side to side. Scanning the footage, she sent the still images to the printer. *Before. After.* Her fingers grappled for a pen. She looked from the footage to the images and back again, uncapping the pen and circling clusters of people. "Controlling for baseline movements, with a margin of error for individual differences in response to chaos, there are gaps *here, here,* and *here,* with slight but consistent movement northwest and southeast among each cluster." Sloane drew a path from Aaron's body to Beau's final position, then ran her finger back over the path she'd drawn.

You drop the knife. You make your way back through the crowd, light on your feet, never hesitating, never stopping.

"Pretend you're picking pockets," Dean told Lia, his gaze fixed on the path Sloane had drawn. "Who are your easy marks?"

"I'm insulted you think I would know," Lia replied, not sounding insulted in the least. She brought her fingertip to the image and tapped one long, painted nail against first one person, then two more. "One, two, and three," Lia said. "If I were picking pockets, those would be my marks."

You're weaving through the crowd. It's dark. Chaotic. People are fumbling for their cell phones. You keep your head down. There's no room for hesitation. No room for mistakes.

I looked at the three people Lia had indicated. *You just killed a man, and you're going to let someone else dispose of the evidence.* From the beginning, I'd seen our UNSUB as a planner, a manipulator. *You knew exactly which mark to choose.*

"That one." I pointed to the second of the two marks Lia had chosen. *Late twenties. Male. Wearing a suit jacket. Mouth pursed in distaste.*

Familiar.

"Thomas Wesley's assistant." Michael recognized him, too. "Not a big fan of the FBI, is he?"

— — —

"We're on it." Agent Briggs wasn't a person to sit on a lead for long. He and Agent Sterling were in transit before we'd even finished briefing them.

"Will it be enough?" I asked. Sloane had gone quiet beside me. No matter how badly she wanted answers, she wouldn't be able to form the question, so I asked it for her.

"*If* the assistant still has it, and *if* it has Beau's fingerprints on it, and *if* forensics can tie it to either the knife or Aaron's blood . . ." Briggs let the number of conditionals in that sentence speak for itself. "Maybe."

Trace evidence. That was what this came down to. Trace evidence had told me my mother's blood was on that shawl. Trace evidence had said those bones were hers.

The universe owes me this, I thought—fiercely, irrationally. Trace evidence had taken my mother away. Trace evidence could give me—give Sloane—this one thing.

"*Maybe* isn't good enough." Lia spoke now, just as much for Sloane as I had. "I want him squirming. I want him helpless. I want him to watch it all come crumbling down."

"I know." There was an undertone in Briggs's voice that told me he wanted the same, wanted it the way he'd wanted Dean's father, once upon a time. "We've got local PD working on tracking down video footage—of Michael at the Desert Rose, of the hours leading up to the fight between Beau and the Majesty's head of security. Something will turn up."

Something has to, I thought desperately. *You don't get to get away with this, Beau Donovan. You don't get to walk away from this unscathed.* If we could obtain physical evidence—and video evidence—the one thing we were missing was witness testimony.

"Tory Howard." I threw the name out there, knowing that I wasn't saying anything that Briggs and Sterling hadn't already considered.

"We tried," Briggs replied curtly. "This is the second time we've arrested Beau. She thinks he's innocent."

Of course Tory wouldn't want to believe Beau had done this. I thought about the young woman I'd profiled again and again. *You loved Aaron. Beau can't have been the one to take him away from you.*

"We're the bad guys here," Briggs continued. "Tory won't talk to us."

You loved Aaron, I thought again, still focused on Tory. *You're grieving.* I thought of the last time I'd seen Tory and let out a long breath. "She won't talk to *you*," I said out loud, "but she might talk to Sloane."

CHAPTER 58

Tory didn't answer the first time we called. Or the second. Or the third. But Sloane had an eerie capacity for persistence. She could do the same thing over and over, caught in a loop until the outcome changed, jarring her from the pattern.

You're not going to stop calling. You're not ever going to stop calling.

Sloane dialed the number Sterling and Briggs had given her in full each time. I knew her well enough to know that she found some comfort in the rhythm, the motion, the numbers—but not enough.

"Stop calling." A voice answered, loud enough that I could make out every word from standing next to Sloane. "Just leave me alone."

For a split second, Sloane stood, frozen, uncertain now that the pattern had been broken. Lia snapped a finger in front of her face, and Sloane blinked.

"I told him. I told my father." Sloane went straight from one pattern to another. How many times had she spoken those words? How often must they have been repeating themselves in her head for her to utter them so desperately each time?

"Who is this?" Tory's voice cracked on the other end of the phone line.

With shaking hands, Sloane set the phone to speaker. "I used to be Aaron's sister. And now I'm not. And you used to be his person, and now you're not."

"Sloane?"

"I told my father that it was going to happen. I told him that there was a pattern. I told him the next murder was going to happen in the Grand Ballroom on January twelfth. *I told him,* Tory, and he didn't listen." Sloane sucked in a ragged breath. On the other end of the phone line, I could hear Tory doing the same. "So *you* are going to listen," Sloane continued. "You're going to listen, because *you know*. You know that just because you ignore something, that doesn't make it go away. Pretending something doesn't matter doesn't make it matter less."

Silence on the other end of the phone line. "I don't know what you want from me," Tory said after a small eternity.

"I'm not normal," Sloane said simply. "I've never been normal." She paused, then blurted out, "I'm the kind of not-normal that works with the FBI."

This time, Tory's intake of breath sounded sharper. A

flicker in Michael's eye told me he heard layers of emotion in it.

"He was my brother," Sloane said again. "And I just need you to listen." Sloane's voice broke and broke again as she spoke. "Please."

Another eternity of silence, tenser this time. "Fine." Tory clipped the word. "Say what you need to say."

I could feel Tory shifting from one mode to another: naked grief to defensiveness to a kind of flippancy I recognized from Lia. *Things only matter if you let them. People only matter if you let them.*

"Cassie?" Sloane sat the phone down. I stepped forward. On Sloane's other side, Dean did the same, until the two of us were standing facing each other, the phone on the coffee table between us.

"We're going to tell you about the killer we're looking for," I said.

"I swear to God, if this is about Beau—"

"We'll tell you about our killer," I continued evenly. "And then you'll tell us." Tory was quiet enough on the other end of the line that I wasn't completely sure she hadn't hung up on us. I glanced at Dean. He nodded slightly, and I started. "The killer we're looking for has killed five people since January first. Four of the five people were between the ages of eighteen and twenty-five. While this could mean that our killer has a fixation on this age group due to a prior experience in his or her life, we believe the most likely explanation—and the one that fits best with the nature of the crimes—is that the killer is young as well."

"We're looking for someone in his early twenties," Dean continued. "Someone who had a reason to target the casinos in general and the Majesty in particular. It's likely our killer has extensive experience with Las Vegas and is used to going unseen. This is both his greatest asset and the fuel for much of his rage."

"Our killer is used to being dismissed," I continued. "He almost certainly has a genius-level IQ, but probably performed poorly in school. Our killer can play by the rules, but feels no guilt for breaking them. He's not just smarter than people give him credit for—he's smarter than the people who make the rules, smarter than the people who give the assignments, smarter than the people he works for and with."

"Killing is an act of dominance." Dean's voice was quiet and understated, but there was conviction in it—the kind of conviction that spoke of firsthand experience. "The killer we're looking for doesn't care about physical dominance. He wouldn't back down from a fight, but he's lost his fair share. This killer dominates his victims mentally. They don't lose because he's stronger than they are—they lose because he's smarter."

"They lose," I continue, "because he's a true believer."

"Beau isn't religious." Tory latched on to that—which I took to mean she recognized just how well everything else we'd said fit her foster brother.

"Our killer believes in power. He believes in destiny." Dean paused. "He believes that something has been taken from him."

"He believes," I said quietly, "that now is the time to take it back."

We didn't tell Tory about the cult. With Nightshade's attention on Vegas, knowing could put her in danger. Instead, I stopped telling Tory about our killer's present state of mind and starting extrapolating backward.

"Our killer is young," I said again, "but it's clear from the level of organization in the kills that these murders have been years in the making."

There was a reason we hadn't been able to pinpoint the UNSUB's age until we'd identified Michael as the intended fifth victim. So much about these kills spoke of planning—experience, grandiosity, *artistry*. To have reached that point by the age of twenty-one . . .

"In all likelihood, our killer has one or more traumatic events in his past—most likely, prior to the age of twelve. These events may have included physical or psychological abuse, but given the lengths the killer is going to"—*to get their attention*. I didn't say those words out loud—"in order to prove himself worthy, it's also likely we're looking for someone who experienced a sudden loss and severe emotional or physical abandonment."

"The cessation of abuse," Dean said with heartrending calm, "would have been as traumatic and formative as what came before."

"Stop." Tory whispered the same thing she'd said when she'd answered the phone, but this time, her voice was rough and low and desperate. "Please, just stop."

"He was killing in a pattern." Sloane spoke suddenly, her whisper a match for Tory's. "It was going to end in the Majesty's theater. February thirteenth, the theater—that was where it was going to end."

"You matter to our killer, Tory." Dean bowed his head. "It was always going to be you—just like it had to be one of your biggest rivals, just like it had to be Camille, just like it had to be a young girl with dark hair that first night."

"Just like it had to be Aaron," Tory choked out, her voice no longer a whisper.

Michael caught my gaze. He held up a pad of paper. *On the verge,* it said. I gave a nod to show that I understood. Whatever we said next had the potential to push her one way or the other—to believe or fight back against every word we said, to help us nail Beau or throw up a wall.

I chose my words carefully. "Have you ever seen Beau draw a spiral?"

That was a gamble, but the violence we'd seen these past few days was years in the making. If our profile was right, if Beau *had* been working toward this for years, if his sick needs and plan could be traced back to an early trauma . . . *You planned and you dreamed and you practiced. You never let yourself forget.*

"Oh, God." Tory broke. I could hear the exact moment she shattered. I could almost *see* her sinking to the ground, pulling her knees to her chest, the hand holding her phone dropping to her side.

Dean caught my eyes in his. His hand made his way to my shoulder. I closed my eyes and leaned into his touch.

I did this to you, I thought, unable to get the picture of Tory out of my mind. *I broke you. I shattered you, because I could. Because I had to.*

Because we need you.

"He used to draw them in the dirt." Tory's voice was hoarse. I wanted to tell her that I knew how it felt to have your insides carved out. I wanted to tell her I knew what it was like to feel hollow—like there was no grief left to be had. "Beau never drew on paper, but he used to draw spirals in the dirt. No one ever saw them but me—he never let anyone see them but me."

It was always going to be you. Beau would have killed her. She was his family. He loved her, and he would have killed her. He had to, *had* to, for reasons I couldn't quite grasp.

"You need to talk to the FBI," Dean said gently. "You need to answer their questions." He gave her a moment to process his words. "I know what I'm asking, Tory. I know what it will cost you."

From experience. He knows from experience. Dean had testified against his father. We were asking Tory to do the same to Beau.

"I heard our foster mother talking about him once," Tory said after an extended silence. "I heard her say . . ." I could hear the effort it took for her to even form the words. "They found Beau half-dead in the desert. He was six years old, and someone just left him there. No food, no water. He'd been out there for days." Her voice shook slightly. "No one knew where he'd come from or who left him. Beau couldn't tell them. He didn't say a word, not to anyone, for two years."

No one knew where he'd come from. Like dominoes, falling one by one, everything I knew about Beau's motivation, about the murders, began to shift.

YOU

They think they can arrest you. They think they can charge you with murder. They think they can put you in a box. They have no idea—what you are, what you have become.

They have no proof.

There's talk of security footage at the Desert Rose, the day you anointed the one who was to become your fifth. The same pawn store that caught Victor McKinney assaulting you on camera has provided footage of you there hours before, loosening the brick. The FBI claims they have a plastic baggie with your fingerprints on it. They claim to be scanning it for Aaron Shaw's blood.

Tory is talking. About teaching you hypnosis. About what little she knows of your past.

You won't be in here forever. You'll finish what you started. You'll take your seat at the table. The ninth seat.

Nine.

Nine.

Nine.

Four more, and then you will be finished. Four more, and you can go home.

CHAPTER 59

Agent Sterling and Agent Briggs sat in the interrogation room opposite Beau Donovan. He was wearing an orange jumpsuit. His wrists were handcuffed together. A public defender sat beside Beau, continually advising his client not to speak.

Back at the safe house, Lia, Michael, Dean, and I watched. Sloane had tried to watch, too, but she couldn't.

She'd been wearing the shirt Aaron gave her for three days straight.

We needed a confession. We'd laid out enough evidence to convince the DA to press charges, but to avoid a trial, to be sure that Beau would pay, we needed a confession.

"My client," the lawyer said forcefully, "is pleading the Fifth."

"You have nothing," Beau told Briggs and Sterling, his eyes simultaneously dead of emotion and strangely alight.

"This is the second time you've tried to put me in this box. It won't work. Of course it won't."

"My client," the lawyer repeated, "is pleading the Fifth."

"Nine bodies." Agent Briggs leaned forward. "Every three years. On dates derived from the Fibonacci sequence."

This was the final card we had to play.

"Keep going," Michael told them, his words going to the earpiece both agents wore. "He's surprised that you know about the others. And the way his eyes just darted toward his lawyer? Agitation. Anger. Fear."

Beau's lawyer was an outsider. He didn't know why his client had done what he'd done. He didn't know what had inspired him to kill. We were banking on the fact that Beau might not want the man to know.

One by one, Briggs started pulling pictures out of his file. Kills—but not Beau's. "Drowning. Fire. Impaling. Strangling."

Beau was getting visibly agitated.

"Knife." Briggs paused. That was as far as Beau's pattern had gone. "You would have beaten your sixth victim to death." Another picture.

You weren't expecting this. You weren't expecting the FBI to know. Beau went pale. *The FBI can't know.*

You only meant to hint at age-old secrets. To get their attention. To make them see you.

You never meant for it to go this far.

"Number seven would have been poison," Briggs continued. He laid the last picture down. In it, a woman with blond hair, green eyes, and a face that tended more toward quirky than cute lay on her back. Her mouth was crusted with blood. Her body was contorted. She'd ripped her own fingernails off.

I swallowed as I remembered what Judd had said about Nightshade's poison. *Undetectable. Incurable. Painful.*

"She was my best friend." Agent Sterling brought her fingers to the very edge of Scarlett's picture. "Did they take someone from you, too?"

"They?" the lawyer said. "Who's they?" He gestured angrily toward the pictures. "What is the meaning of this?"

Briggs locked his eyes onto Beau. "Should I answer that question?" he asked. "Should I tell him why we're showing you these pictures?"

"No!" The word burst out of Beau as a snarl.

You don't talk to outsiders. Lia's insight into cult mentality rang in my head. *You don't tell them what they're not blessed enough to know.*

"Get out," Beau told his lawyer.

"I can't just leave—"

"I'm the client," Beau said. "And I said get out. *Now.*"

The lawyer left.

"You're under no obligation to speak with us without your lawyer present," Briggs said. "But then, I'm not convinced you want him to hear about this. I'm not convinced you want *anyone* to hear about this." Briggs paused. "You're right when you said we might not have enough for a conviction."

Sterling picked up where Briggs left off. "But we do have enough for a trial."

"Twelve people on a jury," Sterling said. I recognized her strategy of playing up the numbers, playing into his pattern of thinking. "Dozens of reporters. The victims' families will want to be there, of course. . . ."

"They will destroy you," Beau said.

"Will they?" Sterling asked. "Or will they destroy *you*?"

Those words landed. I could see Beau straining against the handcuffs, straining to keep from turning back and looking over his shoulder.

"Tell him a story," Dean instructed the agents. "Start with the day someone found him in the desert."

Dean and I were used to using our abilities to catch killers. But profiling was just as useful in knowing how to break them.

"Let me tell you a story," Briggs said on-screen. "It's a story about a little boy who was found, half-dead, in the desert, when he was six years old."

Beau's breath was coming quicker now.

"No one knew where he'd come from," Briggs continued.

"No one knew what he was," I said. Briggs repeated my words to Beau.

We weren't positive how Beau had spent those first six years, but Dean had a theory. I'd wondered, days ago, if Dean had seen any of himself when he looked at Beau. I'd thought that if the UNSUB was young, his profile wouldn't be dissimilar from Daniel Redding's apprentices'.

You didn't just stumble across the pattern. You knew to look for it. You spent your whole life looking for it. And the reason you did that lies in those first six years.

"You don't know what you're talking about." Beau's voice was no louder than a whisper, but it cut through the air. "You couldn't possibly know."

"We know they didn't want you." Sterling went for the kill. Beau's murders had taken the cult's pattern to the next level. He'd been appealing to them, attacking them, showing them just how worthy he was. "They left you to die. You weren't good enough for them." Sterling paused. "And they were right. Look at you. You got caught." Her eyes trailed over his orange jumpsuit, his cuffs. "They were right."

"You have no idea what I am," Beau said, his voice shaking with emotion. "You have no idea what I'm capable of. Neither do they. No one knows." His voice rose with each word. "I was born for this. The rest of them, they're recruited as adults, but number nine is always born within their walls. The child of the brotherhood and the Pythia—blood of their blood. Nine."

"*Nine* is a name to him," Dean said. "A title. Tell him it's not his. Tell him he doesn't deserve it."

"You're not Nine," Sterling said. "You're never going to be Nine."

Beau lifted cuffed hands to his own collar. He latched his fingers over his shirt and pulled it roughly off his shoulder. Underneath, etched onto his chest, was a series of jagged cuts, halfway healed and on their way to a scar.

Seven small circles forming a heptagon around a cross.

I stopped breathing. That symbol—I knew that symbol.

"Seven Masters." Beau's face was taut, his voice full of fury. He ran his fingers around the outside of the heptagon. *Seven circles.* "The Pythia." He pressed his finger into the wound and pulled it down the vertical line on the cross. His hand trembled as he went to do the same with the horizontal. "And Nine."

The symbol. I know that symbol. Seven circles around a cross.

I'd seen it carved into the lid of a plain wooden coffin, uncovered at the crossroads on a country dirt road.

"You *wish* you were Nine," Agent Sterling said, still pressing. I felt my limbs going numb. Blackness crept in on my field of vision.

"Dean," I wheezed.

He was with me in an instant. "I see it," he said. "I need you to breathe for me, Cassie. I see it."

The symbol Beau had carved into his own flesh had also been carved into my mother's coffin. *Not possible. June twenty-first. Not a Fibonacci date. My mother died in June.*

On-screen, Beau's hands were still trembling. His fingers tensed. They clawed at his neck. His back arched. And then he fell to the floor, convulsing.

Screaming. I registered the sound as if it were coming from very far away. *He's screaming.*

And then he was gargling, choking on blood as it poured from his lips, his fingernails clawing violently against his own body, against the floor.

345

Poison.

"Breathe," Dean repeated.

"We need help in here!" Sterling was screaming. *Beau is screaming, and Sterling is screaming*—and finally, the convulsions stopped. Finally, Beau was still.

Seven small circles forming a heptagon around a cross.

I forced myself to suck in a breath. And then another and another.

Beau's cracked lips moved. He looked at Briggs in one final moment of clarity. "I don't," he struggled to say. "I don't wish I was Nine." He sounded like a child.

"You've been poisoned," Briggs told him. "You need to tell us—"

"I don't believe in wishing," Beau murmured. And then his eyes rolled back in his head, and he died.

CHAPTER 60

eau was poisoned. I thought the words, but didn't understand them. *The cult killed him. Nightshade killed Beau.* Beau, who'd carved a symbol onto his own chest—a symbol someone else had carved into the box that contained my mother's remains.

"My mother didn't die on a Fibonacci date," I said. "It was June. There are no Fibonacci dates in June, none in July...."

I realized on some level that Michael and Lia were staring at me, that Dean had wrapped his arms around me, that my body had collapsed against his.

My mother had disappeared five years ago—six in June. The person who'd attacked her had used a knife. *It was poison that year. In the pattern, it was poison. Nightshade was the killer. The knife was New York, six years before that.* There wasn't supposed to be another one for twenty-one years.

Nothing about my mother's death fit the pattern—so why was the symbol etched onto her coffin?

I struggled out of Dean's arms and went for my computer. I pulled up the pictures—the royal blue shroud, the bones, my mother's necklace. My finger hit at the keys again and again until the symbol showed up.

Lia and Michael came up behind us. "Is that . . ."

"Seven Masters," I said, forcing my hand around the circles on the outside of the symbol. "The Pythia." The vertical line. "And Nine."

"Seven Masters." Sloane appeared in the doorway, as if the mere mention of numbers had called her to us. "Seven circles. Seven ways of killing."

I pulled my eyes from the screen to look at Sloane.

"I always wondered why there were only seven methods," she said, her eyes swollen, her face pale. "Instead of nine."

Three.

Three times three.

Three times three times three—but only seven ways to kill.

Because this group—whatever it was, however long it had been around—had nine members at a time. *Seven Masters. The Pythia. And Nine.*

"Beau Donovan is dead," Lia told Sloane. "Poison. Presumably Nightshade's."

Sloane's hands smoothed themselves down over the front of the shirt Aaron had given her. She trembled slightly, but all she said was, "Maybe the flower was for him."

The white flower in the photograph that Nightshade had

sent Judd. *White flower.* Something stuck in the back of my brain, like food caught in between the teeth. Nightshade always sent his victims the bloom of a white nightshade plant. *White. White flowers.*

I walked into the kitchen, scrambled until I found what I was looking for. I pulled out the evidence envelope, opened it, removed the photo inside.

Not white nightshade. The photo Nightshade had sent Judd wasn't of a white nightshade bloom. It was a picture of a paper flower. *Origami.*

I stumbled backward and grabbed the edge of the counter for balance, thinking of Beau's last moments, the words he'd said.

I don't believe in wishing.

I saw the little girl in the candy store, staring at a lollipop. I saw her father come and put her on his shoulders. I saw her beside the fountain, holding the penny.

I don't believe in wishes, she'd said.

There was a white origami flower behind her ear.

In my mind, I saw her mother come to get her. I saw her father, tossing a penny into the water. In my mind, I saw his face. I saw the water, and I saw his face—

And just like that, I was back on the banks of the Potomac, a thick black binder on my lap.

"Enjoying a bit of light reading?" The voice echoed through my memory, and this time, I could make out the speaker's face. *"You live at Judd's place, right? He and I go way back."*

"Nightshade," I forced out the word. "I've seen him."

Lia looked almost concerned despite herself. "We know."

"No," I said. "In Vegas. I've seen him here. Twice. I thought . . . I thought I was watching him."

But maybe—maybe he was watching me.

"He had a child with him," I said. "There was a woman, too. The girl, she came up next to me at the fountain. She was little—three, four at most. She had a penny in her hand. I asked if she was going to make a wish, and she said . . ."

I couldn't coax my lips into forming the words.

Dean formed them for me. "I don't believe in wishing." His gaze flicked to Michael's, then to Lia's. "The same thing Beau Donovan said when Sterling told him he only *wished* he were Nine."

Right before he died.

"You said Nightshade had a woman with him," Dean said. "What did she look like, Cassie?"

"Strawberry blond hair," I said. "Medium height. Slender."

I thought of my mother's body, stripped to the bones and buried at the crossroads. With honor. With care.

Maybe they weren't trying to kill you. Maybe you weren't supposed to die. Maybe you were supposed to be like this woman—

"Beau said the ninth member was always born to it. How did he phrase it?"

Dean stared at a point just to the left of my shoulder and then repeated Beau's words exactly. "The child of the brotherhood and the Pythia. Blood of their blood."

Seven Masters. A child. And the child's mother.

The woman at the fountain had strawberry blond hair. It would be red in some lights—like my mother's.

Nine members. Seven Masters. A woman. A child.

"The Pythia was the name given to the Oracle at Delphi," Sloane said. "A priestess at the Temple of Apollo. A prophetess."

I thought of the family—the picture-perfect family I'd looked at, knowing to my core that it was something I'd never have.

Mother. Father. Child.

I turned to Dean. "We have to call Briggs."

CHAPTER 61

The man we knew as Nightshade stared back at me from the page. The police artist had captured the lines of his face: strong jaw, thick brows, dark hair with just enough curl to make his remaining features look boyish. The wrinkles at the corners of his eyes told me he was older than he looked; light stubble masked the fullness of his lips.

You came to Vegas to take care of a problem. Watching me, tormenting Judd—that, you enjoyed.

I felt someone take a seat next to me at the kitchen table. The FBI had taken the sketch and run with it. They were monitoring the airport, bus stations, traffic cameras—and, courtesy of Sloane, the casinos' security feeds.

You look like a thousand other men. You don't look dangerous.

The man in the sketch looked like a neighbor, a coworker,

a Little League coach. *A dad.* I could see him in my mind, hoisting the little red-haired girl up onto his shoulders.

"You've done everything you can."

I tore my gaze from the police sketch to look at Judd. *This man killed your daughter,* I thought. *This man might know what happened to my mother.*

"Trust Ronnie and Briggs to do what *they* can," Judd continued.

A manhunt didn't fall under Naturals' jurisdiction. Once the FBI figured out who the man in the picture was, once we had a name, a history, information, maybe we could be of some use, but until then, all we could do was wait.

By then, a voice whispered in the back of my head, *it might be too late.* Nightshade might disappear. Once he left Vegas, we might never find him again.

Judd wouldn't get justice for Scarlett's death. I wouldn't get answers about my mother's.

Beside me, Judd let himself look at the police sketch— *made* himself look at it.

"You do what you can," he said, after seconds of silence had stretched to a minute, "to make sure your kids are safe. From the second they're born . . ." He stared at the lines of Nightshade's face, the ordinariness of it. "You want to protect them. From every skinned knee, from hurt feelings and punk kids who push smaller ones into the dirt, from the worst parts of yourself and the worst parts of this world."

This man killed your daughter. She died in pain, her fingernails torn, her body contorting—

"Briggs saved my life." Judd forcibly shifted his eyes away from the man in the picture and turned to look at me. "He saved me, the day he brought me Dean."

Judd's right hand slowly worked its way out of a fist. He closed his eyes for a moment, then reached for the picture of his daughter's killer and turned it facedown.

You do what you can to make sure your kids are safe.

This was Judd, trying to protect me. This was Judd, telling me to let it go. I thought about the little red-haired girl, about Beau Donovan, about *seven* and *nine*, the symbol carved into my mother's coffin, the pattern of murders stretching back over years and generations.

I didn't want anyone's protection. *I want Nightshade. I want answers.*

Judd responded like I'd said the words out loud. "You have to want something else more."

"Home isn't a place, Cassie. Home is the people who love you most." Standing on the back porch, looking out at the safe house backyard, I let the memory wash over me. I lost myself to it. I needed to remember. I needed my mom to be my mom—not a body, not bones, not a victim—*my mom.*

We're dancing, right there on the side of the road. Her red hair escapes the scarf. It frames her face as she moves—wild and free and absolutely unabashed. I spin in circles, my hands held out to the side. The world is a blur of colors and darkness and snow. She tilts her head back, and I do the same, sticking out my tongue.

We can shed the past. We can dance it off. We can laugh and sing and spin—forever and ever.

No matter what.
No matter what.
No matter what.

I didn't want to forget—the smile on her face, the way she'd moved, the way she'd danced like no one was watching, no matter where we were.

I sucked in a breath and wished—fiercely, vehemently—that I didn't understand how a stranger could have looked at her and thought, *She's the one.*

They were watching you, I thought. *They chose you.*

I'd never asked myself what my mother's killer had chosen her *for*. I thought of the woman I'd seen with Nightshade—the little girl's mother. *Do you know what he is?* I asked the woman, holding the image of her in my mind. *Are you a part of this group? Are you a killer?*

Seven Masters. The Pythia. And Nine. I thought of the hundreds of people who'd passed through my mother's shows. *Seven Masters.* Had one of them been there? Had they seen her?

Did you expect my mom to go willingly? I asked them silently. *Did you try to break her? Did she fight you?*

I looked down at my wrists, remembering the feel of zip ties digging into them. I remembered being stalked, hunted, trapped. I remembered Locke's knife. I remembered fighting—lying, manipulating, struggling, running, hiding, *fighting*.

I was my mother's daughter.

They didn't know what they were getting into with you, I thought, my mother still dancing in my memory, fearless and free. My mom and Locke had grown up with an abusive father. When my mom got pregnant with me, she got out. She left her father's house in the dead of night and never looked back.

"Dance it off."

My mother was a survivor.

The back door opened. After a moment's pause, Dean came to stand behind me. I leaned back into him, my hands held palms up in front of me, my eyes on my wrists. Webber had bound them behind my back. *Did they bind your arms, Mom? Did they give you a chance to win your freedom? Did they tell you that yours was a higher purpose?*

Did they kill you for fighting?

By the time they killed you, did you want to die?

"I've been trying to imagine," Dean said, "what this is like for you. And instead . . ." His voice caught in his throat. "I keep imagining seeing her, choosing her, taking her—" Dean cut off abruptly.

You hate yourself for imagining it. You hate how easy it is to put yourself in the mind-set of my mother's killer—or killers.

You hate that it makes any kind of sense at all.

"I imagine taking her," I told him. "I imagine being taken."

I swallowed. "Whatever this group is, they operate by certain rules. There's a ritual, an uncompromising tradition. . . ."

Seven Masters. The Pythia. And Nine.

Wordlessly, Dean reached around my body. He took my right hand in his. His thumb grazed my wrist, exactly where Webber's zip ties had dug into my flesh.

Like mother, like daughter—

All thoughts cut off as Dean lifted my wrist to his lips, pressing a soft, silent kiss to the once-abused skin. He closed his eyes. I closed mine. I could feel him, breathing behind me. I matched my breaths to his.

In. Out. In. Out.

"You don't have to be strong right now," Dean told me.

I turned, opened my eyes, caught his lips in mine. *Yes. I do.*

Like mother, like daughter—I was a fighter.

My neck arched. I pulled back from Dean, my face less than an inch from his.

"You should really put a tie on the door or something." Lia sauntered onto the back porch, utterly unremorseful about interrupting us. "Serial-killing cults and citywide manhunts aside, a little discretion on the PDA front goes a long way."

I took that to mean Lia hadn't received any updates on the case. Briggs and Sterling hadn't called. *Nightshade's still out there. The FBI is still looking.*

"Lia." Dean's tone clearly requested that she vacate the premises.

Lia ignored him and focused on me. "I told Michael to put on his big-boy pants," she informed me. "I think the near-death experience might have put a damper on his downward spiral, and besides . . ." Lia met my gaze. "I told him it was your turn."

There was a beat of silence as I absorbed the full meaning of Lia's words. She was here for me. Michael was here. Sloane—shattered, grieving Sloane—was here.

Briggs saved my life, Judd had said. *He saved me, the day he brought me Dean.*

I wanted Nightshade behind bars. I wanted answers—but when I let myself, I wanted *this* more. Dean and Lia and Michael and Sloane—*home is the people who love you most.*

Forever and ever.

No matter—

"Guys." Michael stood frozen at the back door. Behind him, I could see Sloane, dark circles ringing her eyes.

I knew, then, that there was news. The thudding of my heart, the roar in my ears—I knew there was news, and I was terrified to let Michael say a single word.

"They got him."

Nightshade.

The man in the picture.

They got him.

"The woman?" I heard, as if from a distance. *My voice. My question.* "The little girl?"

Michael shook his head, which I took to mean that they hadn't been with Nightshade.

The Pythia. The child.

My heart raced as I thought of the man I'd seen, the man I'd remembered.

You killed Judd's daughter. You killed Beau. You know why that symbol was carved onto my mother's coffin.

"What aren't you telling us?" Lia's voice was low. *"Michael."*

I couldn't read Michael the way he would have been able to read me, but in the second it took him to reply to Lia's question, his expression was enough to knock the breath from my lungs.

"Nightshade stuck Briggs with some kind of needle." Michael looked from Lia to Dean to me. "Injected him with something. They don't know what."

My mouth went dry and the roaring sound in my ears surged. *Poison.*

CHAPTER 62

One last trick up Nightshade's sleeve. *Your grand finale. Your au revoir.* I'd been worried that the FBI wouldn't catch him. It hadn't occurred to me, even for a second, to worry about what might happen once they did.

Undetectable. Incurable. Painful. I didn't want to remember what Judd had said about Nightshade's poison, but the words kept repeating themselves in a loop in my head.

"Cassie." Judd appeared, his face grim. "We need to talk."

What else was there to say?

Undetectable. Incurable. Painful.

Sloane's lips were moving as she silently went through a list of every poison known to man. Dean had gone ashen.

"He claims there's an antidote," Judd said. Our guardian didn't specify who "he" was. He didn't have to.

Nightshade.

"And what does he want?" Dean asked hoarsely. "In exchange for that antidote?"

I knew the answer—knew it based on the way Judd had said my name, the number of times I'd seen Nightshade, the time he'd spent watching me.

My mother fought, tooth and nail. She resisted whatever it was you people wanted from her, whatever you wanted her to be.

I looked from Dean to Judd. "He wants me."

I stood on one side of a two-way mirror and watched as guards escorted the man I'd identified as Nightshade into the room on the other side. The man's hands were cuffed behind his body. His hair was mussed. A dark bruise was forming on one side of his face.

He didn't look dangerous.

He didn't look like a killer.

"He can't see you," Agent Sterling reminded me. She looked at me, her own eyes shadowed. "He can't touch you. He stays on that side of the glass, and you stay here."

Behind us, Judd placed one hand on my shoulder. *You won't put me in the same room as Scarlett's killer,* I thought. *Not even to save Briggs.*

I tried not to think about Briggs and instead focused on the man on the other side of the glass. He looked older than he had in my memory—younger than Judd, but significantly older than Agent Sterling.

Older than my mother would have been, if she'd lived.

"Take your time," Nightshade said. Even though I knew he couldn't see me, it felt like he was looking directly at me.

He has kind eyes.

My stomach twisted with unexpected nausea as he continued. "I'm here when you're ready, Cassandra."

Judd's grip tightened slightly on my shoulder. *You'd kill him, if you could,* I thought. Judd wouldn't have lost a single night's sleep over snapping this man's neck. But he didn't make a move. Instead, he stood still, with me.

"I'm ready," I told Agent Sterling. I wasn't, but time was a luxury we didn't have.

Judd met Agent Sterling's gaze and gave a curt nod. Sterling stepped to the side of the room and hit a button, converting the two-way mirror in front of us to a clear pane.

You can see me, I thought as Nightshade's eyes landed on mine. *You see Judd. Your lips curve slightly.* I kept my face as blank as I could. *One last card to play. One last game.*

"Cassandra." Nightshade seemed to enjoy saying my name. "Judd. And the indomitable Agent Sterling."

You watched us. You get off on Judd's grief, on Sterling's.

"You wanted to talk to me?" I said, my voice unnaturally calm. "Talk."

I expected the man on the other side of the glass to say something about Scarlett or about my mother or about Beau. Instead, he said something in a language I didn't recognize. I glanced at Sterling. The man opposite us repeated himself. "It's a rare snake," he translated after a moment. "Its venom is slower-acting than most. Find a zoo that has one, and you'll find the antivenom. In time, I hope." He smiled, and this time, it was chilling. "I always have had a certain fondness for your Agent Briggs."

I didn't understand. This man—this killer—had brought me here. He'd used the only bargaining chip he had to bring me here, and now, having seen me, he was handing it in?

Why? If you enjoy tormenting Judd and Sterling, if you want to leave them with the taste of fear in their mouths, with the bitter knowledge that the people they love will never be safe, why cure Briggs?

"You're lying," Agent Sterling said.

We should have brought Lia, I thought. And a second later: *I shouldn't be here.* The feeling started in my gut and snaked its way out to my limbs, weighing them down.

"Am I?" Nightshade countered.

"Incurable. Painful." I spoke the words out loud without meaning to, but didn't pull back from talking once they'd made their way out of my mouth. "You wouldn't just hand away your secret. Not this easily. Not this fast."

Nightshade's eyes lingered on mine a moment longer. "There are limits," he admitted, "to what one might say. Some secrets are sacred. Some things you take to the grave." His voice had taken on a low, humming quality. "But then, I never said your Agent Briggs had been afflicted with *that* poison."

That poison. Your poison. Your legacy.

"Go." Judd spoke for the first time since the man who'd killed his daughter had been brought into the room. He met Sterling's gaze and repeated himself. "He's telling the truth. *Go.*"

Go get the antivenom.

Go save Briggs.

"We're done here," Sterling said, reaching for the button on the wall.

"Stop." The word burst out of my mouth. I couldn't draw my gaze away from the killer's. *You brought me here for a reason. You do everything for a reason—you all do.*

Nightshade smiled. "I thought," he said, "that you might have some questions for me."

I saw now, the game he was playing. He'd brought me here. But staying? Listening to him? Asking him for answers?

That was on me.

"Go," Judd told Sterling again. After a split second's hesitation, she did as he said, dialing her phone on the way out. Judd turned back to me. "I want to tell you not to say another word, Cassie, not to listen, not to look back."

But he wouldn't. He wouldn't make me walk away. I wasn't sure he could walk away himself. *You can look at the files,* Judd had said, back when this all began, *but you're not doing it alone.*

Neither one of us was doing this alone now.

"Beau Donovan." I turned back to the monster waiting patiently on the other side of the glass. I couldn't make my mouth form the words to ask about my mother, not yet. And I couldn't—*wouldn't*—bring up Scarlett. "You killed him."

"Was that a question?" Nightshade asked.

"Your people left him in the desert fifteen years ago."

"We don't kill children." Nightshade's tone was flat.

You don't kill children. That was a rule they lived by. A sacred law. *But you have no problems leaving them in the desert to die of their own accord.*

"What was Beau to you? Why raise him at all, if you were going to turn him out?"

Nightshade smiled slightly. "Every dynasty needs its heir."

My brain whirred. "You weren't raised the way Beau was."

The rest of them, Beau had said, *they're recruited as adults.*

"The term *Master* suggests an apprentice model," I continued. "I'm assuming Masters choose their own replacements—adults, not children. The cycle repeats every twenty-one years. But the ninth member, the one you call Nine—"

"Nine is the greatest of us. The constant. The bridge from generation to generation."

Your leader, I filled in. Beau hadn't just been born in their walls. He'd been born to lead them.

"You left him to die," I said.

"We do not kill children," Nightshade repeated, his voice just as flat as it had been the first time he said the words. "Even if they prove themselves unworthy. Even when they fail to do what is asked and it becomes clear they will never be able to take the mantle to which they were born. Even when the way must be cleared for a true heir."

What did they ask you to do, Beau? What kind of monster were they molding you to be? I couldn't let my mind go down that path. I had to concentrate on the here and now.

On Nightshade.

"And the little girl?" I said. "The one I saw you with. Is *she* worthy? Is she the new heir? A *true* heir?" I took a step forward, toward the glass. "What are you doing to her?"

I don't believe in wishing.

"Are you her father?" I asked.

"The girl has many fathers."

That answer sent a chill down my spine. "Seven Masters," I said, hoping to jar him into telling me something I didn't know. "The Pythia. And Nine."

"All are tested. All must be found worthy."

"And that woman I saw with you? She's worthy?" The question tore out of me with quiet force. *My mother wasn't worthy.*

My mother fought.

"Did you take her, too?" I asked, my mind on the woman I'd seen. "Did you attack her, cut her?" I continued, my heart pounding in my chest. "Did you torture her until she became one of you? Your *oracle*?"

Nightshade was quiet for several moments. Then he leaned forward, his eyes on mine. "I like to think of the Pythia more as Lady Justice," he said. "She is our counsel, our judge and our jury, until her child comes of age. She lives and dies for us and we for her."

Lives and dies.

Lives and dies.

Lives and dies.

"You killed my mother," I said. "You people took her. You attacked her—"

"You misunderstand." Nightshade made the words sound reasonable, gentle even, when the room around him was charged with an unholy energy.

Power. Games. Pain. This was the cult's stock-in-trade.

I reached for a piece of paper and drew the symbol I'd seen on Beau's chest. I slammed it against the glass. "This was on my mother's coffin," I said. "I don't misunderstand anything. She wasn't part of the pattern. She wasn't killed on a Fibonacci date. She was attacked with a knife the same year you were 'proving yourself worthy' with poison." My voice shook. "So don't tell me that I don't understand. You—all of you, one of you, I don't know—but you *chose her*. You *tested her* and you found her unworthy."

They didn't kill children. They left them to die. But my mother?

"You killed her," I said, the words rough against my throat and sour in my mouth. "You killed her and stripped her flesh from her bones and buried her."

"*We* did no such thing." The emphasis on the first word somehow managed to break through the haze of fury and sorrow clouding my mind. "There can only be one Pythia."

Every instinct I had told me this was what Nightshade had brought me here to hear. This was what he'd traded his last remaining bit of leverage to say.

"One woman to provide counsel. One woman to bear the child. One child—one *worthy* child—to carry the tradition on."

One woman. One child.

You killed her.

We *did no such thing.*

All are tested. All must be found worthy.

My mother had been buried with care. With remorse. I thought of the woman I'd seen with the little girl.

One woman. One child.

I thought about how a group could possibly persist for hundreds of years, taking women, holding them, until captive became monster. *Lady Justice. The Pythia.*

I thought about the fact that the woman I'd seen by the fountain hadn't taken her child. She hadn't run. She hadn't asked for help.

She'd smiled at Nightshade.

There can only be one Pythia.

"You make them fight." I wasn't sure if I was profiling or talking to him. I wasn't sure it mattered. "You take a new woman, a new Pythia, and . . ."

There can only be one.

"The woman," I said. "The one I saw with you." My voice lowered itself to a whisper, but the words were deafening in my own ears. "She killed my mother. You *made her* kill my mother."

"We all have choices," Nightshade replies. "The Pythia chooses to live."

Why bring me here? I thought, aware, on some level, that my body was shaking. My eyes were wet. *Why tell me this? Why give me a glimpse of something I'm not blessed enough to know?*

"Perhaps someday," Nightshade said, "that choice will be yours, Cassandra."

Judd had been standing ramrod stiff beside me, but in that instant, he surged forward. He slammed the heel of his hand against the switch on the wall, and the pane darkened.

You can't see us. I can see you, but you can't see us.

Judd took me by the shoulders. He pulled me to him, blocking my view, holding me, even as I started to fight him.

"I've got you," he murmured. "You're okay. I've got you, Cassie. You're okay. You're going to be okay."

An order. A plea.

"Two-one-one-seven." Until Nightshade spoke, I hadn't realized the speaker was still on. At first, I thought he was saying a Fibonacci number, but then he clarified. "If you want to see the woman, you'll find her in room two-one-one-seven."

The Pythia chooses to live. The words echoed in my mind. *Perhaps one day, that choice will be yours.*

Room 2117.

CHAPTER 63

The hours after Nightshade's interrogation blurred into nothingness. Sterling called to say that Briggs had received the antivenom. She called to say that he was expected to make a full—if slow—recovery. She called to say they found the woman.

They found the little girl.

Fewer than twenty hours after Nightshade had named my mother's killer, I stepped into room 2117 at the Dark Angel Hotel Casino. You could smell the blood from fifty yards away. *On the walls. On the floor.* The scene was familiar.

Blood. On the walls. On my hand. I feel it. I smell it—

But this time, there was a body. The woman—strawberry blond hair, younger than I remembered—lay in her own blood, her white dress soaked through. She'd been killed with a knife.

Wielded by Nightshade, before he was captured? One of

the other Masters? A new Pythia? I didn't know. And for the first time since I'd joined the Naturals program, I wasn't sure I *wanted* to know. This woman had killed my mother. Whether she'd had a choice, whether it was kill or be killed, whether she'd enjoyed it—

I couldn't be sorry she was dead.

The little girl sat in a chair, her small legs dangling halfway to the ground. She was staring blankly ahead, no expression on her face.

She was the reason I was here.

The child hadn't said a word, hadn't even seemed to see a single one of the agents who had come into this room. They were afraid to touch her, afraid to remove her by force.

I remember coming back to my mother's dressing room. I remember there was blood.

I made my way through the room. I knelt next to the chair.

"Hi," I said.

The little girl blinked. Her eyes met mine. I saw a hint—just a hint—of recognition.

Beau Donovan had been six years old when he'd been abandoned in the desert by the people who'd raised him, deemed unsuitable for their needs.

Whatever those needs might be.

You're three, I thought, slipping into the girl's perspective. *Maybe four.*

Too young to understand what was happening. Too young to have been through so much.

You know things, I thought. *Maybe you don't even know that you know them.*

Beau had known enough at the age of six to uncover the pattern once he was older.

You might be able to lead us to them.

"I'm Cassie," I said.

The child said nothing.

"What's your name?" I asked.

She looked down. Beside her on the ground, there was a white origami flower, soaked in blood.

"Nine," she whispered. "My name is Nine."

A chill ran down my spine, leaving nothing but fury in its wake. *You're not a part of them,* I thought, fiercely protective. She was just a baby—just a little, little girl.

"Your mommy called you something else," I said, trying to remember the name the woman had used that day at the fountain.

"Laurel. Mommy calls me Laurel." She turned to look at the woman on the ground. Her face held no hint of emotion. She didn't flinch at the blood.

"Don't look at Mommy, Laurel." I moved to block her view. "Look at me."

"That's not my mommy." The little girl's tone was dispassionate.

My heart thudded in my chest. "It's not?"

"The Master hired her. To watch me when we came here."

Laurel's chubby baby hands went to an old-fashioned locket around her neck. She let me open it. Inside, there was a picture.

"That's my mommy," Laurel said.

Not possible. The necklace. The bones. The blood—it was her blood. The tests said it was her blood.

I felt the world closing in on me. Because there were two people in the photo, and Laurel looked exactly the same in the picture as she did today.

It was recent.

That's my mommy, Laurel had said. But the woman in the picture was my mother, too.

I always knew—I always *thought*—that if she'd survived, she would have come back to me. Somehow, some way, if she'd survived—

"Forever and ever," Laurel whispered, each word a knife in my gut. "No matter what."

"Laurel," I said, my voice hoarse. "Where is Mommy?"

"In the room." Laurel stared at me and into me. "Masters come, and Masters go, but the Pythia lives in the room."

EPILOGUE

I stood in front of the tombstone. Dean stood beside me, his body lightly brushing mine. The others stood behind us in a semicircle. *Michael and Lia and Sloane. Sterling and Briggs and Judd.*

The remains the police had recovered from that dirt road had been released to the family. To my dad. To me. My father didn't know that the remains weren't my mother's. He didn't know that she was alive.

Masters come, and Masters go, but the Pythia lives in the room.

We had no idea who the woman we'd just buried in my mom's grave was. The necklace she'd been buried with, the blood on the shawl—those had been my mother's.

The Pythia chooses to live, Nightshade had told me, knowing quite well that my mother was the one who'd made that choice.

I didn't know how long it was after my mother had been taken that she had been forced to fight for her life—again. I didn't know if it was standard operating procedure for these men to stage a woman's death before they took her.

All are tested. All must be found worthy.

What I did know was that my mother was alive.

Masters come, and Masters go, but the Pythia lives in the room.

My mother hadn't been killed. She hadn't been buried at the crossroads with care. She'd buried her predecessor. *My mom's favorite color. Her necklace. Traces of her blood.* From the beginning, Dean and I had seen the funeral rites as rife with remorse. *My mother's.*

"Are you ready?" Dean asked, his hand on my shoulder.

I stared at the tombstone marked with my mother's name a moment longer. For Laurel's sake, the cult needed to think we hadn't put the pieces together. They needed to think that I believed I'd buried my mother. They needed to think that we hadn't read much into the fact that the woman I'd mistaken for Laurel's mother was actually a nanny, a disposable Las Vegas native Nightshade had hired earlier that week.

They needed to believe that the FBI had put Laurel into protective custody because of her connection to Nightshade, not her connection to me.

We don't kill children.

I thought of Beau, wandering the desert, and pushed back the bitter taste in my mouth. "I'm ready," I told Dean. I turned, meeting each of the others' eyes, one by one. *Home is the people who love you.*

I was ready to go home. To do whatever it took to find the Masters. To protect Laurel. *Forever and ever.* To find my mother. Find the Pythia. Find the room.

No matter what.

ACKNOWLEDGMENTS

Over the course of the Naturals series, I've been lucky enough to work with multiple incredible editors who are experts at asking the right questions and are just as invested in these characters and this story as I am. In particular, *All In* owes a great debt to Lisa Yoskowitz, who was so passionate about this book that I couldn't wait to sit down and write it for her, and Kieran Viola, who knows exactly what a writer needs to hear. I am also incredibly grateful to the fabulous Julie Moody, who has been with this series since the very first book, and to Emily Meehan, Dina Sherman, Jamie Baker, Seale Ballenger, Mary Ann Zissimos, and the rest of the folks at Hyperion for all of their support!

As always, I'd also like to thank my amazing team at Curtis Brown: Elizabeth Harding, Ginger Clark, Holly Frederick, and Jonathan Lyons, as well as Sarah Perillo and Kerry Cullen. I am incredibly blessed to work with people who are not only good at their jobs, but also exceptionally lovely people, and I am extremely thankful for you all!

With the Naturals series, I've also gotten the chance to meet readers all over the country, and I'd like to give a shout-out to the hardworking folks behind the North Texas Teen Book Festival, the Rochester Teen Book Festival, the Texas

Teen Book Festival, the Southwest Florida Reading Festival, and the Miami Book Fair for hosting me in the past year. The amount of work you all put into bringing readers and authors together is astounding, and I am profoundly grateful for it.

I could not survive as a writer—let alone thrive—without the support of some of the most wonderful and brilliant women I know. Thanks go to Ally Carter, Elizabeth Eulberg, Carrie Ryan, Rachel Vincent, Rose Brock, and Sarah Rees Brennan, for Rose Fest in all of its incarnations, and special thanks go to Rachel Vincent for Panera Thursdays, Ally Carter, who knows exactly how hard thrillers (and series!) can be to write, and Sarah Rees Brennan, for reading an earlier draft of this book on very short notice. Thanks also to my colleagues and students at the University of Oklahoma, Ti30, NLPT, and everyone else who kept me sane during the writing of this book.

Finally, I owe my family more than I could ever say. My mom and dad are among the very first readers of all of my books, and I would not be where I am today without them. I am also extremely grateful to my husband, Anthony, for being my best friend, support system, sounding board, and the love of my life. And thank you also, Anthony, for keeping me from stressing too much when I was doing some final tweaks on this book while preparing for our wedding! Finally, thank you to my wonderful siblings, nephews, and niece: Justin, Allison, Connor, Jeana, Russ, Daniel, Gianna, Matthew, Joseph, Michael, Lindsey, Dominic, and Julian. You guys are the best!

TURN THE PAGE FOR A PREVIEW OF THE NEXT THRILLING INSTALLMENT OF THE NATURALS SERIES!

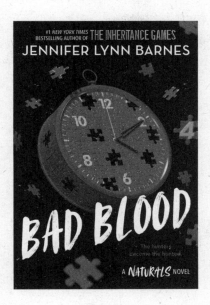

This time, the Naturals aren't just hunting serial killers. They're being hunted.

When Cassie Hobbes joined the FBI's Naturals program, she had one goal: solve her mother's murder. But now everything Cassie thought she knew about that night has been called into question. The people holding the truth captive are more powerful—and dangerous—than anything the Naturals have faced so far. And as Cassie and the team work to uncover the mysteries of a group that has been killing in secret for generations, they find themselves racing against a ticking clock.

With the bodies piling up, Cassie, Dean, Lia, Michael, and Sloane have to decide what they're willing to risk for a case—and for each other.

All your burning questions are answered in this shocking conclusion to the Naturals series.

YOU

Without order, there is chaos.

Without order, there is pain.

The wheel turns. Lives are forfeit. Seven masters. Seven ways of killing.

This time, it will be fire. Nine will burn.

So it has been decreed, and so it must be. The wheel is already turning. There is an order to things. And at the center of all of it—all of it—*is you.*

CHAPTER 1

The serial killer sitting across from me had his son's eyes. The same shape. The same color. But the glint in those eyes, the light of anticipation—*that's wholly your own.*

Experience—and my FBI mentors—had taught me that I could delve further into other people's minds by talking to them than by talking about them. Giving in to the urge to profile, I continued to appraise the man across from me. *You'll hurt me if you can.* I knew that, had known it even before coming to this maximum security prison and seeing the subtle smile that crossed Daniel Redding's lips the moment his gaze met mine. *Hurting me will hurt the boy.* I sank deeper and deeper into Redding's psychopathic perspective. *And the boy is yours to hurt.*

It didn't matter that Daniel Redding's hands were cuffed together and chained to the table. It didn't matter that there was an armed FBI agent at the door. The man in front of me was one of the world's most brutal serial killers, and if I let him past my defenses, he would burn his mark into my soul as surely as he'd branded the letter *R* onto the flesh of his victims.

Bind them. Brand them. Cut them. Hang them.

That was how Redding had killed his victims. But that wasn't what had brought me here today.

"You told me once that I would never find the man who killed my mother," I said, sounding calmer than I felt. I knew this particular psychopath well enough to know that he would try to get a rise out of me.

You'll try to burrow into my mind, to plant questions and doubts so that when I walk out of this room, a part of you goes with me.

That was what Redding had done months ago when he'd dropped that bombshell about my mother. And that was why I was here now.

"Did I say that?" Redding asked with a slow and subtle smile. "It *does* sound like something I might have mentioned, but . . ." He lifted his shoulders in an elaborate shrug.

I folded my hands on the table and waited. *You're the one who wanted me to come back here. You're the one who set the lure. This is me, taking the bait.*

Eventually, Redding broke the silence. "You must have something else to say to me." Redding had an organized killer's capacity for patience—but only on his own terms, not on mine. "After all," he continued, a low hum in his voice, "you and I have so very much in common."

I knew he was referencing my relationship with his son. And I knew that to get what I wanted, I'd have to acknowledge that. "You're talking about Dean."

The moment I said Dean's name, Redding's twisted smile deepened. My boyfriend—and fellow Natural—didn't know that I was here. He would have insisted on coming with me, and I couldn't do that to him. Daniel Redding was a master of manipulation, but nothing he said could possibly hurt me the way every word out of his mouth would have shredded Dean.

"Does my son fancy himself in love with you?" Redding leaned forward, his cuffed hands folding in imitation of my own. "Do you tiptoe into his room at night? Does he bury his hands in your hair?" Redding's expression softened. "When Dean cradles you in his arms," he murmured, his voice taking on a musical lilt, "do you ever wonder just how close he is to snapping your neck?"

"It must bother you," I said softly, "to know so incredibly little about your own son."

If Redding wanted to hurt me, he'd have to do better than trying to make me doubt Dean. If he wanted what he said to haunt me for days and weeks to come, he'd have to hit me where I was most vulnerable. Where I was *weak*.

"It must bother you," Redding parroted my own words back at me, "to know so incredibly little about what happened to your own mother."

The image of my mom's blood-soaked dressing room surged to the front of my mind, but I schooled my face into a neutral expression. I'd set Redding up to hit me where it hurt, and in doing so, I'd steered the conversation exactly where I wanted it to go.

"Isn't that why you're here?" Redding asked me, his voice velvety and low. "To find out what I know about your mother's murder?"

"I'm here," I said, staring him down, "because I know that when you swore to me that I would never find the man who killed my mother, you were telling the truth."

Each of the five teenagers in the FBI's Naturals program had a specialty. Mine was profiling. Lia Zhang's was deception detection. Months ago, she'd pegged Redding's taunting words about my mother as true. I could feel Lia on the other side of the two-way mirror now, ready to separate every sentence I got out of Dean's father into *truth* and *lies*.

Time to lay my cards on the table. "What I want to know," I told the killer in front of me, enunciating each word, "is exactly what kind of truth you were telling. When you guaranteed me that I would never find the man who murdered my mother, was that because you thought she'd been murdered by a *woman*?" I paused. "Or did you have reason to believe that my mother was still alive?"

Ten weeks. That was how long we'd been looking for a lead—any lead, no matter how small—on the cabal of serial killers who'd faked my mother's death nearly six years earlier. The group that had held her captive ever since.

"This isn't a casual visit, is it?" Redding leaned back in

his chair, tilting his head to the side as his eyes—*Dean's eyes*—made a detached study of mine. "You haven't simply reached a tipping point, my words haven't been slowly eating away at you for months. You know something."

I knew that my mother was alive. I knew that those monsters had her. And I knew that I would do anything, make a deal with any devil, to bring them down.

To bring her home.

"What would you say," I asked Redding, "if I told you that there was a society of serial killers, one that operated in secret, killing nine victims every three years?" I could hear the intensity in my own voice. I didn't even sound like myself. "What would you say if I told you that this group is steeped in ritual, that they've been killing for more than a century, and that *I* am going to be the one to bring them down?"

Redding leaned forward. "I suppose I'd say that I wish I could be there to see what this group will do to you for coming after them. To watch them take you apart, piece by piece."

Keep going, you sick monster. Keep telling me what they'll do to me. Tell me everything you know.

Redding paused suddenly, then chuckled. "Clever girl, aren't you? Getting me talking like that. I can understand what my boy sees in you."

A muscle in my jaw ticked. I'd almost had him. I'd been *this* close. . . .

"Do you know your Shakespeare, girl?" Among his plethora of charming qualities, the serial killer across from me had a fondness for the Bard.

" 'To thine own self be true'?" I suggested darkly, racking my brain for a way to reel him back in, to *make* him tell me what he knew.

Redding smiled, his lips parting to show his teeth. "I was thinking more of *The Tempest*. 'Hell is empty, and all the devils are here.' "

All the devils. The killer across from me. The twisted group that had taken my mother.

Seven Masters, a voice whispered in my memory. *The Pythia. And Nine.*

"From what I know of this collective," Redding said, "if they've had your mother for all these years?" Without warning, he surged forward, bringing his face as close to mine as his chains would allow. "She might be quite the devil herself."

TURN THE PAGE TO START ANOTHER UNPUTDOWNABLE SERIES FROM JENNIFER LYNN BARNES!

Don't miss this *New York Times* bestselling "impossible to put down" (Buzzfeed) novel with deadly stakes, thrilling twists, and juicy secrets.

Avery Grambs has a plan for a better future: survive high school, win a scholarship, and get out. But her luck changes in an instant when billionaire Tobias Hawthorne dies and leaves Avery virtually his entire fortune. The catch? Avery has no idea why—or even who Tobias Hawthorne is.

To receive her inheritance, Avery must move into the sprawling, secret-passage-filled Hawthorne House, where every room bears the old man's touch—and his love of puzzles, riddles, and codes. Unfortunately for Avery, Hawthorne House is also occupied by the family that Tobias Hawthorne just disinherited. This includes the four Hawthorne grandsons: dangerous, magnetic, brilliant boys who grew up with every expectation that, one day, they would inherit billions. Heir apparent Grayson Hawthorne is convinced that Avery must be a con woman, and he's determined to take her down. His brother Jameson views her as their grandfather's last hurrah: a twisted riddle, a puzzle to be solved. Caught in a world of wealth and privilege, with danger around every turn, Avery will have to play the game herself just to survive.

CHAPTER 1

When I was a kid, my mom constantly invented games. The Quiet Game. The Who Can Make Their Cookie Last Longer? Game. A perennial favorite, The Marshmallow Game involved eating marshmallows while wearing puffy Goodwill jackets indoors, to avoid turning on the heat. The Flashlight Game was what we played when the electricity went out. We never walked anywhere—we raced. The floor was nearly always lava. The primary purpose of pillows was building forts.

Our longest-lasting game was called I Have A Secret, because my mom said that everyone should always have at least one. Some days she guessed mine. Some days she didn't. We played every week, right up until I was fifteen and one of her secrets landed her in the hospital.

The next thing I knew, she was gone.

"Your move, princess." A gravelly voice dragged me back to the present. "I don't have all day."

"Not a princess," I retorted, sliding one of my knights into place. "Your move, *old man*."

Harry scowled at me. I didn't know how old he was, really, and

I had no idea how he'd come to be homeless and living in the park where we played chess each morning. I did know that he was a formidable opponent.

"You," he grumbled, eyeing the board, "are a horrible person."

Three moves later, I had him. "Checkmate. You know what that means, Harry."

He gave me a dirty look. "I have to let you buy me breakfast." Those were the terms of our long-standing bet. When I won, he couldn't turn down the free meal.

To my credit, I only gloated a little. "It's good to be queen."

———

I made it to school on time but barely. I had a habit of cutting things close. I walked the same tightrope with my grades: How little effort could I put in and still get an A? I wasn't lazy. I was practical. Picking up an extra shift was worth trading a 98 for a 92.

I was in the middle of drafting an English paper in Spanish class when I was called to the office. Girls like me were supposed to be invisible. We didn't get summoned for sit-downs with the principal. We made exactly as much trouble as we could afford to make, which in my case was none.

"Avery." Principal Altman's greeting was not what one would call warm. "Have a seat."

I sat.

He folded his hands on the desk between us. "I assume you know why you're here."

Unless this was about the weekly poker game I'd been running in the parking lot to finance Harry's breakfasts—and sometimes my own—I had no idea what I'd done to draw the administration's attention. "Sorry," I said, trying to sound sufficiently meek, "but I don't."

Principal Altman let me sit with my response for a moment,

then presented me with a stapled packet of paper. "This is the physics test you took yesterday."

"Okay," I said. That wasn't the response he was looking for, but it was all I had. For once, I'd actually studied. I couldn't imagine I'd done badly enough to merit intervention.

"Mr. Yates graded the tests, Avery. Yours was the only perfect score."

"Great," I said, in a deliberate effort to keep myself from saying *okay* again.

"Not great, young lady. Mr. Yates intentionally creates exams that challenge the abilities of his students. In twenty years, he's never given a perfect score. Do you see the problem?"

I couldn't quite bite back my instinctive reply. "A teacher who designs tests most of his students can't pass?"

Mr. Altman narrowed his eyes. "You're a good student, Avery. Quite good, given your circumstances. But you don't exactly have a history of setting the curve."

That was fair, so why did I feel like he'd gut-punched me?

"I am not without sympathy for your situation," Principal Altman continued, "but I need you to be straight with me here." He locked his eyes onto mine. "Were you aware that Mr. Yates keeps copies of all his exams on the cloud?" He thought I'd cheated. He was sitting there, staring me down, and I'd never felt less seen. "I'd like to help you, Avery. You've done extremely well, given the hand life has dealt you. I would hate to see any plans you might have for the future derailed."

"Any plans I *might* have?" I repeated. If I'd had a different last name, if I'd had a dad who was a dentist and a mom who stayed home, he wouldn't have acted like the future was something I *might* have thought about. "I'm a junior," I gritted out. "I'll graduate next year with at least two semesters' worth of college credit. My test scores should put me in scholarship contention at UConn, which has one of the top actuarial science programs in the country."

Mr. Altman frowned. "Actuarial science?"

"Statistical risk assessment." It was the closest I could come to double-majoring in poker and math. Besides, it was one of the most employable majors on the planet.

"Are you a fan of calculated risks, Ms. Grambs?"

Like cheating? I couldn't let myself get any angrier. Instead, I pictured myself playing chess. I marked out the moves in my mind. Girls like me didn't get to explode. "I didn't cheat." I said calmly. "I studied."

I'd scraped together time—in other classes, between shifts, later at night than I should have stayed up. Knowing that Mr. Yates was infamous for giving impossible tests had made me want to redefine *possible*. For once, instead of seeing how close I could cut it, I'd wanted to see how far I could go.

And *this* was what I got for my effort, because girls like me didn't ace impossible exams.

"I'll take the test again," I said, trying not to sound furious, or worse, wounded. "I'll get the same grade again."

"And what would you say if I told you that Mr. Yates had prepared a new exam? All new questions, every bit as difficult as the first."

I didn't even hesitate. "I'll take it."

"That can be arranged tomorrow during third period, but I have to warn you that this will go significantly better for you if—"

"*Now.*"

Mr. Altman stared at me. "Excuse me?"

Forget sounding meek. Forget being invisible. "I want to take the new exam right here, in your office, right now."

Kim Haynes Photography

JENNIFER LYNN BARNES

is the #1 *New York Times* bestselling author of more than twenty acclaimed young-adult novels, including the Inheritance Games trilogy, *The Brothers Hawthorne*, *Little White Lies*, *Deadly Little Scandals*, *The Lovely and the Lost*, and the Naturals series: *The Naturals*, *Killer Instinct*, *All In*, *Bad Blood*, and the novella *Twelve*. Jen is also a Fulbright Scholar with advanced degrees in psychology, psychiatry, and cognitive science. She received her PhD from Yale University in 2012 and was a professor of psychology and professional writing at the University of Oklahoma for many years. She invites you to find her online at jenniferlynnbarnes.com or follow her on Twitter @jenlynnbarnes.